To the three musketeers
Oliver, Graham, and Audrey

"Two Romes have fallen. The third stands. And there will be no fourth. No one shall replace your Christian Tsardom!"

Letter composed by the Russian monk Philotheus in 1510 to their son Grand Duke Vasilli III.

delta: noun, Mathematics,
an incremental change in a variable, as Δ

Prologue

She was thirty-eight years old and a virgin. Her parents had seen to that. They had selected her when she was only ten to be the guardian of the flame. Her life was laid out in front of her before it even started. It had not been a bad life; in fact, it was quite pleasurable. She was worshipped and held a very high position in Roman society. She even had her own box at the Coliseum with the five other virgins. But, as with the clouds in the sky, things always change.

Julia and the five Vestal Virgins guarded the flame in the Temple of Vesta. The virgins and their ancestors had guarded the flame for a thousand years. The temple was a fifteen-meter-wide, circular edifice in the Foro Romano, supported by twenty Corinthian columns. It was one of the oldest structures in Rome and was used to store important records and business documents for safekeeping. There was an opening to the east pointing towards the sun, the origin of fire. The flame burned continuously inside. It was said that if the flame ever went out, Rome would fall. The year was 298 AD. Vesta was the goddess of fire, the goddess of the hearth—the fire that kept an ancient home alive. She was worshipped originally in the

1

circular huts the Roman tribes built in the area, hence the circular design of the temple. The goddess kept Rome alive as long as they kept their covenant with her to keep the flame burning. At least, that was what the people were led to believe.

Julia also had a covenant with Rome, although not of her choosing. Her parents had offered her as a virgin to guard the flame when she was ten. The virgins came from very high-placed families in Roman society. It was an honor to have a daughter selected to guard the Temple of Vesta. In return for thirty years of celibacy, upon their fortieth birthday, the virgins were allowed to marry and received a huge dowry from the state. They had statues made in their likeness that were placed in the gardens around the temple. However, if a virgin broke her vow of celibacy to the Empire, the consequences were dire.

The Vestal Virgins lived in a multi-room structure right outside of the temple. The site was the most holy in Roman culture and was placed squarely in the center of Foro Romano, where it all began. This was where the first tribes of the ancient valley met to trade along the lowlands of the river. It was where Romulus was suckled by the she-wolf after being abandoned by his parents. Any free Roman citizen could take the fire to his home, and the temple therefore represented the hearth of Rome.

It was early evening when the visitor came to call on Julia. He was a younger man, a servant dressed in servant's clothes, and quite handsome. She met him at the gate to the temple grounds to talk after he had sent a request in to the College of the Vestals to speak

2

with her. The senator's aide could come no further. "Tonight at midnight, Senator Thor will pay you a visit. He has something to give you, something that needs to be guarded, even from the emperor himself. This is the safest place in Rome. Please meet him." The visitor left without explaining further. Julia was left wondering at the gate for some time but finally retired to her room.

Julia was troubled. She would have to be very careful. This meeting was very dangerous for both her and the senator. She knew things were changing in Rome. The corruption was rampant. The emperor was claiming for himself more and more power. The Roman order and process that had survived for centuries was giving way to raw corruption and tyranny.

The Senate had long been relegated to the periphery. Originally the body was set up by the early Roman kings and came from the historical group of elders the tribes organized to help govern themselves. In fact, the word senate is derived from the Latin word senex, which means *old man*. Once Rome became a republic, the power of the Senate grew exponentially. However the republic was long gone. All power was now held by the emperor. No longer was he seen as an equal to the average citizen in Rome; he was a god. However, he was becoming more and more corrupt, cut off from communication with his subjects and events throughout the Empire. He received information filtered by his court with which he constantly feared revolt and death. His actions were not those of one concerned about the future of the Empire but of one concerned with staying in power. While he concentrated on giving out favors, the barbarians advanced to the north.

Night fell. At the appropriate time, Julia rose from her bed and left her chambers, moving as quietly as possible. She made her way out into the warm night. She could see the light from the flames of the hearth in the Temple of Vesta licking the ceiling of the ancient structure. She was scared. However, she trusted the senator and knew he was a good man; she would meet him despite the danger.

She made her way silently across the garden between the wading pools and stopped near the stone fence on the other side. Her white evening clothes stood out like a ghost under the full moon. The cicadas sang a rhythmic song of joy to the white orb in the sky. The Roman Forum was silent.

"Julia," a voice whispered. "I am here." She turned and walked toward the sound. The senator stepped from the shadows. "Thank you for coming," he said softly. He was old, probably over seventy, which was ancient for a Roman man. His eyes were flanked by deep crevices in his skin, and his hair was a wispy white. He walked with a pronounced stoop. He was dressed in a tunic made of expensive cloth with large, colorful stripes, identifying him as a senator.

"I came as you requested. What is so important? I cannot stay long," Julia declared.

"I don't have much time," he said and handed her a small, stone tube typically used to store documents. It was capped at both ends and sealed. "You must guard this with your life. It is the past and the future of Rome. Do not place it in the temple with all of

4

the other royal documents. Keep it with you at all times. Tell no one. It is safe here I believe. No one will bother you. When you are older, pass it on to one of the other virgins with a sacred oath to guard it with her life as I request you to do."

She took the container. It was surprisingly light. There was a lanyard attached at both ends. She put the cord around her neck, and the scroll dangled between her breasts. She moved it under her night clothes so it could not be seen. "I will do as you ask," she replied, "because I believe you are a good man that wants what's best for Rome. I have seen you fight to restore Rome to its former glory and justice. I trust you." Julia had heard of the senator's reputation as being kind and wise, although they had never met in person. She looked him in the eyes one last time then looked around the courtyard, frightened that she would be discovered. "I must go."

With that reply she turned and walked back across the gardens. The senator disappeared into the night. What neither of them saw was another young girl, barely fourteen, also in a white night dress in the garden, hiding behind a column at the Temple of Vesta. She was Cornelia, one of the other five virgins. She had been guarding the flame through the night. Cornelia was still young but quite adamant in her opinion of herself and the importance of her role in Roman society. She was new to the temple and rather passionate about her duties. Cornelia was also a budding woman and felt subconsciously angry about not being able to talk to the young boys she frequently saw looking at her. She was jealous of the other girls in society and really quite angry about it. She knew

5

that it was not permitted to meet male Romans without a chaperon, especially at night, and decided to take her anger out on Julia, as it was the only avenue she had, however misguided. Had Julia broken her vow of celibacy to the temple? She would need to report this to the authorities. She was certain she would be well rewarded by the emperor.

The next day, Julia rose late in the morning after a fitful sleep. She had not slept well after the meeting with the senator, and sleeping with the scroll draped around her neck would take some getting used to. She moved to the window and drew the curtain to let in some light. Strange, her morning servant was not next to her when she woke. That had never happened before. Her servant had taken care of her every need flawlessly for years. Since she had slept late, she was hungry. There was no breakfast by her bed either as she had grown accustomed to over the last twenty-eight years. A twinge of fear rose up her spine. She walked to the door to the outside chamber and opened it.

Her heart melted in terror as she saw the Praetorian guards outside of her sleeping quarters, waiting for her. The ten soldiers were in full ornamental battle gear and had no thoughts of allowing this girl to get away after the emperor's instructions. The emperor had a habit of decimating soldiers he surmised were not loyal. The practice consisted of killing one in ten men in a unit in order to ensure discipline. No, they would not let her get away. In fact they would enjoy this task.

"No, please, I can explain!" she shrieked and dropped to the floor, sobbing. Denouncing a virgin for incest against the state was a serious offense. The emperor used this opportunity shrewdly to blame this treason for his recent failures in battle and deflect blame from himself.

The guards picked her up off the ground and tied her hands behind her back. "It is too late for you; it has already been decided. You have broken your vow to Rome and the Temple of Vesta." Julia screamed in horror, as she knew what was awaiting her. She wailed as they dragged her by the hair from her bedroom and out of the College of Virgins. The pain added to her fear but was nothing compared to what she was about to experience.

The soldiers carried her to the cobblestone road outside the temple grounds in the center of Foro Romano. The crowds had already gathered, as the word had spread fast of what was to happen. This was even better entertainment than the gladiators in the Coliseum. No one wanted to miss the show. They were used to the emperor providing routine ghoulish spectacles to divert attention from their miserable and declining living conditions. The crowd was excited.

First she was whipped by a thick cane fifty times. The back of her white clothes became stained with blood. She was close to unconsciousness but hoisted onto a funeral cart and tied to a stake emanating from the center. A pail of cold water was thrown in her face to wake her up in order to enjoy the procession. Soon she was again screaming in horror and shock at what was happening. She

7

had done nothing wrong! She had been true to Rome; she no longer even had any sexual feelings. Those had vanished long ago. She had been true to her oath. But today it didn't matter.

The cart wound its way through the center of the ancient city and slowly made its way outside of the massive walls to the place where the dead were buried, to the Campus Sceleratus, a small rise near the gate. Roman citizens lined the streets to witness the spectacle. Some were empathetic and sad, others were enjoying the cruel procession and used the occasion to start another decadent binge of drinking, drugs, and sex. The corruption of the Roman ethos was almost complete.

Julia had fainted with shock in the now hot sun. Her head hung limp on her shoulder as her body was supported by the cords strapping her to the pole. Soon the procession stopped. Another bucket of cold water from the nearby aquifer was thrown on her to wake her up. She looked up and hoped she had awoken from a nightmare but stood in shock as she realized it was not the case.

Her parents and family were screaming and crying behind a wall of soldiers protecting the executioner. The wealthy family, once close to the emperor's court, would now be banished. Their lives changed forever. They would be lucky to escape with their lives and would soon be making hurried plans to flee the city.

The soldiers untied her from the cart and dragged her by her bound hands to the hillside below. The ropes around her wrists and the rocks on the ground cut into her skin. She pleaded with them to listen to the truth, but they ignored her. They led her to an open tomb. They stopped in front of the crypt, and a Roman judge walked up to her and began to speak.

"You have broken your sacred vow to Rome. You will now accept the consequences of your pleasure of the flesh." At this point, Julia was too weak to protest. The soldiers walked into the crypt and placed an oil lamp on one of the slabs next to a decaying body. The air smelled of death, as one of the bodies was fresh from burial a week before. The soldier adjusted the wick and lit the lamp. Beside the lamp he placed a loaf of bread and a cup of water. Then they brought Julia into the tomb and pushed her to the floor. She was mumbling in an incomprehensible manner.

The rock was then moved to close the tomb. The last vestige of light twinkled out as the stone was rolled across the opening. Julia's voice was drowned out to the outside world, and her screams whispered like death on the wind.

No one noticed the richly dressed man standing in the crowd. If they did notice, they did not speak to him. The power emanating from his stature made it clear he was not to be spoken to, although no one recognized him as a local. He was dressed in a way which was foreign to Roman society, but it was obvious he was a man of sophistication. If they had noticed him, they would have seen he was smiling.

One hundred years later, Emperor Theodosius I extinguished the fire in the hearth of the Temple of Vesta as he proclaimed it inconsistent with Christianity, now the official religion of Rome. A few years later, Rome fell to the barbarians.

Chapter One

The words just wouldn't come. He sat at the wooden table on the old, rickety, spindle chair, his eyes attempting to focus on the laptop. The chair creaked beneath him. He had been meaning to buy something new to sit on, but in reality he just couldn't part with an old friend. It had been two months, and it was now like they were married. His body had molded a depression in the soft wood of the seat. How could he get a new chair? It was not going to happen.

The words still wouldn't come. Sometimes when he started to write, the words gushed out of him like a hot geyser, not tonight. He leaned forward on his elbows into the table and stared at the blue and white screen. He began to make out the pixels in the coloring. The table swayed slightly below him with the force of his weight and screamed in pain. Nothing. Today was not going to be the day he made progress. He just didn't know where to take the story. He needed inspiration.

So inspiration it would be. Rafe stood up. He wavered slightly as he stood and grabbed the table to steady himself. Glancing at the bottle of Chianti on the table, he could see it was half empty. Another dead soldier stood next to it. He should have been really drunk, but he wasn't. A couple bottles of wine a day saw to that. His tolerance was impressive.

Next to the first bottle was a picture of his kids. *I miss them, bad.* He turned away and pushed the thought out of his mind. *Actually, I'm the happiest I've been in a long time!* And he really was. The divorce had been over for six months now. Oh, of course he still had the raging phone calls, usually in the evening when she was drunk. But the good thing was he didn't have to be in the same room anymore. He had been taught not to hit a woman. So he had taken it—for years. It almost destroyed him. *No more.*

Rafe made his way confidently to the balcony door as he had been doing for two months now and opened it. The smell of the sea embraced him like a foggy morning. But it was evening. The sun was setting. The sun was setting on Venice. His balcony overlooked one of the canals meandering off the main drag. He could hear the taxi boats plodding along, their engines sounding like a growling lion. It seemed they never stopped. Venice, like any major city, had an extensive public transport system, except hers was on water. Luckily his building was tall, taller than most around him, and his view was spectacular from the top floor. He could see the clock tower in St. Mark's Square in the distance. The balcony was quite large, and he had started a nice collection of herbs and other plants growing in the Venetian sunlight and salty air. It was a heavenly location for a writer. It was just what Rafe needed to find some peace. He just wanted to write and be left alone for a while.

12

He turned and made his way back across the main room to the exit and started down the several flights of stairs, emerging along the canal into the evening shortly after. It was going to be a beautiful night. The gondolas for hire were taking full advantage of the perfect conditions for a moonlit cruise. After a few twists and turns and five minutes later, he arrived at his favorite restaurant along the water. The nightlife here was fantastic." It was when the real Venetians came out to play, avoiding the horde of tourists during the day.

Rafe sat at a table in the outdoor seating area, and soon a waiter was describing to him in Italian the specials for the evening. He understood only half of what was said but shook his head in agreement. "Surprise me," he said in English. The waiter smiled and started shouting instructions to the chef as only an Italian could do. Soon the food starting coming and didn't seem to stop.

In spite of all his problems, and besides missing his kids terribly, Rafe really *was* happy. This place enthralled him. *Maybe I will never leave Venice.* The authentic Italian seafood meal went down easy, and the courses were never ending. He found himself apologizing to the overweight, female proprietor why he just couldn't eat anymore. He paid the bill and spent an hour wandering through the passageways of the floating city, marveling at the history. The walk helped to digest his meal. The best thing to do in Venice was to get lost. He was on an island for God's sake, so it wasn't really being lost. He could find his way back eventually. But the pleasure was in finding a new street and meeting new people and watching the Venetians do their thing in their element, which was the evening. Soon he was doing just that as he found himself chatting with a local businessman who owned a tobacco shop. He enjoyed a fine cigar and became fast friends with the gentleman. *This is how I always find inspiration.*

Eventually, he decided to go back to his flat and get some writing done. Maybe the evening stroll would stir his imagination. He could still see St. Mark's in the distance, and he oriented himself to the bell tower. Soon he would come out near his home. Rafe found himself walking along a foreign canal in a neighborhood he did not know. It was strangely quiet and almost deserted. He enjoyed times like these, finding new places in his new favorite city, listening to the noises of the night. Rafe reveled in the fact he had no schedule and no one telling him what to do. He was completely in control of his own destiny, and he loved it.

He gazed at the ornately decorated palaces lining the canal and tried to imagine the history of the owners hundreds of years ago. The parties they threw, the beautiful women who lived there, all of this danced through his mind. He casually stopped along one such palace, long since deserted due to the mold creeping up to the upper floors from the constant flooding. He paused to take in the structure. It was times like these that inspiration came.

Venice was sinking. Slowly, very slowly, but sinking just the same. The buildings were constructed on wooden pilings sunk into the mud and clay centuries before. The foundations of the city's structures rested on this wooden support. The earth delayed the process of decay, but slowly these pylons were deteriorating. Artesian

14

wells sunk in the early twentieth century to feed local industry were discovered to be adding to the structural problems, hastening the sinking of the city's support. As the city's elevation shriveled, the floods came more often and the damage grew exponentially. Many of the palaces along the waterways were deserted, or at least the first floor, due to mold and other hazards from the encroaching sea.

The population of Venice was now mostly older, as families with children had moved out long ago because of the safety hazards and expense of living on the island. The Italian government had spent hundreds of millions of euros to stop the decomposition of the city but could only slow not alter nature's course. Seawater had a nasty way of eating into a foundation over time that no amount of human intervention could stop. The future of Venice was in doubt in the long run. Today, however, Rafe enjoyed the scenery and wondered about the past.

As the evening light dimmed, out of the corner of his eye, Rafe noticed a strange glow emanating from the base of the palace. It was an orange, fiery color wafting through the water like cream in a coffee. He walked over and looked closer. The strange, colored light angrily turned bright red and then was gone. He shrugged and kept walking. *Must be the wine.* Darkness set in for the rest of his trip home.

His head hurt but not too much. His body was used to the alcohol. He was terribly thirsty however. The sun was peeking through the venetian blinds and stabbing him in the eyes. He awoke but didn't want to move. This was his favorite part of the day. He could just lie in bed until he couldn't lie there anymore. Rafe reached for a glass of water on the nearby table and downed it quickly. Then he closed his eyes. *I wonder what time it is. But, I don't really care.*

Rafe Savaryn was a world traveler. He loved exploring different civilizations, new and old. He wrote books about those experiences and taught history at a small Ivy League school in the northeastern United States. He especially loved European history. His family had emigrated from the Ukraine during the previous generation, and he still felt he had roots in Eastern Europe. "If you don't know history, you're doomed to repeat it," he always told his incoming classes.

Rafe spent several months a year in different, far-off corners of the globe. Previously he brought his family, but on this trip he was alone, due to the divorce. He enjoyed finding places that no one in the West knew much about, places that experienced a deep history that had been lost to the ages. Learning about the past gave Rafe great pleasure, as it helped him understand the present. This was the secret of his books and why he had become such a successful writer.

One of his earliest memories as a child was running across an expansive, open terrazzo with a large statue in front of him. He was obliviously happy and his mother was chasing him from behind, calling for him. He remembered her explaining to him about the statue and how important it was to history. Rafe ignored her and kept running. He remembered reaching the statue and seeing a tall, bronzed man riding a horse. As he grew older, he had always

16

wondered where that place was. *Perhaps that is why I'm always searching and writing, hoping one day I'll run into that statue again. Perhaps that is where my curiosity for the past began.*

But his favorite place in the world was Italy. And his favorite city in Italy was Venice. To live among the houses where the Italians had fled from the barbarians during the Dark Ages after the fall of the Western Roman Empire, and built a city on the marshy islands, was heavenly for him. He felt as if he dined with da Vinci when eating among the locals in the late evening. He reveled in the atmosphere. Today was going to be no different.

An hour later, his side began to ache from lying in bed, and Rafe sat up, throwing off the matted sheets. He walked to the balcony and once again threw open the doors. He breathed in the sea. It was a daily ritual he enjoyed. He checked on his herb garden and then walked to the bathroom. Rafe took a short, cold shower to revive himself, quickly dressed, grabbed his laptop, and headed out of his flat and down the stairs. Today was the perfect day to write. He enjoyed the exercise as he strolled through the waking city. Soon he was sitting at a table in St. Mark's square, the tourists and the pigeons milling all around him. The ideas came and he began to write.

Hours later he came up for air. His eyes burned from staring at the screen, and his wrists ached from typing. He had finished five thousand words. *Quite the productive day if I do say so myself! Almost makes up for the horrible writing day yesterday.*

Rafe was in Venice to write a novel, a novel about the Renaissance. *And what better place to do that than here?* He looked at the bell tower rising forcefully high above all of the other structures. He remembered as a child his parents had a painting of St. Mark's Square hanging over the fireplace. He always wondered where the place was. Now he knew and he was sitting here. He experienced a form of déjà vu.

The sun was now slowly heading toward the horizon, and the light began to fade. Shadows made their way across the cobblestone. The tourists began to make their way to the boats. The dueling jazz and classical music orchestras across from each other in the plaza took turns playing to the locals and the tourists left on the island for the evening. The scene was magical. Rafe ordered his first drink of the night, and his mind wandered off into the past laid out before him.

He was jerked back to reality when he heard a young, female voice ask, "Is this chair taken?" Rafe, startled, turned to face the owner of the voice on his left side. A young woman not more than thirty sat next to him and signaled to the waiter for a drink. "I'll have what he is having," she said as the waiter arrived.

Rafe raised his eyebrow and said, "Very confident of you."

"You want me to stay, don't you?"

Rafe looked her over. She was young, thin, beautiful, and elegantly attired in a little black dress, her dark shiny hair rained down around her shoulders and framed her delicate face.

"I think I do," Rafe responded, a smile creasing his lips. She was of Italian descent he guessed, and her accent was deadly attractive. "Well this is a pleasant surprise," he added.

"I like to be spontaneous." They chatted about nothing for fifteen minutes or so, and Rafe smiled, as she was quite witty.

The first drinks went down easy, and Rafe signaled for another round. She began to speak but stopped as the drinks arrived and waited until the waiter was out of earshot.

"Do you like me?" she asked coquettishly.

"Yes, I do."

"Well, here's the deal. You take care of me and I'll take care of you."

"I figured it was something like that. The oldest profession?"

"I like to call it being a courtesan. I only work with high-end clients."

Rafe thought about it for a minute. The full moon shone down across the square, illuminating the pearls around her dark neck. *What the hell.* He reached into his wallet and pulled out several five hundred euro notes. Money was not a problem for Rafe. He was a very successful writer. He slid the notes across the table. "Will this do?"

She smiled. "I'm yours for the night."

They walked hand in hand through the darkened alleyways, occasionally stopping for a bite to eat or a drink at the many restaurants and bars dotting the landscape of Venice. Rafe enjoyed having some company for once. It had been several months since the divorce, but it had been years since he was happy with a woman. He realized he had been missing female companionship. *Rational, happy, fun companionship that is.*

Soon the hour was very late. He stopped in a darkened doorway that was indented several feet into the building, providing a very private space for exactly a moment like this. He pulled her close and felt her young, toned body under her dress. Her full breasts pressed against his chest. She kissed him and threw her arms around his neck, pressing her body into his. They embraced for several minutes.

They both were startled by a loud splash. Rafe looked up across the canal to the palace on the other side. Even in the dark, he could see the mold making its way up to the second floor like something out of a drive-in movie. The light from the full moon covered the water in a milky glow. Rafe looked around and realized he was at the same spot where he had seen the fiery water the night before. He walked over to where he had heard the object hit the water and looked around. He heard another noise below as the water was disturbed. He then realized part of the upstairs balcony of the abandoned palace was crumbling and pieces of stone were falling into the water.

They both peered into the water where the stone had entered as the ripples emanated from the entry point. Slowly an orange, fiery glow like the flame of a candle appeared as a small circle and then grew, spreading across the water like an oily flame. "What is that?" she gasped.

"I don't know, but I think I saw it last night as well." He leaned over the canal to try to get a better look. The mist turned a raging red and then vanished as quickly as it came.

"That's the weirdest thing I've ever seen!"

"Yeah, it's really weird. I just don't have any idea what it is!" Rafe stared a little longer and then turned away. "Come on, let's go."

They walked silently the short distance to his flat, climbed the stairs, and entered his studio. He kicked off his shoes and went out on the balcony.

"Do you have a name?" he asked.

She walked out with him and looked out over the moonlit city. "Cecilia. It's an ancient Roman name. I like it. My parents did good. And I know your name is Rafe." His eyes widened. "Don't worry, I always check out my clients."

She walked over to him and began unbuttoning his shirt. When she had finished, she pulled his shirt out of his trousers with his belt still buckled, exposing his stomach and chest. Her delicate hands caressed him.

She lightly kissed his chest then looked up at him. "You know next time, you're going to have to let me bring a friend." She bent lower to where her mouth was a couple inches above his belt buckle. "We both should be licking right here." Her tongue touched his skin. Rafe closed his eyes.

When Rafe awoke, the bed was a wreck but she was gone. *Oh well, at least it was worth the money. I feel like notching my bedpost or something.* He rose from the bed, looked out the balcony, and went through his morning ritual. This time, however, there were blackened clouds in the distance billowing down from the sky. He could hear the thunder and see the occasional flash of lightning. The storm was moving fast towards Venice, and he could see the people below scurrying to bring their things inside before the rain started. Just like that, the rain started pouring down in buckets. The clouds were violently churning and spewing thunder and lightning. He barely had time to shut the balcony doors.

Just then, the door jerked opened to his flat. Cecilia walked in carrying a tray with two cappuccinos and some pastries and fruit. She had changed into another knee-length sun dress from the small bag she had been carrying. "Breakfast is served!" she said. She looked out the balcony door windows. "Wow, that's an angry storm!"

"I thought you were gone for good."

"No, just thought I'd be nice to you and serve you something to eat. You were so gentle with me last night. And I had another thought. I thought maybe I'd just stay with you a while. You know, get to know each other. I like you."

"I'm not paying you any more money."

"I'm not asking, am I?"

'I guess not."

"You can just buy food. What do you think? I'm a kind of spur-of-the-moment person anyway."

"Well, I had fun last night that's for sure. So stay a while. But don't bug me, I've got to write."

"Yes, I know. The famous writer." She put the food down on the table next to his computer, walked over to him, pushed him back on the bed, and pulled her dress over her head. "You can start writing in thirty minutes."

She lay next to him with her head on his shoulder, her dark hair pushed up into his face. "You smell good but I need to write now, if I have any energy left."

"Of course, I'm not stopping you."

"So what's a nice girl like you doing what you're doing?"

"Aahhh, the big question. Well I'll tell you. I don't do it very often but I need money, and it's an easy way for me to get it. Capiche? I'm a perpetual student and I have to eat. Can you understand? Plus I like to travel, buy things, and meet interesting people. Does that make sense? I hope so, because it's the truth."

"Sure, it makes sense. I'm not judging you. I took you up on your offer, didn't I? Everybody has a price. What are you studying?"

"I'm an expert on the Roman Empire. Soon I will be rich and famous. I hope anyway. I give a lot of speeches now around Italy on the subject already. I'm quite the intellectual, believe it or not."

"I'm impressed! Maybe you can help me with parts of the book I'm writing."

"See, I knew you'd want me to hang around. Tell me about yourself, cowboy! I mean I know you are a famous writer and everything. I read an article that you'd be spending some time in Venice, writing your next novel."

"So that's how you found me? Ha. I remember that article. I was angry they wrote it. The guy caught me at a cocktail party in New York and presto, off-the-record comments show up in print. Well, what do you want to know?"

"Here's my big question. Why are you alone?"

"Let's save that question for another day."

Chapter Two

Rafe sat typing away at his laptop at a cafe overlooking the water near the fish market in Venice. It was a beautiful day and he was thrilled to be alive. He loved to sit in the middle of the crowds and imagine how life would have been centuries before. He tried to visualize how the remnants of the Roman population fled the barbarian advances from the north during the Dark and Middle Ages and took refuge in the marshlands off the coast, slowly building up the city over hundreds of years to become a major economic power, the most powerful city-state in all of Europe at one point.

The doge, or duke, as the Venetian leader was called, ruled the Adriatic as a major naval power during the early second millennium, building and operating thousands of ships and training accompanying crews. Venice even threated the Eastern Roman Empire at one point, sacking its capital Constantinople and occupying hundreds of Islands along the Adriatic coast, creating her own Latin empire. It wasn't until Christopher Columbus discovered the New World and opened up alternative trading routes that the power of Venice began to wane. A long and costly war with the Ottoman Empire served to irreversibly force her into decline. Venice was also an important republic during the Renaissance. She flourished as an independent city and patron of the arts until Napoleon Bonaparte conquered her in the late eighteenth century. The city-state became part of the Kingdom of Italy in the late nineteenth century.

The smell of fresh fish dominated the air, and sea gulls soared overhead in endless patterns, diving to pick at the discarded carcasses of the fish as they were cleaned and thrown in the trash bin near the alleyway. This was not a touristy area of the city, although some did come here to see the local atmosphere. The boats off-loading their catch came and went, and the market was bustling in the midday heat. Rows and rows of all different types of seafood were on display, nestled in a thick bed of ice. The Venetian women combed through the offerings, trying to find the best selection of fish to feed their families. Occasionally a tourist would wander into the market and request a picture with the mounds of whole specimens piled in the containers of ice, only to be shooed away by the market proprietors. This place was for selling fish, not for catering to tourists. Speed was of the essence to sell the entire catch, as the shelf life of a dead fish was limited before its freshness could not be guaranteed. Rafe tried to transfer all of the activity around him to his novel. There was nothing like seeing and describing events real time. It was a favorite technique of his.

There was not a cloud in the sky. It was as if all the rain the day before had washed away any hint of bad weather. He spent the previous day writing and was again quite productive. Cecilia had left him alone and let him work. That is until the sun began to set.

Rafe looked up from his computer as the memory of her body returned. *Wow,* he thought. A sea gull swooped down over him and caught him by surprise. The scene was transposed immediately to his book. He attempted to capture the motions of the bird's wings, the sound of its call, and the aggressiveness of its attack while it attempted to acquire a scrap of seafood. He couldn't type fast enough.

It was late in the afternoon, and Cecilia had gone back to check out of her hotel and get her things. *I guess she's staying with me for a while. I'm probably crazy but what the heck.* He decided he had written enough for the day and paid his bill, downed the last bit of wine in his glass, stood up, and headed back towards his flat. He checked his word count and noticed he had only written a couple thousand words for the day. However, the prose was high quality and Rafe was satisfied.

The sun was beating down hard, and it was a scorching day. The tourists on the main drags were out in force, and he could hardly make his way down the crowded thoroughfare. It was no use. He decided to take an alternate route away from the well-traveled, popular parts of Venice. Soon he was on an alleyway along a canal devoid of people. Rafe felt relaxed and happy. *That's probably because of Cecilia. How strange is that? In other words, what the heck are you doing? Well, it feels right. One day at a time, I guess.*

A group of sea gulls again flew overhead making a god-awful racket, shattering his bubble of self-absorption. It was like they were trying to get his attention. He noticed they began to circle over the canal a few meters ahead. Instantly Rafe realized where he was. He was at the palace again. The palace filled with mold and the home of the fiery water. He walked to the edge of the concrete and peered into the green canal. There were no colors floating around, as it was the middle of the day and the light was bright. But there was something else. Rafe could see something attached to the wall of the palace about ten feet below the water, some type of symbol. He couldn't make it out, as the canal rippled on the surface and clouded his field of vision.

He felt drawn to this place. *I'm supposed to be here—how strange,* he thought to himself. The images below the surface beckoned him. He desperately tried to make them out through the trembling, murky water. It was no use. He sat on the edge of the canal and let his legs dangle over the side, frustrated, trying to decide what to do.

Screw this. Rafe looked around to his left and right and confirmed the alleyway was deserted. He quickly pulled off his clothes to his boxer shorts, looked around to check once again, and dove into the water. The salt filled his nose and eyes, and they burned. He made his way down to the symbol on the palace foundation. The light became less and less visible as he swam about ten feet under the surface. He arrived eye level with the image and stared as long as he could as his breath ran out. Rafe felt curiously alone and not alone at the same time. He stared at the image of the lion's head atop a naked man's body. A snake was wrapped around the torso with its head sitting atop the lion's mane. The body held two keys in its hands. The image had four wings protruding from his back,

28

and a lightning bolt flashed across his chest. Rafe stared at the picture hewn into the stone. The lion's mouth was open and was terrifying. He needed to surface but he was held there. Something wouldn't let him go. He felt at home. Like the image was familiar, but he had never seen it before, of that he was sure. He felt light-headed and his lungs were bursting. *Surface you idiot!*

At the last moment, he used what strength he had, flailed his arms and legs, and kicked to the top. As his head broke the surface, the air exploded out of his lungs, and he sucked whatever molecules of oxygen he could manage. After several moments of regaining his breath, Rafe slowly swam overhand to the edge and pulled himself to the side of the canal and onto the walkway. He was exhausted. He lay there for several minutes, recovering. The image of the beast was still in his mind. Rafe could have sworn as he swam away that the face had turned red and blood oozed from the mouth of the lion.

It was some time before Rafe returned to his flat. The experience had jarred him. He had walked around the city for a couple hours, trying to make sense of it. But nothing made sense, he was confused. He opened the door to the flat as the sun began to set and the light was beginning to disappear from the balcony glass doors.

"I was beginning to think you wouldn't be coming back," said Cecilia as he noticed her lying on the bed. She was dressed in nothing but a terry cloth robe. Yet, his mind was still foggy from what had happened.

"I really don't know what just went down," Rafe responded.

"What do you mean?"

"As I was walking back from the fish market after writing there for several hours, I ended up back at the palace where we saw that strange glow in the water a couple days ago. It was the weirdest thing! I felt drawn to it, like I was supposed to be there. Then I saw something under the water mounted onto the stone foundation. It was an image of some sort. I couldn't see It clearly, so I dove in, just like that."

"Just like that?"

"Yeah, really strange, isn't it? And I almost stayed down too long, staring at it. I mean I really almost drowned. It felt like I was supposed to be down there, even though I knew I had to surface."

"Really? What was the image?" she asked.

"Like nothing I've ever seen before." Rafe walked to his writing table and pulled a blank piece of paper from a notepad. He began to draw. A few moments later, he handed the drawing to Cecilia. "Like this."

She gazed at the rendering. "I've seen this before!"

"Where?"

"I don't know. I can't remember. But I know it has something to do with the Roman Empire. Can I use your phone?"

"Why?"

"I know someone who will know what this is." She took the phone from his hand as he held it out for her. She dialed.

30

"Fernando, hello, it's me Cece from Rome. Yes, it's good to hear from you as well. Listen, I don't have time to talk, but I want to send you an image, okay? I'll scan it and email it right over. I know I've seen it before but I can't place it. It's of ancient origin. Thanks, luv! Call me back at this number, okay?" She clicked off the phone and spoke to Rafe. "We've helped each other out from time to time. He is head of archeology at the Maritime Museum in Barcelona. I know he will be able to tell us what this is." She placed the image Rafe had drawn on the scanner and hit the button. The device began to hum. Shortly after, she logged in to her email from Rafe's computer and fired off the image. "Now we just wait!"

"Should I be jealous?" *Because strangely I am.*

"I'm not even going to answer that," she responded with a smile.

Embarrassed for asking, Rafe changed the subject. "So tell me more about your work."

"I have been studying archeology at Sapienza in Rome for some time now. There is always another class to take. I've focused on Roman society. It's quite fascinating. Several months ago, I was asked to give a speech on the subject at a diplomatic event in Rome. I have some contacts in the corpo diplomatic, and they were having an event, so they asked me to speak. I thoroughly enjoyed it. Since then, I've received multiple invitations. My talk is on why Rome collapsed. I'm even going to be paid for my next speech in Florence in a few weeks. It seems I've found my calling."

"Then I guess you won't have to hit up strange men in St. Mark's Square?" He regretted saying it right after the words left his mouth. He could see the look of shame sweep over her face.

"Hey a girl's got to survive, right? Anyway, I don't see you complaining. It takes two to tango."

"You're right. As I said, I'm not judging." There was an awkward silence between them. The phone rang unexpectedly and loudly, thankfully shattering the uncomfortable moment.

Cecilia answered. "Pronto, aaah Fernando, let me put you on speaker phone, okay? And speak English? I have a friend here as well." She placed the phone on the rickety table after hitting the speaker button.

"Where did you find this?" asked Fernando.

"Let's just say we found it in Venice," Cecilia responded.

"Well, I would like to know more at some point about where. It's a symbol of an ancient religion that we don't know much of anything about. It was very secret. It's called Mythraism. We do know it was mostly contained within the Roman legions. It seems they built underground temples wherever they garrisoned. The origins of the religion are unknown. There is some evidence that links it back to a god worshipped in Persia thousands of years ago, but the links are not definite or clear and mostly theory. There are a few symbols associated with this movement. This is one of them. The other primary one you see consistently is a statue of a soldier slaying a bull with a spear. Beyond that, we know nothing."

"But why would we find it here in Venice?"

"That's a good question, as Rome was long gone when Venice was built—that's why I want to know more. But today is your lucky day. I suggest you come to Barcelona. We've been doing some more excavation under the naval dockyards here in part of the museum space. We've found more of the old Roman city of Barcinoi. I suggest you come here and look immediately."

"But why do we need to do that?" she asked. "Can't you just tell us what you've found?"

"Because day after tomorrow, we are opening a two-thousand-year-old, underground temple we believe to be Mythraic."

After buying the plane tickets rather quickly, Rafe found himself leading Cecilia into the Venice evening to find a quaint, out-of-the-way restaurant for the evening meal. They made small talk for a while, enjoying a fine bottle of Pinot Noir and reveling in the discreet privacy of the small establishment. The place was tucked into the side of a fifteenth-century military structure; previously the area had been used as an armory or something of that sort. It was perched about ten meters above the canal below and the associated walkway beside it. It was one of Rafe's favorites. He had stumbled upon it rather accidently one day while wandering around the city. It was quite remarkable he had found his way back so easily, as it had been weeks ago. Cecilia was enchanted.

"You are full of surprises!" she gushed. "This place is marvelous."

"Yes, I thought you'd like it."

"So you never answered my question."

"What question was that?"

"Why are you alone?"

Rafe said nothing for a while then spoke. "It's a long story."

"We've got all night."

"I'm divorced. My ex-wife and I got married rather quickly. You see it was the great sex and all. Four months. Can you believe that? I was living high on Wall Street and she was my goddess. I was her hero. We turned out to be neither. Anyway, right after we were married, one evening, she became really violent. She totally changed. It was as if she wanted to get married quickly to not let me know what she was really like. It was scary. I mean like glazed-over eyes, talking in tongues kind of scary. Really dangerous stuff. I had no idea what to do. I was taught growing up you never hit a woman. But she was physically, emotionally, verbally, you name it, out of control abusive. It got worse and worse. And I took it. I took it for years. A year later, our first child was born. That was interesting, since the sex had stopped completely after we tied the knot, except for the occasional roll in the hay once a year. Anyway, things went downhill even more after that. I tried to keep her happy but it was no use. She was unhappy inside. Only later did I find out about the abuse she suffered as a child. Well, some years later we had another child, trying to put a happy face on this disaster, but it ended anyway. The divorce was final six months or so ago. I was literally exhausted. I needed a break. So here I am."

"Quite the story. I'm sorry for you."

"Don't be, as I told you, I'm the happiest I've ever been in my life. I wake up with a smile on my face every day. When you've been through what I've been through, to have a chance at a somewhat normal life is breathtaking. And, I have my kids. They are my sun, my light. I cherish them. My little girl is only four years old. She is a blessing."

"Do you miss them?"

"Of course, I talk to them almost every day, but this sabbatical has done wonders for me. I'm a new man. So, what about you? No boyfriend, sugar daddy?"

"Oh, there have been a few, but no one special right now. I dated a member of parliament for a couple years, went to all of the fancy parties and official events. But it got boring after a while. It was all about him, not about me. So I broke it off. Now I just focus on my career and traveling, when I can."

Rafe's phone rang. "Hello?" he answered.

"Hi, Daddee!"

"Hello, my little princess, how are you today? I miss you very much!"

"Daddy, I learned a fun song at school today. Do you want to hear it?"

"Yes, of course, my darling." Rafe listened as his daughter sang Twinkle Twinkle Little Star. His heart melted.

Chapter Three

As the Airbus jet approached Barcelona, Rafe stared out of the aircraft window, lost in thought. He vaguely noticed the hills surrounding the ancient city as the aircraft started its approach. The topography was striking, as the highlands were covered in a dark green whereas all the land below them was a drab brown. The affect was mesmerizing and reminded him of a camouflage paint job on a tank. He awoke from his trance when startled by the bump of the landing gear being lowered and the flight attendants preparing for landing. His thoughts returned to the present.

After taxiing for what seemed like an eternity, Rafe and Cecilia finally walked off the jetway into an opulent, modern airport rebuilt to showcase the Olympics several years back. The addition of the new Terminal 1 in 2009 expanded the facility even further. The floors and glass walls were gleaming, and the duty-free shopping and other amenities were somewhat overwhelming. Cecilia resisted the temptation to browse the shoe stores as they walked past. Rafe found himself comparing it to the third world infrastructure of NYC and was embarrassed. Eventually they made their way out of the airport, bypassing customs and immigration, as they were still inside the European Union. They found the car the museum had sent waiting outside the terminal. The thirty-minute ride went by fast as they drove towards the sea and the old city. The vegetation had changed radically from Italy and was more barren and drab, almost like a desert.

As they entered the center of the metropolis, Rafe marveled at the cleanliness and order of Barcelona. It thrived with an energy of youth, art, and design. He concluded it was a special place, a place he had not yet visited. They passed through the Eixample—the modern district—where the dreamy creations of Gaudi and other artists were on full display. Soon they were driving slowly down the Rambla, the main boulevard leading to the water and the old shipbuilding port. Eventually, after dodging thousands of people idling their way to the sea, they arrived at the water and could drive no more. The monument to Christopher Columbus' likeness adorned the roundabout in front of them. Here, he had told the Spanish monarchy of the New World. And from here, the Spanish monarchy projected power around the globe as one of the first truly global empires before succumbing to the financial burden of supporting its far-off colonies and financing multiple wars around the globe.

The car pulled into a garage behind the old naval dockyards to the right, which now housed the museum. Fernando bounded out to meet them.

"Hello hello, my friends. Thanks for coming! I didn't think you should miss this! I've got lunch waiting for you inside in my office. Then we will get to the festivities! Welcome!" He kissed Cece on both cheeks in a little too friendly of an embrace. Rafe felt himself slightly annoyed. *Where is that feeling coming from? You hardly know her.*

Barcelona had been the maritime center of the Spanish Empire back in the day. In the reign of King Ferdinand and Queen Isabella, and in the heyday of Christopher Columbus, thirty galleys a year were hewn and built here next to the Mediterranean to buttress the sea power of the magnificent Spanish fleet. The site of the facility built to house this construction had long ago been relegated to other purposes, such as artillery storage for the Spanish Army. However, with the coming of democracy in the late twentieth century, the army gave the dockyards back to the city. Only then did the excavations begin and the researchers realized what they had—not only fifteenth-century dockyards but much more lay underneath.

The city of Barcino was a Roman colony two millennium ago. Soldiers who were too old to fight the far-flung battles of the empire settled there. Spain was an important colony of Rome and provided food, olive oil, wine, and metal to the rest of Roman civilization before being overrun by the Germanic tribes as the Western Roman Empire deteriorated. However, the impact of Roman society on the Iberian Peninsula was enduring.

The old Roman city was a strategic trading port on the Mediterranean, existing underneath the foundation of the follow-on empires, undisturbed. Slowly, it was being rediscovered. The museum now boasted open-air pits in the stone floor scattered among the fine specimens of maritime history, allowing visitors to view recently found remnants of lost Rome.

Fernando led them into a conference room near his office, and they enjoyed a variety of tapas brought in from a local restaurant. Shrimp, Greek salad, cheese, ham, olives, and other appetizers adorned the table. Rafe was quite enjoying himself, as the conversation was entertaining and stimulating. Everything was washed down with a pleasant bottle of Rioja, which made him extra happy.

After Cecilia and Fernando exchanged discussions about their various research projects for another twenty minutes, Fernando abruptly changed the subject. "Okay, my friends. Let's get on with the business of the day." He got up from the table, and Rafe and Cece followed. He led them into the open expanse of the museum. Rafe immediately noticed a reconstructed copy of a galley that was the centerpiece of the current exhibition on Spanish sea power. It was massive and took up the majority of the open hall. Cecilia and Rafe followed Fernando around the vessel to a far corner of the monstrous, covered ship construction facility, and there they found a makeshift set of wooden stairs heading down into the cavern below that had been recently excavated. Slowly they negotiated the wooden staircase and entered a small space that had been carved out of the soil. There etched in the dirt on the far wall was the outline of an arched entranceway. The copper door was still attached and had blocked the outside elements for two thousand years. On the face of the door was a man with the head of a lion, a serpent wrapped around his body, with the head of the snake resting on the lion's mane. The figure held two keys, and his mouth was open in a terrifying pose.

The image was similar to the one Rafe had seen below water and sketched for Cecilia. He was mesmerized by the engraving, drawn to it. The face of the lion seemed to be looking directly at him, beckoning him. Cecilia waved her hand in front of his face to get his attention. "Rafe?" she asked. "Are you with us?" He had to tear his gaze away from the image.

"Yes," he responded. "Let's see what's in there."

The ancient hinges supporting the door were in fairly good condition, and it was obvious nothing had been disturbed. The copper had turned almost a pastel blue over the centuries. The soil was still packed into the cracks around the door as an earthly seal. Fernando motioned to his workers, and they appeared with a satchel of small tools in order to pry open the lock. After around thirty minutes of delicate work, the metal gave way easily, and the ancient chamber was ready to be opened.

"Are you ready?" asked Fernando. "After this, I want you to tell me where you found the image. It's your price of entry," he said with a smile. He pushed on the door. It swung forward elegantly. They peered inside. The height of the doorway was rather small, as humans were much shorter back then. Cecilia was amazed at what she saw.

There was a long alleyway down the middle of the small room. Stone benches were attached on each side against the wall. At the opposite end of the table, between the benches, there was an altar. Above was a large image of a man riding a horse and slaying a bull. On the walls of the rectangular room were all types of other images of battles and of strange creatures. It would take years to discern all of the data they could claim from this find. Fernando and Cecilia were overjoyed and beside themselves with excitement. She turned to Rafe with elation in her eyes, but it was short-lived. Rafe was staring at the altar. A look of horror gripped his face. On the altar under the image of the bull was a small frame. It was leaning against the wall facing them. Inside the frame was a picture of his four-year-old daughter, Clare.

Cecilia looked at where Rafe was staring. "That's my daughter!" he shouted. "Who put that there? Is this some kind of trick? Who are you people?" He waited for a response. Cecilia and Fernando were too shocked to offer one. They said nothing. Rafe went to the altar, grabbed the picture, looked at it with fear, and then left the vault, not caring about the ancient artifacts surrounding him.

They had been down in the excavation site for almost an hour now, and Rafe had no cell reception. He bounded up the stairs and made his way toward the exit of the museum; he had to call his daughter. His phone began buzzing insistently in his pocket as the coverage connected. He looked at the screen, there were a dozen missed calls. They were from his ex-wife. His heart sunk. Rafe dialed.

41

"Melanie, it's me."

His ex shrieked into the phone. "She's gone! She's gone! They took her! It's all your fault!"

"What are you talking about?" queried Rafe. But he knew in the depths of his heart she was gone.

"It's Clare, she's gone, you son of a bitch! It's all your fault!"

"Melanie, calm down and tell me what happened!"

There was a pause on the phone. Rafe waited. "I was at home and it was a nice day. I let her go play in the backyard. Then my friend Rachel called, and I started talking to her for a while. Then when I hung up, I looked in the backyard and she was gone. The police have been here for over an hour. Like I said, it's all your fault, you son of a bitch!"

Rafe ignored as usual the accusations coming from left field. He was used to her deflecting blame. "How long were you on the phone?"

"Only about an hour." Rafe winced. Panic welled up inside him.

"My angel," he muttered to himself. "Let me talk to the police. I'm coming back to the States immediately."

After a short conversation with the police detective at his former home, Rafe bounded back inside to the excavation site. Fernando and Cecilia were coming up the ladder and entering the main museum floor.

"What have you done with her!" he demanded. Again they looked shocked.

"What are you talking about, Rafe?" asked Fernando.

"My daughter, she's missing. And coincidently I find her picture in this tomb of yours that supposedly hasn't been opened for two thousand years. A little hard to freakin' believe, don't you think?" He grabbed Fernando by the throat and threw him into the wall. "Where the fuck is she?" he screamed, his face an inch from Fernando's.

Cecilia pulled him off of Fernando, grabbed both his shoulders, and looked him in the eyes. "Rafe, I don't know what's going on, but I can tell you Fernando has nothing to do with it. I have known him for years and he is a good person. Do you understand me? Now let's go back to the conference room and talk this through so we can figure out a way to help you and decide on the best course of action. Okay?"

Rafe was shaking with worry and fright. The police knew nothing. Cecilia tried to comfort him. How could he go back to the States after what had happened here? Who could he trust? What the hell was going on? Fernando had brought out a bottle of whiskey to help calm his nerves. Rafe downed a few shots, felt a little better, and tried to think. Finally he looked sternly at Fernando and spoke.

"How did her picture get in there?"

"Honestly, Rafe, I have no idea. That vault has not been opened for two thousand years. You saw the hinges and the lock. They were too fragile to be opened, shut, and opened again. I don't know what to tell you. I'm baffled."

"Someone is playing a trick on me. A horrible trick. I've got to figure it out." They all fell quiet until Fernando broke the silence.

"Tell me about the discovery of the image. Where did you find it?"

Rafe recounted the story. Fernando listened and finally spoke. "You've been chosen."

"What do you mean, chosen?" asked Rafe incredulously.

"It seems pretty obvious to me. I've studied this religion for years, and there is not much known about it. But it does seem that individuals were *invited* into it. Otherwise, no one knew it existed. That's why the temples are all underground. It seems to me, someone at least wants you to *think* you were chosen."

"But what does this have to do with my daughter?" asked Rafe angrily.

Cecilia spoke, "Well, I say we all try and figure this out. However, I'm not sure where to start."

"Tell me about this god they worship," said Rafe quietly.

"That's the thing," started Fernando. "No one knows much about this religion. It's all speculation. It's considered a mystery religion because, as I mentioned, you had to be asked to join. Everything was done in secret. It is believed by some that the Roman Mythraic god stems from the pre-Zoastrian god Mithra. Mithra was the god of contracts, the god of the sun, the god of good things. In fact, they believed Mithra could provide salvation. Others believe the god is related to a demon worshiped in Persia thousands of years ago. The one thing we are sure of is that Roman Mythraism competed with Christianity in its first few hundred years, until Emperor Constantine allowed Christianity to become the dominant religion in Rome." Fernando paused for a moment and then continued. "We also know there were seven stages of enlightenment. Each phase had its own symbols. Again, we are mostly guessing what it all means because nothing was written down. The one remnant of Roman Mythraism that you can see and touch today is the underground temples. There are hundreds if not thousands of them spread around the former empire, wherever the legions lived. The religion flourished primarily among the soldiers and diplomatic personnel."

Rafe could only think about his daughter. "I've got to get some fresh air and think." He left the room alone and walked out into the warm night air, his soul tormented with anguish.

Rafe walked along the Rambla in a trance. The street was the connection from the shipyards to the city hundreds of years ago during the height of the Spanish empire. It was a wide pedestrian walkway lined with artisans and cafes. In one section of the thoroughfare, in front of the old pubs, one could actually see holes in the concrete that the prostitutes had worn into the pavement with their high heels, waiting on the sailors coming off the ships.

His angel had been kidnapped. He didn't notice any of the people walking around him. The tourists and the locals mingled together. The cafes and restaurants were humming with business, but he didn't notice. He kept walking. Sometime later he was halfway up the wide pedestrian corridor towards the Plaza de Catalonia when he realized he was outside the Boqueria Market. The open-air market had its beginnings a thousand years prior as an outdoor straw market near the gate to the old city. Today, the market was a planned facility showcasing all types of local food merchants. As the evening set in, the market was full of tourists and local buyers alike trying to decide amongst the dazzling array of food. There were vegetable stands teeming with fresh produce, chocolate venders, pastries, fresh seafood, butchers, and small stands selling various types of prepared dishes. He could barely make his way down the open corridors and much less get the attention of the shop merchants. It was a madhouse and had probably been this way for over a thousand years. Rafe decided to wander in. He was not sure why.

He strolled among the throng of people in a daze. The smells of all the different foods washed over him. However, his thoughts were on Clare. *Why had someone taken her? Was it for ransom?* He couldn't even imagine any more sinister reasons. He became angry and started to panic.

Someone has taken my daughter. I'm going to find them, and kill them.

Rafe stopped in the middle of a back corridor; the smell of fresh-cut fish hovered around him, and he realized he was in the middle of the seafood part of the market. Middle-aged women were picking up large, uncut salmon and other species, looking them over for a possible trip home for dinner. At that moment,

Rafe achieved a clarity of purpose. He had to get his act together so he could help his daughter. He had to be strong. God knows, his ex was not going to be. *Should I go back to the States? But something is going on here. I can feel it. The answer is here. For some strange reason, I'm supposed to be here in Barcelona. I was supposed to find the picture. Yes, I'm being chosen. But for what?*

Rafe turned and made his way back to the front of the market towards the exit to the Rambla. As he exited the throng of shoppers, he noticed the street was full of people watching the performance from the sex museum on the balcony above—a Marilyn Monroe look-alike was entertaining the crowd below, flashing her eyelashes and allowing them to look up her dress. Except one person was not watching. Rafe saw a handsome, well-dressed man looking at him from across the wide expanse of the pedestrian walkway. He wore a stylish, black, Spanish-looking leather coat and boots. There was a rugged strength about him. Even in the dim light he could tell he was staring at him. It was if he and Rafe were the only two people in the whole world. The roar of the crowd was silenced around him. It was eerie, and he felt a chill go down his spine. The man was in his late fifties with salt-and-pepper hair and piercing, green eyes, which were drilling right through him. Rafe felt cold. *He knows something. He knows about Clare!* Rafe took a chance and broke into a sprint toward the man, rage etched in his face. The man saw his rapid movement, turned to melt into the crowd, and disappeared. Rafe gave chase and quickly reacquired him running down one of the side streets that made its way back to the plaza to the north.

"Stop!" yelled Rafe. The man turned his head and then darted onto another side street. Rafe followed, running furiously, closing on him slowly. The crowd moved away from the center of the alley to provide him room as he ran. He could see the man's black coat flapping behind him as he furiously tried to get away. The man turned right around a corner, entered another wide plaza, and disappeared from view, but not before something fell from his coat pocket as he turned.

Rafe reached the place where he had entered the plaza and looked around. The man was nowhere to be found. The plaza was empty. He was gone. Dejected, Rafe continued to search the side streets of the square but finally returned to where they had entered the plaza. The wind had blown the piece of paper the man dropped towards an open pit in the center of the expansive space. The paper was dangerously close to being blown in the pit, which was surrounded by a wrought iron fence. Rafe then realized the pit was the excavation of the ancient Roman acropolis from the old city of Barcino. The tombs were now illuminated by a faint glow of man-made lights. The effect was ghoulish. He could make out the Roman writing on the gravestones. He reached down to pick up what had dropped from the man's pocket. It was a tourist map of Rome.

Chapter Four

Rafe walked quickly back down the Rambla towards the Maritime Museum. He noticed no one. He didn't care about anyone else. He was only concerned with Clare. *How could this happen?* He remembered her sitting in his lap when she was about two years old, clinging to him like a refugee. He was her world and she was his. *I will not allow anything to happen to her.* His anger turned to something darker, something more Machiavellian. *I could easily kill someone for this!*

He was jerked back to the present. *What to do?* One thing he was certain of, the man was trying to tell him something. He wanted Rafe to see him and follow him. *Is it the map?* Rafe took the folded-up map out of his pocket. It was the kind of map you get free at a hotel, printed on cheap paper that was already worn and tearing at the folded seams. It seemed as though soon it would turn to dust. He stopped at a café, sat down, and ordered a glass of wine to calm his nerves. He put the map on the table, so it was bathed in light, to discern what he was supposed to realize.

The paper had been folded so as to highlight a certain part of the ancient Roman city, the Foro Romano. The Forum was the center of Rome, where all the legal, judicial, and political events and decisions took place. The Coliseum stood massively tall outside its perimeter. The Forum had been lost to the ages until excavated by an English archeologist named Edward Gibbon in the eighteenth century. He then proceeded to write the classic series *The Decline and Fall of the Roman Empire*. Although now in a state of ruin, visitors could still see the columns and remnants of the temples and buildings. It was quite a magnificent place. Rafe had been there once as a child.

He looked closer at the map and noticed that it had been folded to highlight one certain place in the ancient metropolis. It was now directly in the center of the folded square. It was the Circus Maximus.

Three hours later, after some time to think at the café and another stroll through the pedestrian walkway, Rafe returned to the museum, which had long since closed. Fernando had left the main doors open, and he and Cecilia sat inside near the ticket counter, sharing a bottle of wine. The light was retreating from the day as the sun started to set. They stood as he finally entered.

Cecilia spoke first. "Are you okay?"

"No I'm definitely not okay!"

"What can we do?" she added.

Fernando spoke, "Rafe, I understand your anger and frustration; however, you have to understand that we have no idea how this happened. It is a mystery to us as well. That being said, I can speak for the museum staff that we will do everything in our power to help you. Our resources are at your disposal. I can feel your anguish and it pains me greatly. I cannot imagine losing a daughter, as I have two myself."

The fight had gone out of Rafe. He was tired with grief. "She is not lost. She is just misplaced. And thank you for your offer. I will let you know if I need you. However, right now, you can tell me all you know about this place." He put the map on the ticket counter and pointed to the place that was obviously highlighted.

Cecilia responded. "It's the Circus Maximus. It was used for sporting events in the old city throughout the ages. Eventually, the Coliseum overtook it for popularity, but chariot races were held there until the fall of Rome. It's a wonderful arena hewn into the hillside overlooking the Forum, a massive structure. It's complete with its own set of tunnels, caverns, vaults, and temples constructed to support the area. It's a fascinating place."

"Well I'm going there," said Rafe.

"Why? Where did you get this?" asked Cecilia incredulously.

"Let's just say someone wants me to go there." Cecilia stared at him, not understanding.

Fernando spoke, "There is a Mythraim there. It's in an underground cavern under the arena. The public is not allowed to access the temple. It is closed off."

"Funny, what a coincidence," Rafe quipped.

"I'm going with you," declared Cecilia.

"Suit yourself," said Rafe, his voice full of distrust.

Rafe stared at Cecilia, who was sleeping soundly on the hotel bed. They had found a room for the night at a local establishment. Rafe could hear the tourist crowd still partying on the Rambla below with the usual crowd of locals, even though it was well into the early morning hours. He could not sleep. It seemed Barcelona couldn't sleep as well.

He had learned everything he could online about the Circus Maximus. The only thing to do now was to go there. There were no flights to Italy until early the next morning.

He decided to call his ex-wife for an update on Clare's disappearance.

"So you're not even coming back to help me, you fucker? I'm gonna kill you, or better yet my dad's gonna kill you! How dare you leave me here to take care of this? Of course, that's par for the course, I took care of everything, you loser! Fuck you!" She hung up the phone after at least telling him there was no more news and the police had no leads. Rafe thanked the stars again he was no longer in that relationship. He stared out the window towards the old city of Barcino, wondering how that ancient time could be connected to him now and the disappearance of his daughter. Nothing came to him.

So, he then booked two tickets online to Rome from Barcelona the next morning. All of a sudden, he was very tired. Rafe stripped down to his underwear and slid into bed beside Cecilia. She slid close to him and put her arms around him. "We'll find her," she said softly as she drifted back to sleep. Rafe lay awake for an eternity until finally drifting off from exhaustion, only to be awakened by the alarm on his phone a few hours later.

The flight to Rome was uneventful. Rafe had no idea what he was doing or why. He only knew that he was sure it was the right thing to do. Someone wanted him here, he was confident of that, someone who wanted to tell him about Clare. The anxiety he felt was overwhelming. She was so young and helpless. She needed him and he couldn't find her. He was letting her down. Slowly his anxiety turned to rage. *I'm coming, my angel. Just tell me where you are somehow!*

Rafe was jerked back to reality as the plane thudded onto the runway. Soon they were in a taxi headed into the old city. Rome was like any modern urban area; the sprawl emanated out from the original outline of the planned community. Rome had an uneasy relationship with the northern city of Milan. She had a reputation of living off the efforts and hard work of the northern Italians. The financial muscle of Milan and her fashion credentials stood in contrast to the decaying economy of Rome. Many of the people in the city lived off the government dole.

The taxi left them outside the ticket booth for the Foro Romano. They were able to buy tickets quickly, as there was no line; it was late in the day. "It's only open for one more hour," explained the ticket agent. "Are you sure you don't want to come back tomorrow? There is a lot to see and one hour is not much time."

"Yes, we're sure," Rafe replied. The middle-aged woman rolled her eyes, took his credit card, and handed him the tickets. She had tried to warn the foreigner.

They entered the fenced-in area and made a left to go up towards Palatine Hill and the expansion of the old city, which emanated from the Forum. As the centuries had progressed, wealthy Romans built more and more palaces expanding out from the center of the metropolis. The Circus Maximus was one of these projects that sat on the far end of the plateau. It took about fifteen minutes of walking to get there. Both of them had broken a sweat in the late day heat.

They arrived on the southeastern edge of the arena and gazed out over the open, sunken space. It was an oblong-shaped course surrounded by a stone wall rising on all sides. In the center were old statues and gardens, where the emperor's guests had sat and enjoyed the festivities while watching whatever sporting event was taking place. An oval track followed just inside the curved walls.

Rafe pulled out his map and found the directions he had drawn to the Mythraim, courtesy of Fernando. They found the stone stairway down the western wall and retreated down into the catacombs of the facility. Soon they were immersed in a labyrinth of tunnels and underground spaces that supported the arena. Slaves had worked here tirelessly to supply the food, water, and other commodities needed to entertain the festivities above. They worked their way through the labyrinth, following the tourist map, and finally arrived at a passageway, which was marked for the Mythraim. They could go no farther. The passageway was blocked with a wrought iron gate. A sign in Italian read *Do Not Enter, For Official Personnel Only!*

The light from the setting sun was growing faint as the day was winding down. Rafe tried to see past the gate but it was no use, since it was not lit. He looked at the lock and made a plan on the spot. "We're coming back tonight," he told Cecilia then turned to leave.

"Whatever you say. How are you going to get in?"

"Leave that to me," Rafe said commandingly.

They arrived by taxi to their new hotel a few kilometers north of the Coliseum. Rafe immediately left to find a store to buy supplies. He returned an hour later with a crowbar and a small, battery-operated drill and an attachment—a metal saw bit. He also had two small penlights with green light filters installed. He was ready. He began placing the items in his pockets. "Now we wait," he told Cecilia. He turned on the TV to an American news channel and went into the small kitchenette to make some coffee. It was going to be a long night. He could hear the anchorwoman spreading the dreary news of the day from North America. He walked back into the bedroom, where Cecilia was napping on the bed. Rafe could make out her shapely body under the sheet. *No!* he thought to himself. *Not until I find Clare.* His sexual appetite was gone.

The anchorwoman droned on. *Americans on food stamps hit sixty*

55

million this month; government disability payments are also rising to record rates.
Unbelievable, thought Rafe as he carefully poured his espresso.

Hours later, Rafe and Cecilia exited the metro several blocks from the Coliseum. The sun had set hours ago and the moon was high in the sky, providing an amount of natural light bright enough to allow them to proceed on foot to the fenced-in area of the Foro Romano. Upon arrival, Rafe scanned the area for the darkest portion of the metal barrier. He had perused the entire area before they had previously left and searched out the location of the security guards watching the complex. There was a new shift in place, but they stood in approximately the same place.

They made their way to the space between the floodlights on the eastern side of the restricted grounds. Here they could operate without fear of discovery. Rafe quietly moved a trash receptacle towards the fence and motioned for Cecilia to stand on the can. He pushed her from below over the wrought iron section of the barrier. She landed on her feet with a thud. He quickly followed. They had entered undetected.

Quickly the two intruders melted into the foliage-covered portion of the hill and oriented themselves to the land. Rafe was basically operating on memory as he guided her to the Circus Maximus. Upon reaching the site, they detoured around to the eastern wall where the catacombs were located. Rafe switched on the small, green penlight to read the guideposts and confirmed their location. After retracing their steps from earlier in the day, they soon arrived at the entrance to the channel to the Mythraim. They were completely alone. Everything was quiet.

Rafe pulled out the small drill, mounted the saw bit, and proceeded to attack the flange holding the lock on the gate. He reasoned the lock would be made of steel and impossible to cut. That was not the case with the old iron gate. Cecilia held the filtered penlight to provide illumination as Rafe worked. After almost twenty minutes of using the small circular saw, the metal gave way. The door swung open. They stealthily stepped into the darkened corridor.

The passageway led downward into the earth, and Rafe could feel the temperature drop as they descended slowly, guided by the light of the penlight. The green light produced an eerie glow, which bounced off the stone walls, bathing them both in an unnatural color. Eventually they reached the end of the tunnel. There, waiting on them, was a copper door, long turned green by the air, which served for the opening to the Mythraim. It had been recently disturbed and was slightly ajar. Rafe looked at Cecilia and then slowly pulled open the door, not knowing what to expect. He shined the penlight forward.

The temple was very similar to the one he had seen in Barcelona. It was bigger and more ornate but basically the same. It was an elongated, rectangular space with a long, single, stone bench and table running the length of both sides and facing the long wall. There was an altar at the far end with a stone etching of a soldier riding and slaying a bull above the stone. There were no pictures of his daughter or anything else he recognized; however, there was something on each table. There were baskets and stone pottery along each wall, as if there had recently been a feast. Rafe walked over to the baskets and peered inside. There was food, bread, fruit, and water in the pottery. Rafe touched the bread in one of the baskets. It was fresh and warm. Plates of half-eaten portions dotted the waiste-high slab.

Rafe and Cecilia searched the Mythraim for any other evidence but found nothing. Rafe was frustrated, time was slipping away. Who knows where his Clare could be by now. "I know I was supposed to be here! Someone just had a feast here! I don't get it!"

"Well there's nothing here that indicates anything about Clare."

"Let's go search around, maybe we will find something, or someone." They headed back down the darkened corridor and left the passageway into the moonlit night. Rafe doused the penlight, threw the saw and crowbar down the embankment far away from them, and followed the signs to the Circus Maximus.

As they silently crept closer, Cecilia grabbed Rafe's shoulder, stopping him, and whispered, "Listen!" From far above they could hear a mumbling noise. "It sounds like a chant of some kind," she said.

"Yes I hear it too. Let's go!" Slowly they made their way up the twisting and turning paths to the top of the hillside. The chant became louder and louder. Finally they broke onto the surface and carefully snuck up to the opening to the arena. The sound was loud now. They were exposed against the moonlight.

"Holy shit!" whispered Cecilia. Torches were placed in a circular pattern around a platform in the middle of the arena down below. Surrounding the torches were at least one hundred people dressed in white, hooded robes. They were mumbling some kind of chant. On the platform was a hooded figure in a black robe. He had a stone altar in front of him and held a long knife, which glinted in the dancing light of the torches. Rafe could not make out the person's face. There was a live animal on the altar with all four legs bound together. It looked like a baby goat and was baying loudly with fear, trying to move unsuccessfully. The chanting became louder as the tension mounted. The dark, hooded figure held the knife with both hands and raised the blade high in the air above the animal. The chanting increased with a crescendo of expectation. The white-robed figures in the audience waved fists in the air and chanted even louder, demanding consummation of the sacrifice. The dark, hooded figure plunged the knife into the animal, which screamed and then became silent. Blood spurted upward and splashed the executioner's dark robe with red splotches. The crowd erupted with delight and raised their fists in the air with satisfaction. Rafe felt sick to his stomach. He thought of Clare. *No!* he said to himself.

"I'm going down there," he declared.

"Are you kidding? You'll get killed yourself!" replied Cecilia.

"I don't care. My daughter is here somewhere. I'm not going to let this happen to her. You stay here and get help if something happens to me. Don't move unless you have to. If something bad goes down and we get split up, I'll meet you at the hotel if I can. If I'm not there in twenty-four hours, go home and forget about me."

"I'm not forgetting about you and I'll be here when you return." Cecilia slinked away into the shadows.

Rafe glanced around the arena below the ledge. He saw small spaces carved into the sides, which were used to store food or other commodities two thousand years ago. He then noticed a man in business clothes arrive in the arena from the northwestern end and enter one of the spaces carved into the earth. He emerged a moment later clothed in a white robe. "I'm going there first!" Rafe declared as he pointed in the direction of the cave.

"Good luck!" whispered Cecilia from her place of concealment.

Rafe crept down the stone staircase at the far end of the arena and blended into the shadows created by the bright full moon above. He stayed in the darkened recesses of the space along the far wall and slowly made his way to where he saw the man exit in the robe. Finally arriving, he peeked into the cave-like area. The ceremony in the middle of the Circus Maximus was going on as fierce as ever, as another animal had been brought out for the slaughter and the chanting again became louder. The animal screamed in fear, it's eyes wide with terror.

Inside the cavern were multiple white robes hanging from a rod attached at both ends of the ceiling. Rafe was alone and walked in as if he belonged and slipped into one of the robes. He emerged from the cavern looking exactly like the other participants in this dark charade. Rafe desperately wanted to get a look at who was

60

in the black robe on the platform. He had to get something out of this crazy trip to this cradle of history. He had to find his daughter no matter the risk to himself. Soon he was blended into the crowd as the chanting became louder and louder. The dark-robed figure again raised the blade high in the air over the bound, screaming animal. The knife was plunged into the heart of the beast, who screamed louder in pain. After the animal quit moving, the shadowy figure became perfectly still and eventually reached her hands up to the hood covering her head. She slowly pulled the hood down, revealing her face. Rafe was mesmerized, as she was very beautiful. He felt as if he recognized her in some way. At that moment, the crowd became deathly quiet. She stared directly at Rafe. She pointed at him and beckoned her hands toward herself, as if she wanted him to come onto the altar. The entire white-robed crowd turned to look at him. "Come to me, join us!" she said softly to Rafe as he stood there exposed and filled with anxiety. The Circus Maximus became very quiet and still.

Rafe froze then spoke, "Who are you and where is my daughter?" he demanded.

Before she could answer, someone in the crowd pointed to the ledge where Cecilia was highlighted in the moonlight as she strained to hear what was happening in the Circus Maximus below. She was discovered.

The woman on the altar looked upwards and saw her. "Seize her!" she ordered.

"Run!" Rafe called out to Cecilia as he pulled off the robe and sprinted from the gathering towards the stone stairs leading up to the edge of the arena.

Cecilia darted from the precipice towards the trails to the catacombs below.

Rafe had somewhat of a head start towards the staircase and managed to reach to the platform leading away from the arena before the robed figures following him could stop his progress. One hand grabbed his ankle as he reached the top and he fell. Kicking violently, he was able to free himself from his assailant and knocked the robed figure down into the other sacrifice participants who were climbing the stairs as well. They were entangled in each other's robes, and the brief respite gave Rafe time to lose himself in the trails below to the labyrinth of tunnels.

Since he and Cecilia had just been in the area, he remembered the way off Palatine Hill. Upon seeing him approach, Cecilia left her hiding place and joined him as he sprinted down towards the gate. Suddenly he stopped and turned towards her. "They will be waiting for us there. We need to lose ourselves for a while somewhere else. Follow me!"

Rafe made a left turn as they neared the gate area, and quickly they found themselves in the middle of the ancient Forum itself. They kept running past the Temple of Vesta toward the Temple of Saturn. As they neared the old riverbed where Rome began, Rafe turned quickly to the left and ducked into a stone altar of some sort and hid behind a waist-high bench that looked like a kitchen island surrounded by a stone wall. There were piles of cut flowers that reached to his shoulders thrown all around the area. Rafe motioned to Cecilia, and they ducked under the stone pedestal and pulled the flowers around them for concealment.

Once their hearts had stopped pounding, Rafe listened in the stillness for any followers. He could hear none. "We need to stay here a while. I'm sure they are searching for us," he stated. The moon shone above like a searchlight, illuminating their location.

"I'm sorry, Rafe, tell me about your daughter," Cecilia whispered.

"Later maybe, not now. I still don't even know you. We'll wait here a couple hours and then leave from the other direction towards the opposite gate."

"You can trust me, really. Do you know why all of these flowers are here?" she asked innocently.

"Yes. This is a shrine. This stone table above us is where they burned Julius Caesar's body after he was assassinated."

Chapter Five

Rafe and Cecilia arrived back at the hotel late the next morning after silently sneaking out of the historic, controlled area before dawn. Rome was still awake, but the police were more concerned with rowdy, late-night partiers that guarding the Roman Forum. Unable to hail a taxi at that hour, they walked the two kilometers back to the lodging sector, dodging the occasional gang of revelers staggering from the bars. Finally they were able to relax after a tense time in the Foro Romano. Rafe locked the hotel room door, and they climbed into bed to get some rest. Neither one of them had slept much the previous evening, being worried about their assailants finding them and about what was happening to Clare. Sleep came easy for both. However, Rafe woke up several hours later, his dreams having been filled with sacrifices and the face of his daughter. He couldn't bear to go there. That was not going to happen to Clare. He sat up in bed and glanced nervously out the window into the street. Everything looked normal, though he knew that was not the case. *At least there are no people in hooded robes out in the street waiting for me.* Cecilia was fast asleep. *Let her sleep,* he thought. *I honestly don't know what to do,* he admitted to himself. *I'm*

64

at a complete loss and don't know where to turn. I need to speak to someone I can trust, but who? Rafe pondered who he would call, all the while knowing who that person would be.

Rafe continued to gaze out the window for a long while, his mind spinning. Eventually he closed the curtain, picked up his phone, and dialed a number he knew by heart. The phone rang and a male voice answered. "Yes."

"It's me. I need to talk to you."

"Come to the Rock. I'm staying near the normal place. Meet me there tomorrow at 4:00 p.m.. Come alone." The phone went dead. *Well that's done,* thought Rafe.

No longer able to sleep, he made some espresso with the coffeemaker in the hotel room and sat down at the table to make plans, opening his laptop. Quickly he confirmed flight reservations to Gibraltar for two and selected a room at a small inn on the side of the mountain he had known for years. He then pulled out a picture of Clare he had in his wallet. His heart melted. He could look at it no more. Rafe sat for several minutes in silence. He then turned on the television, muted the sound, and flipped to the American financial channel, where he normally followed the markets. There was a documentary showing about the European debt crisis and the associated civil unrest. Rafe dropped his coffee cup on the table, spilling the remaining fluid while staring at the television screen. Cecilia briefly awoke but soon rolled over and went back to sleep. The anchorwoman narrating the pretaped documentary was the woman he had seen in the black robe at the altar in the Circus Maximus several hours before.

Rafe's eyes continued to be locked on the television long after turning it off. His mind was spinning out of control. It was as if he had been thrown into a parallel universe and did not know how to function. The whole world had been turned upside down. *What is happening? And why is it happening to me?* Rafe continued to sit, thinking about the situation for some time. His anxiety was overwhelming.

Eventually the sun came up, and the light began to peek through the closed shades covering the hotel room windows. Cecilia started stirring in the bed around mid-morning. Rafe had hardly slept at all and he looked like it. He kept the espresso machine humming. "I've got to figure out what is going on," he said aloud as the sun was now firmly planted in the overhead sky, signaling the day had begun.

Cecilia finally woke and found Rafe staring out the window. As her eyes adjusted to the conditions in the room, she asked, "What time is it?'

"It's 10:30 local time. You need to get up and get dressed and get ready to go."

"Where are we going?" she asked groggily.

"I'll tell you on the way to the airport. We're going to see a friend of mine. So get up and let's get moving."

"You haven't slept at all, have you?"

"Why does that matter?"

"Because you need to be your best, if not for you, then for Clare."

"You let me worry about myself, and Clare also for that matter."

"Suit yourself," Cecilia responded curtly and made her way to the bathroom.

Twenty minutes later, she emerged showered and refreshed. Rafe had packed and was still in the clothes he had worn before. He went into the bathroom and splashed water on his face.

"Let's go," he ordered coldly.

Once again Rafe awoke as the small aircraft landed with a thud. He had tried to stay awake and think of Clare, but his body had shut down on the flights from Rome to Madrid and then on to Gibraltar. Cecilia was next to him, reading a book, her hand affectionately on his leg.

I've been an asshole, he thought. *She's been good to me and I've been treating her like the enemy.* He moved his hand on top of hers. She looked up and smiled at him. Eventually the aircraft stopped taxiing and the door to the cabin opened, allowing the passengers to off-load via mobile stairs and then walk to the small terminal beyond. *She's connected to everything that's happening in some way, but I just don't know how. Maybe she doesn't know either. We both have to figure it out.*

Rafe looked around the airfield as they walked to the seemingly provincial, one-story facility. The Rock of Gibraltar loomed behind them to the south. It was a massive formation rising from the flat terrain around it, reaching upwards and outwards like the chin of an outlandish, masculine cartoon character. Rafe could smell the sea.

Located at the bottom of the Iberian Peninsula and guarding the entrance to the Mediterranean, Gibraltar was ceded from the Spanish to the English in the 1713 Treaty of Utrecht and had been a thorn in Spanish/English relations ever since. Twice the population of Gibraltar had voted to refuse to be brought under Spanish control. Once an important base for the Royal Navy, now the Rock mainly subsisted off tourism and financial services. Even the Romans and Carthaginians had settled Gibraltar thousands of years ago. Rafe had seen it all before, for Rafe had been to Gibraltar several times to meet Neal.

Neal was an agent with MI6. He had recruited Rafe years ago and continued to be his handler. Rafe was a natural target, as he was a famous author. Powerful people loved famous authors. They would invite them to their parties and other social functions in order to make themselves look important and connected. Rich and powerful people always loved the arts. In addition to being famous, Rafe was an attractive man, so doors opened for him, they always had. *I just made the wrong decisions with those opportunities,* he would often think. *Just picked the wrong women, that's why I'm alone.*

Rafe was also second-generation Ukrainian-American. His parents had immigrated to the U.S. during the Cold War. He spoke fluent Ukrainian and Russian. So when the Orange Revolution broke out in Ukraine after the fall of the Soviet Union, Rafe was a natural figure for MI6 to use to gain information about who to trust in the opposition movement. Rafe had made frequent trips to Eastern Europe during that time, wining and dining with Ukrainian centers of influence. His relationship with Neal was a good one; they had looked after each other's safety and interests. They trusted one another. There was, however, a distance between them, a professional distance. They would never be great friends.

Rafe and Cecilia made their way through immigration at the small terminal, collected their bags, and walked out into the warm night air. The smell of the ocean was never far away. A taxi stand was in front of the airport exit, but the line was nonexistent. They were able to hail a cab right away.

"Take me to the Oglethorpe," Rafe barked to the driver.

"You haven't even told me what we are doing here," Cecilia said as they drove upwards into the densely populated but small city at the base of the Rock.

"And I'm not going to yet," he replied. He said nothing else until they reached the hotel.

The drive to the hotel took about twenty minutes. Initially the road leading up into the crowded district was wide and accommodated several lanes of traffic. As they neared the top of the inhabited area, the road became thinner, and at some points the taxi had to pull over to let another car pass from the opposite direction. Eventually, they pulled into a small turnoff and parking area in front of the ground-floor check-in area of a large hotel that sprawled upwards on the mountain. Cecilia looked upwards and marveled at the mountain buttressing the hotel against the sea. A bellman took their bags and Rafe checked in to the room.

"Let's have a drink in the bar before we do anything," Rafe suggested. They negotiated the winding steps upwards from the front desk of the hotel and soon were in an expansive lounge area overlooking the Atlantic Ocean arrayed in front of them. The entire western wall of the hotel bar area was glass, and the room was decorated with historical artifacts of Gibraltar nautical history. The other side of the Rock, on the eastern opening to the Mediterranean, simply ended at the sea and was not populated.

"Nice view!" remarked Cecilia. "So what are we doing here?"

"I have to meet a friend. You're going to stay here in the bar until I get back." Rafe was not worried about being polite at this point. His daughter was all that mattered.

"So I get to stay here and drink? What if some handsome guy comes along?"

"You may indulge yourself if you like. I won't be long. An hour or so," he said uncaringly. Cecilia looked hurt but Rafe really didn't notice. He glanced at his watch; it wasn't time yet, so he ordered another round. An hour later, Rafe left the bar, leaving Cecilia wondering and waiting for his return.

Rafe meandered slowly down the small streets, being careful not to get run over by the advancing traffic. Occasionally, he would dart into a side alley and emerge a block or two down the road. It was his way of making sure he wasn't being followed. It was not as if he had received any training from MI6. He just did as he was told. He wasn't in a hurry. Soon he neared his destination.

Rafe arrived in an expansive square nestled against the mountain rising above it. The area was ringed with shops and cafes and filled with the local populace. It seemed like there was some local fair or similar event of some kind taking place in the area. Rafe mingled among the throng of people, pretended to be interested in the festivities, and eventually drifted to the far edge of the square and selected an outdoor seat in the approaching shadows at an Italian cafe hidden in the corner. He sat down and waited. Rafe heard mostly British accents, however, not a proper London English. There was a Mediterranean flair to the way the people talked. It seemed to be a rather unique way of speaking. The patrons of the shops were oblivious to Rafe.

Fifteen minutes later, Neal arrived. "Good to see you, Rafe. You look good. Much better than the last time I saw you." Neal was dressed like a collegiate professor, corduroy sport coat and all. He even had the elbow patches. He was in his late forties, had graying long hair, and stylish glasses. Neal was of average height and in good shape physically.

"Why thank you, boss, you look good yourself, like a true campus radical. So what swashbuckling case are you working on now? Or is it just some boring environmental terrorist or something like that?"

"You always were the cynical one," responded Neal. "As a matter of fact, I'm saving the world, but you wouldn't know anything about that. You're hanging out in Venice and traveling all over Europe with a strikingly beautiful, young woman. Yes, yes, don't look so surprised. We do keep tabs on our people you know."

"I'm impressed. Do you know anything about what I'm up to? What's going on?"

"I can't say that I do, Rafe. Obviously that is why you wanted to meet. And as it usually happens that I am the one who wants to meet and not you, I surmise there is something wrong and it's important. So why don't you properly get me up to speed?"

Rafe laid out all that had transpired over the last few days since he had met Cecilia and seen the image under the water in Venice. Neal listened intently, occasionally asking questions and taking a few notes. "What's the girl's full name?" he asked. Rafe told him and Neal pulled out his phone. Seconds later he began speaking. He gave Cecilia's name and description over the phone and asked for a quick report on her background and activities. Neal also asked for information on Fernando. He hung up and then turned to Rafe.

"So you meet her for a few days of great sex and invite her into your life? Seems a little quick, don't you think?" asked Neal.

"Yes, you could say that. I've thought about that myself, but she has been helping me figure out what's going on. I really didn't have any other leads at the time. But yes, things have been quite coincidental. Frankly I don't give a fuck if I can find out more about Clare. I really don't have any other leads besides her."

"We will of course do what we can to help, Rafe. I'll see what I can find out from the Yanks, but it seems like this is taking place in our sandbox. I will say this, you need to be *very* careful, no matter how beautiful she is."

"Yeah, I figured that one out on my own. I do appreciate your help however. What do you suggest I do?"

"Stay put here for a day or so. Let me find out some information on these people and on the woman in New York. It's all quite shocking. I'll be in touch tomorrow, okay? So stay put for a few days?"

"Okay thanks." Rafe got up to leave.

"And one more thing, my friend," added Neal. "You are definitely being led to the slaughter here. We just have to figure out why and by whom."

"Find my daughter," said Rafe. "I'll sacrifice myself for her. That's all I care about."

The walk back to the hotel was uneventful.

Rafe found Cecilia sitting alone at a table overlooking the ocean. She had moved across the bar and was gazing out at the white caps cresting the waves. She looked ravishing in her tight-fitting sundress. Rafe had almost forgotten how gorgeous she was.

"Ah, back from your secret mission?" she asked as he walked up to the table. "Still not going to tell me?"

"Sorry, no I'm not going to tell you. Maybe someday but not now. I hope you weren't too lonely while I was gone?"

"No, I'm fine. I did kind of miss you however. Even though we've only known each other for a few days." She smiled seductively.

"Growing attached to me already, huh?" Rafe responded. "Usually it takes a girl a few weeks before she can't live without me," he said sarcastically. He was growing more and more depressed over Clare's disappearance and not knowing where to turn for information. He signaled for the waitress to bring him a drink.

Cecilia reached out and held Rafe's hand. "Look, Rafe. We're going to find her, okay?" She then reached over to her purse and pulled out a brochure. She handed it to him. "Look what I found on my table while you were gone. Someone placed it there when I went to the bathroom for a couple minutes. Obviously they wanted us to see this. Seems like there is an ancient Mythraim from the Roman days here in Gibraltar."

Chapter Six

Rafe and Cecilia lay together in bed. Rafe was leaning against the headboard, and her head rested on his chest. Her silky, black hair billowed up into his face. She smelled wonderful and felt warm and soft. She caressed his skin as the sun set on the Mediterranean Sea through the open balcony to their room. A warm breeze wafted up the curtains through the opening. Rafe could see the ships slowly moving into the port on the western side of Gibraltar through the man-made barriers. He couldn't help thinking that thousands of years ago, the view was not that altogether different. Only today the ships were modern. The fatigue of not sleeping for days washed over him.

"Rafe, you need to rest and relax. You can't do anything for Clare in your condition. You're so wired you're gonna burn yourself out. You need sleep," she said softly.

"I can't get her out of my mind. I can't stop thinking about what is happening to her. I don't know what to do. She's my angel."

Cecilia sat up and faced him. She was wearing one of his T-shirts and nothing else. He again noticed how stunningly beautiful she was, but he didn't know if he could trust her.

75

"I'm waiting on a phone call," Rafe added. "Then we will make some decisions."

Cecilia kept on speaking. "Tomorrow we'll go to the Mythraim and see what we can find, okay? There must be some clues there. We need to try and find out how Clare, and you for that matter, are connected to this ancient ritual."

"Yes, that seems like a reasonable plan. Obviously someone wants us to go there. But it's a shot in the dark, so I've asked for some help from a friend. I'll know more tomorrow I hope. Then we can decide what to do as I said."

"Rafe, don't be afraid of me. I'm on your side. I want to help you." She moved forward and kissed him. Rafe tensed his body and turned is head.

"Not until she is found."

She pulled his face back towards her own. "Look at me. You need to relax and sleep or you can't help Clare." She put the palm of her hand against his cheek. "Trust me and let me help you."

Rafe began to soften. "First thing in the morning we go to the temple when it opens."

"Of course." Cecilia pushed him back on the bed and climbed on top of him.

Rafe woke up as the sun again peeked through the curtains partially covering the outside balcony. He felt refreshed and his mind had cleared. His resolve and determination had returned. He rose from the bed and walked outside on the balcony as he had many times before in Venice. *I wish I was back there just writing a book and Clare was safe at home,* he thought to himself. *My how things have changed in a few short days.* The port was starting to come to life as the morning sun rose higher in the sky. Ships were lined up in the harbor, waiting to off-load their cargo. The longshoremen worked the cranes, efficiently removing the containers and other cargo from the decks of the ships. *I'm going to find you, Clare.* Rafe walked back into the hotel room. Cecilia was sleeping peacefully, wrapped up in the cotton sheets. He stared at her a while. She scared him with her passion. He'd never been with a woman like her. He'd never felt such power while make love, such strong emotion and force. It was almost like she was a goddess. No, she was not like any other woman he had ever loved. She was off the charts. He touched her arm and shook her gently. "Come on, it's time to get moving. The sun is up. I want to get there as soon as it opens."

Cecilia stirred and mumbled, "Okay, give me twenty minutes to get ready."

They left the hotel and got into the rental car parked in front of the lobby, which Rafe had ordered the previous evening. It was a small Mini Cooper, perfect for negotiating the tiny roads of Gibraltar. They drove through town and then towards the Rock, eventually accessing the Queen's Road, which led towards the lower nature reserve and the southern base of the mountain. Soon they were parked at the entrance to the Jews' Gate Cemetery and heading out on foot, following the signs to the Mediterranean Steps.

The man-made steps were built by the British two centuries before to provide access to the gun emplacements constructed around the Rock. The steps were literally chiseled out of the Rock by British soldiers. The path meandered to O'Hara's Battery, almost to the summit. However, Rafe and Cecilia were not going all the way to the top of the mountain. Forty-five minutes later, halfway up the path, they broke off to an alternate stone stairway that led up to a man-made landing hewn out of the limestone. The time was approaching 9:00 a.m. when, according to the brochure, the Mythraim would be opening to the public.

The Rock of Gibraltar was formed when the African and Eurasian tectonic plates collided together millions of years ago, which pushed the substrate up into the open air and exposed the underground geological material. Primarily made of limestone from ocean deposits over millions of years, the rock was weathered and had been eroded significantly throughout the ages. Rafe and Cecilia walked towards a natural tunnel whittled into the naturally sculptured stone, which was blocked off by a steel door, as they followed the signs pointing out the location of the Roman ruins. A local security guard was in the process of opening to start the tourist day. There were no other people around at this early time in the morning, which suited Rafe just fine. They were breathing heavily after the almost hour-long climb and sweating profusely.

"How do we get to the Mythraic temple?" Rafe asked the man as the gate was opened. The guard was surprised to see someone at the tourist site this early in the morning. He finished opening the gate then turned to talk to them, pointing inside the cavern.

"Follow the tunnel down about fifty yards, and you will see a lighted room off to the right.   That's the temple. There is a Plexiglas barrier over the opening, but you will get a good view of the temple and its layout. I'll turn the lights on now."

"Thanks," said Rafe. They entered the passageway. Minutes later, Rafe and Cecilia arrived at the opening to the Mythraim. Although as the guard stated, they could not enter. They were able to see most of the inside of the cavern where the temple was located. There was a plaque posted to the right of the doorway, which described the history and lifestyle of the Roman soldiers who were encamped on the rock two thousand years before. The plaque also described the mysteries of Mythraism.

Rafe visibly relaxed, as there were no pictures of his daughter adorning the altar across the space as he had half expected to see. Cecilia scanned the inside of the temple with a more educated, discerning eye. The layout of the Mythraim was the same as they had seen both times before. The cavern was elongated and had a long, stone table on each side mounted into the wall. A stone bench ran lengthwise of each table. At the far end was an altar with an etching above carved into the stone wall of a soldier slaying a bull with a spear while riding atop the beast. Various scenes of battle were etched into the walls above the tables on each side of the arched cavern. Neither Rafe nor Cecilia said anything for a few minutes as they looked for something which was out of the ordinary.

"I don't get it. What are we supposed to see?" asked Rafe finally.

Cecilia was silent, scanning the interior of the temple. Finally she spoke. "Look over at the rear wall, towards the side of the altar. It's slightly hidden. What do you see?" Cecilia asked.

"It's some sort of symbol of a trident."

"And then to the right of that?"

"I see a double-headed eagle coat of arms. Does that have something to do with Rome? What's significant about that?" he asked.

"Look closer, tell me again what you see."

"Well, there is something between the eagle heads. It looks like a cross or something. Why would they have inscribed a Christian symbol?"

"It's not just a Christian symbol. It's an Orthodox Cross. See the two cross beams above and the two diagonal cross beams below? To be specific, it's a Russian Orthodox Patriarchal Cross. It doesn't belong here. It was added later. Many centuries later."

"How do you know that?"

"Because it's the coat of arms of Ivan Grozny."

"Who the heck is that?" asked Rafe.

"You know him by a different name. He was Ivan IV, the first tsar of all of Russia. He was trying to establish the third Holy Roman Empire after Constantinople fell to the Ottoman Empire. He ruled a thousand years after the fall of Rome.

"I've never heard of him. Why did you say I know him by a different name?"

"Ivan Grozny in Russian means Ivan the Terrible."

"So what the heck is that coat of arms doing there?" Rafe demanded. "And what does it mean? And what about the trident?"

"One thing for sure is I don't know the answer to those questions," Cecilia responded. "I do know that the trident can be traced back to the first Slavic Russian Empire of Kievan Rus'. It included modern-day Ukraine, Belarus, and some of the European parts of Russia. The Rurik dynasty ruled from Vladimir the Great through Ivan the Terrible and beyond, after the seat of Russian power moved to Moscow."

The two of them were back at the hotel, sitting in the lounge, having been served a small lunch. Rafe hadn't touched his food. He put his head in his hands in a sign of despair. "Where do we go from here?"

"I've been thinking of what the symbols we saw could be trying to tell us. The trident was an early symbol of Slavic rule; it even can be traced back to the Vikings who conquered the Russian territory centuries before the tsars united the eastern Slavic tribes. However, it usually is connected with Vladimir the Great's rule in Kievan Rus', the kingdom that preceded the princes of Moscow, before the nomads from the East destroyed its capital, Kiev. Several hundred years later, Ivan the Terrible was the first Russian ruler to unite all of Russia and defeat the Golden Horde of Mongols that had been invading the southern Russian territory. The Russian Orthodox Church was integral to the tsar's rule. Ivan persecuted the nobility that did not fall in line with his wishes. He was famous for frying them in huge, iron skillets. Not a nice guy, hence the name."

"But again how does that tie to a Mythraic temple?"

"As I said before, Ivan and the Russian Church thought they were the natural state to carry on the third Holy Roman Empire after the fall of the Eastern Church to the Muslims. So they copied the Byzantine coat of arms and added the Patriarchal Cross between the eagle heads. They took this very seriously. Later Peter the Great tried to destroy the influence of the church on the Russian state. This caused quite a bit of unrest throughout the country. Peter persecuted the church and the 'Old Believers.' The Soviet Union buried religion altogether, at least officially. Christianity was only reunited with the Russian state apparatus after the fall of the communist government in the 1990s. I wonder if this is somehow trying to tie the old Western Roman Empire to the tsars. But why? I don't have a clue. And how does it relate to you and Clare? It's a riddle of some kind."

"Well, one thing is for sure. Someone wants us to think they are connected."

Rafe's phone rang. He stood up as he answered and walked across the lounge so his call would not be overheard.

"Rafe, it's Neal."

"Yes, go ahead? What have you found?"

"I've checked out the girl. She's who she says she is. She's become a quite recent phenom in academic circles in Rome. Really no criminal record of any kind. Actually quite blank if I may say so myself. So, I don't think she is someone that is out to kill you at least. She's been traveling around Rome speaking a great deal lately. Beyond that, I can't speak to her motivation."

"Great, I feel better about that at least," Rafe commented. *I do really feel better about that.* "What else can you tell me?"

"I've checked into the woman you saw at the Circus Maximus, the television anchor. So far all I have come up with that sparks any questions is her travel schedule. And this interests me very much on multiple fronts. She's been traveling a great deal to the same place over and over for the last few years."

"And where might that be?" Rafe questioned.

"To your old stomping grounds, Rafe. You should also be very interested in this. She's been traveling to Ukraine. She's been flying over and over to Kiev."

Chapter Seven

"Kiev, what the hell is she doing in Kiev?" asked Rafe into the phone.

"We don't know," Neal responded. "I was hoping you could shed some light there. You *are* my spy for the Ukraine you know. That's why you have that fancy, encrypted phone, remember?"

"Yes, don't worry, I remember. How would I know what she's doing in Kiev? And what the hell is she doing dressed up in a robe, slaughtering animals at night in the Circus Maximus at some weird, sacrificial ritual? And where the hell is my daughter? Do the U.S. authorities know anything? Have you discussed this with them?" Rafe's voice was rising steadily.

"Yes, we have made contact. The Yank law enforcement authorities have no leads and especially nothing connecting this woman and her followers to your daughter's disappearance. I have arranged to be contacted immediately if anything is discovered. You'll be my first phone call."

"Thank you," said Rafe somewhat more calmly. "I really appreciate that, Neal."

Rafe was hit with another wave of despondency. They really had no serious leads and he was sick with worry. He felt like he was letting Clare down and wished he could calm her fears and make everything okay. *Hang in there, sweetie, Daddy's coming.* He again felt like he might throw up from anxiety. He paced the floor in the bar; people were starting to stare.

It was good Neal would keep him in the loop. Rafe had no desire to call his ex-wife for information and listen to her rage, so he really was grateful for his friend's help.

"Let me know if anything else happens on your end, okay?" Neal asked.

"Well, there is more to tell." Rafe filled him in on the events of the evening and the following morning at the temple on the Rock. "What do you suggest we do?"

"Do you still have that brochure you were given?"

"Yes."

"I want it. I want to analyze it. And tomorrow, the three of us are going back up the Rock to that temple. As far as this riddle goes, someone wants you to come to them."

"To go where?" asked Rafe.

"Isn't it obvious? Someone wants you to come to the old Kingdom of Rus' and the third Holy Roman Empire. You're going to Kiev." Bewildered by the day's events, Rafe hung up the phone.

This time the sun beat down on them as they started up the stone stairs of the Mediterranean Steps. Neal had met them at the hotel, and they had driven back to the Jews' Gate together. The crowd now was much larger, as the Rock always attracted tourists from Spain and elsewhere on a nice day. The hike up the mountain was a popular method of exercise. The sky was clear without a cloud to be seen, and the slight, cool breeze off the Mediterranean was enjoyable. The tourists came in waves as expected, many unaware of the strenuous effort ahead of them. The apes had long since disappeared with the influx of humans, preferring to scatter to the higher elevations where the tourists didn't tread, only to scamper back down during the evening. Everyone was sweating in the hot air, soaking their clothes, as they negotiated their way higher up the mountain.

Rafe had introduced Cecilia and Neal. Neal did not trust her but agreed her expertise would come in handy for their task. He was not his usual chatty self but rather quiet and reserved. Rafe informed her Neal was just a "friend" yet a powerful one. They left it at that. She didn't seem to mind.

After climbing for approximately thirty minutes, they began to pass caves carved into the side of the mountain face. Some were naturally created by seawater thousands of years before, when the water had been much higher. It was fascinating to think that the ocean had existed at such elevated levels in the ancient past. Others had been created by the myriad of military excursions and sieges which dotted the Rock's history. The Moors, the Spanish, and especially the English created a network of tunnels throughout the limestone mountain. "The ancient mariners used to believe the Rock was a gate to the end of the Earth," Neal stated as they stopped to rest in the shade of one of these caves. "They thought

86

that if you went out into the Atlantic, you would fall off the edge of the planet to the Hell below. Many of these caves were used as altars for offerings to the gods to incur their favor and security as they pass through Hercules' Gate. There is evidence of prehistoric human habitation in these caves as well. It's a great place to hike around when you get some time, but that's for another day."

Neal led the way as they reached the stone landing halfway up the mountain where Rafe and Cecilia had been that morning. The same security guard was still minding the entrance to the tunnel that led to the temple. They rested in the shade of the Rock towering above them for a brief moment then continued towards the hidden passageway.

As they approached, a young man dressed in worker's clothes walked out of the tunnel entrance. He seemed to be of some official capacity and carried himself as such. He spotted Neal and addressed him.

"Are you Neal?"

"Yes, have you accomplished what was requested?"

"I have, the temple is open now. The barrier has been removed."

"Thank you. We will be an hour then you can replace the Plexiglas." Neal then turned to the guard. "No one is allowed in here until we return. Is that understood?"

"Yes, very much, sir."

"Great." He then motioned to Rafe and Cecilia. "Let's go."

The three of them walked down the tunnel and soon were staring again into the temple. The temperature dropped as they walked farther inside the Rock. Their sweat began to evaporate and they were soon more comfortable, even a little cold.

"You know, we don't even know what this religion was about," said Cecilia. "This is fascinating. To think soldiers of Rome actually worshipped here. Worshipped some mysterious entity, thousands of years ago. Right here!"

"They say that humans just forgot during the Dark Ages much of the knowledge the Romans had acquired. We don't even know what we don't know about them and how they created such a magnificent society," added Neal.

"That's why the Renaissance is so fascinating to me," added Rafe. "I almost forgot I was writing a book before all of this started! I want my life back."

"So let's see if we can find something that you guys missed. Let's find what we don't know about this wild goose chase you're on," added Neal. They entered the temple.

He stayed near the door and watched for other people entering the tunnel at the opening. Rafe began inspecting some of the symbols above the table hewn into the left wall. Although, he somewhat felt out of place; this was definitely not his area of expertise. He didn't even know what he was looking for.

Cecilia walked over to the altar and gazed at the coat of arms and the trident etched into the limestone wall behind and to the right. She took out her phone and began snapping pictures. The etchings looked as old as the surrounding symbols that had been placed there centuries before. She bent down and took photos from several angles and then turned to change positions to examine the rest of the space. As she moved to stand, she noticed something out of place near the base of the altar and knelt back down. There was something that had been placed under the base of the stone pedestal. She reached under and pulled it out and gasped.

Rafe heard her reaction, turned, and asked, "What is it?"

Cecilia stared at the object in her hand. "It's an icon. I've seen these before from the Byzantine era, but this one is different. It looks to be in the Old Believer style. It's definitely Kievan Rus'."

"Let me see it." Rafe reached out and took the object. It was a small, eight-inch square piece of thin cypress wood bound by a copper cover. The cover was highly decorated with gold leaf, and elaborately glowing religious figures and symbols jumped off the material. Rafe pulled open the cover and revealed the painting below. The brilliant, complicated painting glowed when exposed to the light.

"Wow," said Cecilia.

"It's a copy of a icon. This one is really old but it's not an original."

"How do you know?"

"Because the originals usually are in museums or in safekeeping at religious orders. See how the figures are simplistic and don't seem realistic? You're right, it's the Old Believer style. Obviously we were meant to find this. It has nothing to do with Roman Mythraism."

"Take it with us. Is there anything else out of order?" asked Neal, yanking Rafe and Cecilia back to their present task. "We can have a history lesson back at the hotel." They searched the temple for twenty more minutes, examining every etching and artifact in the underground cavern. Cecilia took more pictures. They found nothing more of significance.

The three left the temple and exited the tunnel. Neal canceled the order with the security guard and motioned for the worker to reinstall the barrier. Then they started the trek back down the stairs towards Jews' Gate Cemetery. Rafe concealed their find under his shirt. An hour later they had negotiated the mountain and drove back to the hotel. Soon they were back at their hotel room, accompanied by Neal. Once inside, he spoke first.

"I was right. Someone wants you in the Ukraine. Just think, Rafe my friend, someone values your skill and knowledge of Ukrainian culture as much as I do! And I have to say, that worries me very much! How about you start thinking of whom you have been in contact with over the last few years and come up with some ideas of who could be doing this? Are you keeping anything from me? Anything I should know about, mate?"

"Don't be ridiculous. My daughter is missing for God's sake. *You're* starting to piss me off!" replied Rafe.

"Well someone knows a great deal about you and is leading you there. You need to try and figure out who it could be and why. Think!"

"I have thought about it. I have no idea."

"Do you have any connection to the woman at the sacrifice? Even from several degrees of separation?" asked Cecilia.

"Not that I can recall."

"Perhaps we should call the cops and have her confronted? Brought in for questioning in New York?" she added.

"No!" replied Rafe. The answer is not in New York. It is here in Europe. It is somewhere in one of these temples. I can feel it! And Clare is still alive! That I can feel as well. No, we continue on and find out whatever it is that I'm supposed to discover. Then we deal with that when it happens!"

"So you go to Kiev and see what you can find," added Neal.

"Yes, I go to Kiev."

"You mean we go to Kiev! I'm going with you. I happen to care about you, you know," said Cecilia.

"You're welcome to come. I'm sure your expertise will come in handy at some point. And I like having you around as well." *Plus the sex is literally out of this world.*.

"Well, now that we have that settled, can we break up this little love fest? I have to get back to work. I'll be in touch. Take care, Cecilia." With that Neal left the room, shutting the hotel room door behind him.

"Well isn't he charming?" said Cecilia.

After he left, Rafe went straight to his computer and began typing furiously.

"What are you doing?" she asked.

"We're going to take a train to Kiev. I don't want to announce to the world we are arriving by buying an airline ticket. There are no visa requirements into Ukraine, so we can just arrive and will be passed through immigration. I'm checking the schedule and routing. We'll pay in cash at the terminal."

"Sounds like a plan," she responded. "Do we get a sleeper car?" She put her arms around him from behind and kissed his neck.

Chapter Eight

The train lumbered on methodically during the dead of night, singing its passengers to sleep with a deep, rumbling lullaby, rocking them gently. Rafe and Cecilia lay naked in bed, the sheets pulled down around their waists and entangled between their legs. The cooling system was not working very well on this leg of the trip, and they were sweating together in the warm night air. The full moon shone through the portal and lit up the compartment of the sleeper car. Cecilia had drifted off to sleep some time before, but Rafe was still fully awake as he held her. Her body felt warm and soft. *I could get used to this,* he thought. They had grown closer over the last two days, making love intensely and often, and talking late into the evening. Rafe had to admit, It was heavenly, although somewhat overwhelming and maybe even a little bit scary. He couldn't match her power in bed and had never felt anything like it before.

They were starting their third day of the journey. Initially they took a bus from Gibraltar to the nearest train station in Spain. Then there was a two-day patchwork of train rides to finally get to Warsaw,

Poland. They had arrived at Centralna Station late in the evening and enjoyed a nice dinner in the center of Warsaw before catching the next train out to Kiev the next morning. Rafe was amazed at how much the former communist country had changed since his last trip there years before. The center of Warsaw was modern and booming and covered with neon lights. Crowds of young people lined the streets late into the night, enjoying the night life, oblivious to the horrors their parents had felt before them under the Iron Curtain. Rafe and Cecilia rented a nice, luxurious apartment nearby and slept till mid-morning before starting the next leg of their journey.

Now they were on the Ukrainian Express bound for Kiev and would arrive later in the day. It had been a pleasant trip with this beautiful woman by his side, but now Rafe felt the need to deal with the business at hand. His mind moved back to his daughter, and he felt guilty for entertaining the pleasure Cecilia gave him. He sat up in bed. The compartment was steadily, rhythmically moving side to side. There was a romantic component to the motion. *I wish I could enjoy this, but I just can't.*

Rafe got up, pulled on some clothes, and exited the sleeper chamber. Cecilia stirred briefly and went back to sleep, pulling the covers over her head. He walked out into the hallway and down the passage to the door to the following cabin, which happened to be a dining car. He winced as the noise of the train wheels clanking on the rails increased when he turned the handle and pulled open the door. It took a great deal of force to get the hatch open, but soon he was safe in the other car. He sat down at an empty table. The dining area was free of other passengers save an older woman sitting at the other end alone. Food service had ended some time ago. He opened the window next to him to let some of the night air in and stared at the leafy green hills going by in the darkness. *Where are you, my little girl?* The train droned on and on towards Kiev and the old Kingdom of Rus'.

Vladimir the Great was the first ruler to unite the various Slavic tribes located in Eastern Europe in the early eleventh century. He ruled from the city of Kiev in what is today Ukraine. He conquered lands from the Baltic to the Black Sea. Once Vladimir had united the Slavic tribes of Kievan Rus', he decided to choose a national religion. He sent out emissaries to the far corners of the earth to learn about the world's different ways of worshipping their gods. This fact-finding exercise included Islam, Christianity, Judaism, and the gods of the eastern Mongols. In the end, Vladimir chose to emulate the Orthodox Christianity of the Byzantine Empire. His emissaries reported that in Constantinople, "We did not know if we were in heaven or on earth, nor such beauty. We know not how to tell of it." He even married one of their princesses in a first for the Slavic people, who were considered barbarians in Constantinople. The marriage of course took place only after Vladimir converted to Christianity.

The dream of Slavic dominance of Europe, however, was dashed by the Mongol invasion in the thirteenth century. Kiev was completely destroyed. The seat of Russian power fled to the northern city of Moscow to avoid the barbarian invasions, and the kingdom of Kievan Rus' was forever gone; however, the Rurik bloodline lived on in the Russian tsars. Ukraine was invaded and conquered over the centuries by the Poles, the Golden Horde, and even the Soviets. Ukraine had only been an independent nation since the fall of the Soviet Union.

Rafe was startled when he felt a hand on his shoulder and was jolted out of his slumber. Initially he felt threatened but then realized it was Cecilia gently shaking him. The sun shone through the glass near his face. He had fallen asleep at the dining table.

"Hey, stranger, what are you doing here?" she asked caringly. "Why didn't you sleep with me? You know I like that!"

"I couldn't sleep anywhere."

"Baby, you need to get your rest; I've told you this."

"Yes I know, but I can't. Just let me do what I have to do, okay?"

"Hey, I'm on your side. I have an idea. Why don't we get some coffee and talk about what we are going to do in Kiev? Sound like a plan?"

"Yes, that sounds like a plan."

Rafe went back to their sleeper compartment to throw some cold water on his face and freshen up. When he returned, Cecilia had ordered fresh espresso and some soup and sandwiches. "Sorry, the menu is pretty limited. I did the best I could." Rafe was starving and attacked the food.

96

"Whoa, slow down, cowboy. You are hungry like the wolf."

Rafe downed some sparkling water and then some more espresso. "Yes, I am."

"Who do you know in the Ukraine?"

"I know lots of people. But we are not going to talk to them. At least not yet."

"Why not?"

"Because I don't think they will be able to help us. Someone wants me to find something. I don't think I want other people trying to find it as well. If we need to tell people we are here, so be it. But I'm not going to telegraph it all over the country."

"So, then why don't you tell me the plan you have in your gorgeous head?" asked Cecilia.

"Okay, I will." Rafe finished his coffee and then looked at her. "Ah, I feel back among the land of the living. Thank you." Cecilia just looked at him and said nothing; she waited. "Here is what I am thinking," Rafe continued. "Let's start with the icon. The old painters usually came from a monastery or a village in the Russian bush. My point is they stayed in one place for a long time. In fact, the icons were usually named after them. They were fantastic artists, passing the craft down through the generations."

"I don't understand. How does that help us?"

"We find out where this icon was made, and we go there and find out everything we can about the painting, like who was the artist, what was significant about the area, et cetera."

"What do you think we will find?"

"I have no idea. That's what's bothering me. We don't know what we don't know. We are coming in blind and whoever wants us there knows that. I don't like it."

"So we don't tell your friends we are here?"

"Well, Neal knows we are here. I can contact him for help if need be. And no, we won't tell my colleagues in Kiev anything. They have their hands full anyway, and I don't want the political classes to know we are here. Of course immigration will know soon but I can't help that."

"We have six more hours. We also are going to have to be shunted into the gauge-changing shed at Yagodin on the Ukrainian border and jacked up to have our wheels changed from standard European gauge to Russian gauge. The border guards will also be checking our identification during that period. I suggest you try and get some sleep."

"Okay, that sounds like a good idea. This coffee is already starting to wear off, and I'm starting to feel like crap again."

"Thank you," Rafe said softly.

"For what?" Cecilia asked as they lay naked together again in the bed.

"For helping me. For loving me. I apologize for not trusting you earlier. It was a mistake. I'm sorry and thank you."

"Honey, you just need some special attention. It's okay. You're driving yourself mad over Clare, and I don't blame you. I'd probably do the same. I'm just trying to take the edge off a little bit for you. It's my way of helping. I'm here for you. Just trying to be good to you and return the favor of letting me stay with you for a while."

"Well, believe it or not, I'd like you to stay with me for a good deal longer. That is, if it's okay with you?"

"I'm not going anywhere. We have a few more hours to go to until we get to Kiev. Get some sleep. Doctor's orders." Rafe closed his eyes.

The noise awoke Rafe first. For a minute he didn't know where he was. Then he realized the rocking of the train back and forth had stopped. We must be at the border. He reached for Cecilia; she was no longer next to him in bed. The sun was beaming into the cabin. Groggily he sat up after sleeping hard, a deep REM state. "Cece?" he asked. There was no response. Rafe realized something was wrong. He noticed the door to the cabin was ajar and had been broken open; the wood around the doorjamb was splintered. There were signs of a recent struggle; the mirror above the sink was cracked, as if something had slammed against it. Her clothes were strewn on the floor. Rafe was fully awake now. "Cecilia?" he cried out loudly.

Rafe stood up and started throwing on his jeans and a shirt.

"Rafe!" he heard her scream, and then someone put something over her mouth, muffling her shouts for help. Rafe burst from the cabin door in time to see Cecilia being dragged down the far end of the sleeper car hallway towards the door to the next cabin.

"Hey, let her go!" he cried and started after her. Then something hit him in the back of the head, and everything went black. As he fell to the floor, Rafe thought he recognized her assailant. It was the man from the market in Barcelona.

Rafe came to lying again in his bed as the train pulled in to Pasazhyrs'kyi Central Railway Station in the center of Kiev. His head hurt really bad and he didn't feel like moving. Then he thought of Cecilia and also Clare. *I don't understand what's going on! I've got to figure this out! Get up!* Rafe turned to a sitting position and found his clothes and dressed. His vision was slightly impaired from the blow to the head and slowly returned. All of Cecilia's things had been removed. There was no evidence left that she had ever been with him at all. *It wasn't a dream. My head can attest to that.* Going to the authorities would be no use. He was sure of this fact. *This is all on you, Rafe, figure it out.*

He felt the back of his skull. There was a large, tender, painful lump. *I've got to get moving.* Rafe put all of his clothes in his small backpack that he had brought, freshened up his face and hair, and left the compartment. He looked all around. No one was watching him that he could see. He moved several cars ahead internally on the train before exiting, in case someone was watching his sleeper car. Then he prepared to leave the train with the throngs of people heading out onto the platform in Kiev.

Chapter Nine

Rafe quickly exited as the train doors opened, fighting his way through the people attempting to board at the same time, and tried to blend into the crowd as best he could. That meant not staring at the beautiful, young, Ukrainian women walking by him or gazing at the bustling interior of the train station itself. He just hurried along with the large group of travelers, massing toward the exit.

He had left the sleeper car in the relatively new southern railway terminal. This building connected through an overhead tunnel across the main set of tracks to the old Central Station, built in the early twentieth century. The tunnel was wide and complete with multiple eating and shopping outlets. It seemed to be a gathering place for young Ukrainian nationals. The tables at the coffee houses and restaurants were full, and walking to the other side of the tunnel was difficult, as the crowd was thick. Young girls in high heels stood talking on their pink iPhones, oblivious to the human activity around them.

The entire complex including the metro and other local train access points was called the Vokzal, after the Russian word of the same name. The derivation of Vokzal is presumed to be from the

English Vauxhall Station in the center of London. It is rumored that Tsar Nicholas I secretly made trips to London to study the English transportation systems in the nineteenth century and got off the train in London at Vauxhall Station. Assuming Vauxhall meant train station, the word made it back to Russia. A competing theory is the word was derived from the English Vauxhall Pleasure Gardens, which were mimicked in Saint Petersburg, Russia as early as the eighteenth century.

He fought the throng of people to make it through the overhead tunnel, and a couple minutes later, the crowd dispersed into the old Central Station interior. The opening was massive, as the old building boasted a very high, ornate ceiling. He went down the long, central escalator, ignored the stately, Baroque architecture, and soon was outside the huge main entrance. He headed left toward the Vokzalna metro entrance. The walkway was filled with merchant shops and travelers making their way between the two stations. The thoroughfare was lined with shops and small markets of all kinds, trying to grab the attention of travelers making their way between the two buildings.

The central metro station was built during Soviet times and was reminiscent of the Moscow metro with its decorative accoutrements. As with most Soviet metro stations, the pylons were artistically covered with white marble, shining ceramic tiles, and featured depictions of Soviet heroes and symbols. Chandeliers dangled overhead. The station was neat, clean, beautiful, and safe. His timing was good, as a metro train was just arriving in the

102

direction he wanted to proceed. Rafe boarded the train headed east towards the Dnieper River, which ran through the center of the historic city. The station announcements in Ukrainian reinforced to Rafe that he was back in Kiev.

Ancient, medieval Kiev was a trading post on the massive Dnieper River for centuries, as it was located on the trade route from Constantinople to Scandinavia. Towards the end of the first millennium, Kiev became a center of Slavic civilization as the various tribes were joined together under one ruler for the first time. The mighty river had always been a focal point of the Slavic trade and civilization. The western bank, or right bank as called by the ancients, consisted of woodland hills, rivers, and other bodies of water, currently used by Ukrainians for recreation. Only in the last century did building spread to the eastern bank as the metropolis expanded. The buildings were constructed mainly on artificial sand deposit foundations. Kiev was a large, metropolitan, European city and the home to millions of Ukrainians.

Unfortunately Ukraine had not experienced the economic miracle that Poland and other Eastern European nations enjoyed after the fall of the Soviet Union. Ukraine was still in the grip of the Soviet legacy of corruption. Everyone was paid for anything someone wanted to get done. Wealthy oligarchs skimmed billions off the production of the main Ukrainian economic resource, natural gas. This restricted the economy and made life miserable for millions. The drab, dull nature of the city reinforced this reality daily to Kiev's residents.

Rafe exited the subway at Zolati Voroda, or Golden Gate Metro Station. The immense gate to the old city greeted him as he exited the subway and set out on foot in his new surroundings. The structure was a recreation of the wooden gate through the stone city walls during the kingdom of Kievan Rus', before the Mongols destroyed Kiev, and was a monstrous edifice.

The walk to Saint Volodymyr's Cathedral was not very long. He found himself in a rather wealthy section of the city, complete with high-end boutiques and plenty of expensive vehicles. Rafe had not fully told the truth to Cecilia. He was of course not going to contact most of his acquaintances in Kiev. However, there was one exception. Bishop Kovolenko was worthy of this exception. He was one of the few people in Ukraine who Rafe trusted and was one of the only ones he could turn to for help. The bishop was an important source of information for the British on Rafe's previous trips to Ukraine. He would be sensitive to Rafe's need for secrecy in his desperate search for his daughter and now Cecilia. Soon Rafe left the sidewalk and was walking through the plaza towards the entrance of the Cathedral; the red and gray mosaic path led the way. Parishioners were slowly walking in and out of the structure, crossing themselves and looking upwards, wondering at its magnificence.

The whole concept of a Christian cathedral in Medieval Europe was to impress upon the peasantry the absolute supremacy of God. If God could create a majestic building such as this, how puny was mankind in his presence? No expense was spared by the leaders of church and state. The cathedrals across Europe were also sources of pride for the host city and evidence of their advanced civilization. They were meant to impress visitors from other cities as they arrived from other jurisdictions.

The Neo-Byzantine structure was constructed in the eighteen hundreds to commemorate the baptism of Kievan Rus' by Volodymyr the Great nine hundred years earlier. Seven cupolas adorned the yellow and white brick structure. Although the architecture was striking from the outside, the inner beauty was overwhelming. Rafe entered the immense, cavernous hall of worship and was once again struck by the amazing art covering every inch of the interior. Gold leaf glittered from the ceilings, from the icons, and from the altars. Unbelievably artistic paintings, frescoes, and mosaics adorned the walls, and ornate religious symbols were perched for all to see. The massive columns reached for the heavens and held the roof aloft. Opulent designs dominated the curving interior roofline. The bright light streamed into the structure, imposing strategically placed illumination.

The cathedral was built entirely by private contributions and almost destroyed by the Bolsheviks. The structure also narrowly escaped destruction during the Polish-Ukrainian War of 1920. For decades it was used as a museum of religion and atheism by the Soviets. However, during the latter twentieth century, it was one of the few places in the U.S.S.R. that one could visit a working church as the state loosened controls on religion. After the fall of the Soviet Union, the cathedral once again became a full-fledged liturgical site.

Rafe stood still inside the entrance and silently marveled at the beauty above and in front of him. He looked forward to the altar apse and saw the incredibly detailed painting of the Holy Mother of God by Vasnetsov. He saw the worshipers kissing the glass above the relics of saints, which lay in their small coffins, sometimes portions of their skeletons exposed, the bones covered with a leathery remnant of skin, centuries old. Shortly, however, memory of his task returned and he focused again on his errand.

The thought of Cecilia sent a shiver of pain through his body. He again felt an agonizing sense of loss. Two of the most important people in his life had just vanished. The two girls he cared about on this earth were being held by some mysterious cult that he knew nothing about. All he could hope was that they were okay. He felt impotent. *I have to do something and change this dynamic. I have to find a way to get an advantage, and that will require information. So now I will get it.* Rafe continued into the cathedral and found a place to stand with the parishioners to pray. The man he had come to see soon appeared on the altar above and motioned for him to come forward. A short while later, after ensuring no one was watching him, Rafe left his position and piously strolled towards the altar at the rear of the cathedral where several analogla, or lecterns, were located near an iconostasion. He set his backpack on the floor and waited. Soon the bishop made his way toward him to hear his confession.

"Your Eminence, I come to confess my sins," Rafe said first in Ukrainian. All services in the cathedral were conducted in the native language.

"Tell me, my son," the bishop responded, and he read a prayer of absolution.

Rafe waited a few seconds after he finished then reached into his backpack and took out the icon. He slid it across the top of the lectern and kept it covered with a cloth. They were in an area of the cathedral where others did not have a good view of them, but he was taking no chances. There was a long silence after the bishop took the work of art and marveled silently at its beauty.

Finally he said, "Where did you get this?"

"Somewhere far away. Someone made sure I found it. I believe they wanted me to come here."

"Most certainly. When you called and said you wanted to meet, I had no idea you were bringing such a treasure. Do you know what this is?"

"I think it's a copy of an Orthodox icon, Your Eminence."

"You may be correct. It may be a copy of the original. However, the copies were quite valuable themselves." There was a short pause. The bishop slid the icon, once again wrapped in the cloth, to Rafe, who returned it to his backpack. "What do you want from me?"

"I need help. Some people I care about have been kidnapped. For some reason, the kidnapper wants me here—wanted me to have this icon. I need to find out why. Whoever it is has my daughter."

There was another long pause, and Rafe could hear the bishop sigh. "I will pray for you, my son. This icon most likely came from a small village near Volodymyr on the Polish border called Zymne. That is where the artist lived and worked for most of his life, centuries before. That is where you need to go. There is a monastery there, an ancient one. The painting is a rendering of Vladimir the Great's wife, Anna, and was believed to be painted in the year 988. Anna was a Byzantine princess, and the wedding was a big deal in the kingdom and tied together the fortunes of the two empires. She was the real force behind the conversion of Kievan Rus'. She would not marry Vladimir until he converted and then proceeded to ensure the entire Slavic kingdom was baptized. The icon is called Our Lady and is said to have miraculous powers of healing and protection. There are shells from WWII embedded in the walls of the monastery that she is said to have prevented from exploding. There is also a legend that the icon put out the sight of a Catholic man who occupied and destroyed much of the Orthodox symbology there in the early eighteenth century. Yes, you need to go to see the monks. They will know how to direct you further."

"Who should I speak to when I arrive?"

"I will give you my introduction and blessing. That will be enough. Stay here." The bishop left and walked behind a partition only meant for priests. Rafe didn't move. Fifteen minutes later, the bishop reappeared and walked slowly to the lectern. He slid an envelope sealed with his wax imprint to Rafe.

"Show them this. They will help you."

"Thank you," Rafe responded and got up to leave.

"One more thing," the bishop said. Rafe hesitated. "You must be very careful. This icon is worth more than you can imagine. The religious icon has a very special place in Ukrainian and Russian history. It took a lifetime to learn how to paint these masterpieces. In fact, these were said to just appear at magical times and were known to carry mystical powers. Most of the time, the paintings were given the name of the location they were made. The icons were tied to these places and people protected them. There were also many copies made of the most famous ones. People were killed or worse for these. Do you understand? For someone to give this to you, they are luring you to the monastery."

"Yes, I understand, Your Eminence," Rafe replied.

"As I said, I will pray for you. Just be careful, my son."

Chapter Ten

Rafe left the cathedral and walked into the warm afternoon light as the sun started slowly heading towards the horizon. *I guess I'm going to Zymne*, he thought to himself. *I wonder what's the best way to get there? I need to eat and figure out what to do.*

Kiev was bustling all around him as he started back up the hill towards the Golden Gate. This part of the city had escaped the drab remnants of the Soviet existence. There were no dull high-rise apartments here, as there were with most of Kiev. This district looked like any other European capital.

He found a cafe a few streets over that he knew from experience was popular with the locals. Rafe enjoyed revisiting places in foreign cities that he had found enjoyable in the past, especially in Europe. The locals usually knew where to eat and get great food without spending a fortune. The late afternoon crowd was just starting to pick up, and he selected a table outside out of the way of the pedestrian crowd. He sat down and ordered a glass of wine and a menu from the young, Slavic waitress. Being out of the way of the crowd suited him just fine. He needed to relax and find his bearings. His head hurt from the blow he had taken earlier. Luckily, it did not break the skin, but there was a swollen bulge on the back of his skull, which he touched lightly and winced. He needed to think and make a plan for the next couple days.

Clare is missing. Cecilia is now missing. He felt a wave of nausea as he thought of both of them. The situation was making him sick, the anxiety overwhelming. *I guess I'll rent a car and drive out there. Probably will take me half a day, depending on the condition of the roads. I wish I had a weapon. I'll have to think about that.* Rafe's phone rang. He picked it up and accepted the call.

"Hello?"

"Rafe, it's Neal."

"What have you got for me, Neal?"

"I've checked again with law enforcement in the States. There's been no more word of Clare. However, I have asked the FBI to get involved as a favor to us. I'll let you know of any updates."

"Thank you again, Neal, that means a lot."

"No problem, least we could do. And, there's something else."

"What now?"

"We've been searching travel records here in the UK, and we've picked up something quite extraordinary from our database provided by the airlines. It seems we've had other individuals making frequent trips to Kiev."

"And who might these people be and any idea why?"

'No, that's just it. They don't seem to be related to your hooded lady friend in any way. Except that they are fairly prominent in their fields. Some in media, but there are other professions as well, academics, et cetera."

"That makes no sense."

"No, it doesn't. That's why we're going to keep working on this. You'll be my first call if anything more comes to light."

"Thanks, Neal. I've also got some bad news. Cecilia's been kidnapped. It was the man I saw in Barcelona, I'm sure of it. They took her from the train. I'm in Kiev now alone."

"Rafe, I'm really sorry. I'll put our people on this trail as well. What are your plans?"

"I've got some leads here myself. It seems the icon is associated with a monastery out in the countryside. I'm going to take a ride and see what I can find out. I have a feeling, however, that whoever wanted me to find that painting knows I'm coming. I sure would like to have something to protect myself with."

"Where are you currently?" Rafe told him. "Stay there. In one hour, go to the park several blocks over to the west and sit on a bench. Someone will sit next to you and leave you a present."

"Thanks, mate! I knew I could count on the Brits."

"No worries. Let me know what you find at the monastery. And take care of yourself. The good news is if someone wanted you dead, you would be already. Cheers." The phone went dead.

The waitress brought Rafe a glass of wine and a bowl of borscht per his request. The wine went down very easy and he started to relax. *I've got to eat to take care of myself and sustain my energy. Even if I don't feel like eating.* His plan started coming together. After finishing his meal, he paid the bill and left the cafe. A short stroll later, he found himself sitting on a bench in the park square, watching the girls walk by on the path through the center of the grassy area. He was soon joined by an older woman, who said nothing as she sat on the other end of the bench and began to read a newspaper. Ten minutes later, she folded the paper and set it down next to her. Saying nothing, she got up and left, disappearing into the crowd. After he was sure no one was watching, Rafe picked up the folded newspaper and walked in the direction of a hotel he was familiar with. He stuffed the newspaper into his backpack. It was heavy, as something was inside.

Twenty minutes later, he arrived at the hotel located on the corner of a building several blocks away. It was a nondescript place that wouldn't draw attention to him, and no one would suspect him staying there. Usually Rafe stayed at the more luxurious tourist hotels while in Ukraine, but this was not a usual trip. The hotel had seen its better days. The lobby walls were covered in a cheap stone, and the decor was something straight out of an American television set in the 1970s. However, everything seemed functional and clean.

He ordered a rental car for the morning, checked in, and soon was in his room. He locked the door then put his backpack on the single bed and pulled out the folded newspaper and opened it. There he saw a 9mm Beretta handgun and three extra magazines full of ammunition. He stuffed the rounds into his sport coat pocket and put the pistol in the rear of his belt. *Now I feel a little safer.* Rafe grabbed his laptop and made his way down to the hotel bar, where there was WiFi. *Now let's see what I can learn about Zymne.*

113

He sat in the bar in the corner where no one could see what he was looking at on his screen. No one noticed him, except the waitress. She offered him a menu but he waved her off. Rafe just wanted to work for a bit and collect his thoughts. He felt sure he hadn't been followed to the hotel. His plan was coming together. Tomorrow he would show up at the monastery and see what he was supposed to see. At least he would be prepared.

The monastery was built by Vladimir the Great in honor of his chosen religion, Orthodox Christianity, and was perched on the top of Holy Mountain, overlooking the Luh River. He is said to have built two churches and a palace near Zymne, meaning wintry in Ukrainian. The village was located five kilometers south of Volodomyr, Ukraine. Initially several monks secluded themselves in the caves surrounding the area, and eventually a religious community developed. At some point fortifications were constructed but were not sufficient to keep out the eastern invaders who occupied and destroyed Kievan Rus' in the thirteenth century.

Why does someone want me to go there? What am I supposed to find? Is my daughter there? Is Cecilia there? Rafe ordered another drink. There was nothing more to be done tonight. He had to wait until the morning to proceed. A few hours later, Rafe went back to his room and crashed for the night, putting the pistol under his pillow. He slept intermittently, dreaming nightmares alternately of Clare and Cecilia.

The drive to the monastery the next morning was long and arduous. Most of the trip was spent on the main national highway, which was somewhat well serviced. However, once he departed Volodomyr for the local direction to the site, the road turned to a potholed path more than a modern transportation route. The last few kilometers took longer than the first fifty. Rafe was tired when he arrived. He first drove into the nearby village of Zymne and booked another room in a small inn perched on the hillside and surrounded by trees. It was a nice enough place. He would be assured of a good meal by the proprietors, he could tell. He looked forward to that on his return from his visit with the monks.

An hour later, he arrived at the monastery, which was perched on the top of a large hill overlooking the river running below. Rafe marveled at the contrast of the golden domes with the deep green meadows surrounding the complex. Dark clouds were approaching from the north. There was a thunderstorm coming. *Such a beautiful place. I'd like to come back here someday and explore but under different conditions.* The monastery had been fortified at one point, and the massive red brick walls and guard towers were a pronounced addition to the religious architecture. He parked the car and walked inside. He was met by an elderly priest.

"I wasn't expecting anyone quite at this hour," the priest said softly.

"Well, I came rather unexpectedly."

"Very well, follow me." Rafe decided to play along and did as he was told. He deferred showing the blessing from the bishop until it was needed.

The priest led him through the outer building and then through several passageways that seemed to go on forever, deep into the building. He seemed to know what Rafe was here for. At some point the priest stopped, turned, and handed Rafe a long, thin candle and pointed to another lit candle mounted on a stand near a small door. "You'll need the light," the priest said. Rafe dipped the tip of the small candle into the flame. The wick sparked a small glow and the flame slowly grew. Then the priest lit a candle as well and motioned for Rafe to follow him into the adjoining corridor. The priest opened the small, iron door, revealing a low passageway, and slowly started down the darkened steps.   Rafe followed. He immediately realized they were descending into the mountain. Soon they were walking through a tunnel that was carved into the rock. The air grew colder. The walls had been smoothed over the centuries and whitewashed. *We're in the catacombs,* Rafe thought to himself. Soon he passed the miniature coffin of a monk, which lay on a small shelf carved into the rock on the side of the tunnel. Then another. Eventually they passed close to fifty caskets. *Amazing how small these people were a thousand years ago,* Rafe thought to himself. *It's an eerie feeling being down here among all these bodies, even if they are hundreds of years old.*

Centuries ago, the monks would commit themselves to a life of reclusion. Some would even seal themselves in a small cave in order to commit totally to worshiping God. Food and water was placed in front of a small opening every day. If the servants noticed the food was uneaten, they assumed the monk was dead. They would then

116

seal the tomb completely for three years. At the end of that time, they would check if the body had deteriorated. If not, they would consider the monk a saint and prepare the body for burial in the catacombs. If the body did deteriorate, the monk was obviously a sinner, and the skeleton would be scattered among the caves. Since Rafe had been raised an Orthodox Christian, he turned and kissed one of the caskets as he walked by, saying a small prayer for the dead. The priest acknowledged his act with a look of surprise in his eyes. Rafe was not what he thought him to be.

Eventually Rafe and the priest stopped in front of an opening to a cavern naturally eroded into the earth. The priest turned and said, "I haven't seen you here before, but, you should be able to let yourself out. If you need anything, please ring the bell on the wall." He pointed to a long tapestry cord hanging in the corner, attached to a bell. He turned to leave.

"Wait," said Rafe. "Have there been others here before me?"

The priest looked at him in a strange way. "Why yes," he said. "The visitors come here regularly. I assumed you were one of them?"

"Oh yes, I am," replied Rafe. "Thank you."

"There were many here this morning. I thought you had all arrived." The priest smiled, turned, and left. Rafe said nothing and pretended to comprehend what the priest was talking about.

When he was gone, Rafe turned and walked into the cave. There was a sign above the opening with letters in Greek that he did not understand. He wrote them on a notepad he had taken from the hotel. The cave was nondescript and was obviously ancient. There were etchings on the wall from centuries before. It had been the dwelling of many a monk through the ages. There was a small, wooden bed and a writing table, not much else. Rafe carefully looked over the carvings in the wall and could not make heads or tails of most of them. He wrote many of them down in his pad. He glanced up and saw across the room something that got his attention. Carved into the wall near a wooden floor platform, he saw a large trident. It was the same he had seen in Gibraltar, only this one fit, as this was a monastery of Vladimir the Great. Rafe walked over to the etching and examined it. He drew an exact replica on his notepad. *Is this it? Is this what I am supposed to find? I don't understand. This is maddening. I wish Cecilia was here to help me with this.* The thought of her saddened him.

Rafe checked the rest of the cave and found nothing. *Am I at a dead end?* He went back down the passageway and made his way to the exit of the monastery. The priest was closing the main doors as he left. He saw Rafe and looked surprised. "You are leaving?"

"Yes, thank you for your help."

"You are different than the rest," he said as he looked at Rafe warily. "Are you sure you are one of them?"

Rafe pulled the letter from the bishop out of his jacket pocket and handed it to the priest. "I was sent here to find information. You have been helpful. I thank you."

The priest read the letter, and his eyes grew wide then shrank with wariness. "We are retiring for the evening meal and

118

meditation. I will close the doors behind you," he said coldly, aware he had been lied to.

"Thank you again," said Rafe, and he left, walked to the car, and drove back to the hotel, a feeling of frustration washing over him.

He was right about the food. He enjoyed a very nice Ukrainian meal. Rafe enjoyed the cuisine of Eastern Europe. It was very tasty and not as heavy as one would find in Germany and elsewhere. There were lots of freshly cooked vegetables that were usually well spiced, cuts of sausage, and smoked fish. A couple shots from a bottle of local vodka helped wash everything down. After eating, Rafe felt full and relaxed but still frustrated for lack of information.

After the dishes were cleared, Rafe spread the pages from the notepad out on the table in front of him. None of it made sense. Nothing stood out to him as significant. He had gone to his room and retrieved his laptop. Upon opening it, he pulled up his web browser and a translation page. He typed in the Cyrillic letters of the words □ □ □ □ □ μ□ □ □ □ ϖ□ □ □ □ □ . It was not a Ukrainian saying, and the software identified the language as Greek. He hit the translate button into English. A word appeared: *Doorway.* Rafe sat back in his chair. *That does not help me! What am I supposed to understand?* He slammed his fist down on the table. The waitress in the kitchen turned to look at him. He smiled and mouthed the word sorry in Ukrainian. She smiled back and returned to her conversation with the cook, occasionally staring back at him over her shoulder. She was young, cute, and obviously interested in him. *She probably thinks I'm rich and can be her ticket to the West*, he thought.

Rafe stared at the computer screen. *Doorway.*

Later that night Rafe awoke, wide-eyed. His mind was racing, even though he had been sleeping. Something had awakened him. *Was it a dream? I'm going to find out!* He bolted upright in bed and dashed to get dressed, clumsily throwing on his clothes. He left the room in a hurry, slamming the door behind him. Soon he was in the car, racing towards the monastery. The high beams on the rental car barely kept up with his speed as he negotiated the winding, barely paved road. *Doorway.*

Chapter Eleven

The night was pitch-black when Rafe arrived at the gates of the monastery. The moon was nowhere to be found, like it had been plucked from the heavens. Even the stars were absent in the night sky. Rafe could barely see his hand in front of him. He parked the car and shut the door as quiet as possible. There was no noise to be heard. The monastery was deathly quiet. Then he began walking through the massive open gates that connected the fortress walls to the large, wooden entrance of the monastery complex, barely making his way in the low light. Eventually he reached the main building. Rafe touched the door, and it moved ever so slightly inward and released a soft creak. It was open. He pushed the door forward and walked in. Everything was dim and silent. No one was waiting for him. There was a damp, musky small that he hadn't noticed before during the daytime.

He switched on the small penlight he had taken from his backpack and began to retrace his steps from earlier in the day with the priest. It was not difficult. The cavernous halls of the monastery caused the small beam to dissipate, but he easily found the passageways he was looking for. He still could not hear anything moving or anyone awake and soon was in the tunnel leading back into the depths of the mountain. He declined to light a candle as he passed through the small, iron doorway. The bodies of the monks were even more ghastly as he shone the light from his flashlight over the coffins. Occasionally one of the relics had a long dead hand exposed, the skin still wrapped around the fingernails resembling a claw more than a human hand. Rafe shuddered in the darkness. The silence was deafening and somewhat eerie. The click of his boots on the stone floor echoed through the tunnel.

At last he reached the cave, having effectively negotiated the winding maze to his satisfaction. Everything was still dark. Rafe was somewhat spooked, thinking of all the monks who had subsisted here for centuries. *If only these walls could talk,* he thought to himself. Rafe looked for the words written above the archway, found them, and entered the cavern. Soon he was standing in front of the wooden platform where above the trident was etched into the wall. *Doorway,* he thought. Rafe reached down to the platform. It was similar to a wooden pallet, raising the floor above the ground about six inches and providing a more civilized look to the cave. He pulled upwards on the outer edge of the small, stage-like structure. It moved. He pulled harder. It moved farther. Soon he had lifted the pallet and moved the flashlight to illuminate the surface underneath. There, embedded into the earth, was an iron door. Rafe pushed the wooden pallet upwards against the wall of the cave and bent down to examine the doorway he had just found. There were hinges on one side and a handle on the opposite side of the rectangular covering. He

122

reached to the handle and pulled. The door started to move, and he opened it fully until it rested against the floor of the cave opposite the opening. *I'm freaking crazy for doing this,* he thought.

Then he heard something and froze.

He heard something all right. It sounded like voices. Rafe pointed the light into the tunnel below and stared. There was nothing but blackness with a wooden stairway leading into the abyss. *Here we go.* He started down the passageway. The stairway was really nothing more than a very old ladder, the wooden planks bending as he stepped down. Eventually he hit the bottom and stood on the dirt floor of a tunnel. He was completely alone and vulnerable. *I've got to find Clare and Cecilia!* Rafe again pointed the light in the direction of the noise and slowly moved forward, bending slightly so his head would not hit the ceiling.

He walked carefully for about ten minutes as the air grew cold around him. The noises were becoming ever so slightly louder. There was a rumbling under his feet, like a bass speaker pounding out a rhythmic beat. At last Rafe saw a flicker of light ahead and slowed down even further. The sounds were loud now. He switched off his flashlight so he would not be discovered, put his hand against the earth wall, and inched forward, straining to see what was ahead.

Eventually he came to an opening in the tunnel; red and yellow light danced beyond the outlet like some monstrous aurora borealis. Rafe had a vague recollection that he had seen this type of light before, though not as concentrated. Then he realized it reminded him of the scene at the Circus Maximus. Carefully, he moved forward and looked into the space in front of him. He was looking into a cavernous, underground room. There was a large, rock platform fifty yards ahead of him. There was an altar built into the ledge, and a black, hooded figure stood on the ledge next to the altar. Several carcasses of dead animals were thrown to the side. The altar was stained with blood. Torches illuminated the cavern, and the light danced around the stalactites dripping in frozen time from the ceiling. It was a ghoulish scene. In front of Rafe, at least one hundred individuals in white, hooded robes were standing in front of the altar on the cave floor. Drums were beating in the background. Rafe recoiled in horror.

Lying on the altar was a woman. She was wrapped partially in a white cloth, her abdomen exposed. She was young and beautiful. Her long, dark hair flowed down around the end of the altar where her head lay. She was conscious but looked as if she was drugged. She was not moving.

Cecilia! Oh no!

Rafe walked out into the midst of the hooded followers. He no longer cared if he was seen. Another black, robed figure walked onto the altar. He held a long blade; the handle was encrusted with jewels. The two figures pulled off their hoods. The first was the woman he had seen before. The other figure was a man. *I've seen him before as well*, thought Rafe. *But where?*

124

The man walked to the altar and stood before it. He started chanting. The followers responded with a crescendo of rising voices. The climax was coming. The man raised the blade into the air over Cecilia.

Rafe burst through the crowd and screamed, "No!" The man thrust the blade down towards her abdomen, and the crowd roared. Rafe was halfway through the crowd, forcing his way through the hooded figures, screaming as he went. His view of the ceremony was blocked by the ecstatic crowd. Someone grabbed him from behind, and a cloth containing some type of chemical was forced over his face. The lights went out.

Someone was washing his face. He felt the cold rag on his forehead. It felt nice and he hoped it would continue. Dreams of distant events in his past washed over his unconscious mind. His mother's face flashed before him but was gone as quickly as she had come. Slowly, he began to realize all was not well.

As like tiny cuts from a sharp knife, the realization of what had happened slowly returned to his being. Rafe tried to get up but was held down by strong, caring arms. "Not yet, my son. Be still," he heard the voice say. "You've been attacked."

Then he realized it was the priest from the monastery, and the recent events rushed back to his memory. Rafe had a splitting headache and a metallic taste in his mouth from whatever chemical had been used to render him unconscious. *I've got to get up and awake!*

125

He soon realized he was lying in a bed in a chamber in the monastery. There were no personal effects lying about, so he surmised it was some sort of guest room. The only item of decoration was an Orthodox Cross hanging on the wall. "What happened?" Rafe asked as he opened his eyes.

"You tell me, my son," replied the priest. "We found you lying by your car, unconscious. So we brought you inside. That was about an hour ago. It is morning now. Why did you return? Do you remember anything?"

Rafe became fully awake. "Do you have some water?"

"Of course." The priest handed him a cup and he drank rapidly. Then he sat up, getting his bearings as he felt his strength returning. He got out of bed and put on his shoes. Ignoring the priest, he started walking, then running back through the corridors of the monastery towards the cave. A few minutes later, he arrived. The priest followed shortly after.

"What is wrong, my son?" Rafe ignored him.

Rafe darted over to the wooden platform, which had been lowered back to the earth. He pulled hard on the upper lip of the wood and jerked the pallet off the ground, expecting to find the iron door that he had entered the previous night.

Except there was no door. There was only earth. There was no evidence of any entrance. The only thing there was an engraving of a man riding a bull and slaying it with a spear.

Rafe turned and looked at the priest, his eyes betraying his rage.

126

"You'd better start talking and telling me what is going on here!" he demanded. "I want my daughter! Now!"

The priest stared at Rafe and said nothing for a few moments, and then he spoke in a low voice that Rafe could barely hear. The man had to be seventy years old, and his shoulders drooped as he spoke.

"You are not one of them, as I reasoned when I found you next to your car. So I will explain as much as I can. My son, there are things going on here that date back almost a thousand years that you cannot understand. Vladimir the Great founded this monastery centuries ago. He united all of the Slavic tribes under one kingdom. Kievan Rus' was the most powerful kingdom in all of Europe for a brief period. He chose Christianity for his people. He even married a Byzantine princess to unite what was left of the Holy Roman Empire with the Kingdom of Rus'. But it was not to last. Kiev was overrun by the Mongol invasions. We lost everything as a kingdom. The princes of Rus' fled to the village of Moscow far to the north."

"What does that have to do with what is going on here?" he screamed. "And where is my daughter? Last night a woman who I knew was murdered! I knew her dammit! She was good to me! Where is Clare?"

"My son, I do not know the answers to your questions. I do not know where your daughter is, but I can pray for you and her. You see, centuries ago, a group of people entered this place during those terrible days of the invasions. I fear they are still here. I fear they are what you saw last night, and I fear they are what you are trying to find. The people that come here we call the visitors. They come to the monastery in groups, and then they leave sometime later. You see, long ago a pact was made. The monks agreed the visitors could come, and in return, the monks were promised their safety and that they could continue their religious life. I'm afraid this pact still exists. That is all I can tell you because it is all that I know."

Rafe looked at the priest in disbelief. "You mean to tell me they have been coming here for a thousand years?"

"Yes."

Rafe fell to the floor and sat. He was dumbfounded. "Why here? And what happened to the tunnel I saw last night?"

"That I also do not know."

"What do I do now? How do I save my daughter?"

The priest walked over to him and put his hand on Rafe's head. He held out his other hand, and Rafe took from him a small, oval, flat object made of silver. "My son, we found this next to you. Perhaps this will lead you in the right direction."

Rafe took the metal piece and looked at the faint inscription. It was a coin of some kind and very thin, like a dime run through a press. He looked at the priest and said, "Where is this from?"

The priest looked at him sadly and said, "I think that is for you to find out."

Rafe doggedly rose from his position on the floor of the cave. "I'm on this journey that I have been on now for several weeks. I will continue until I find my daughter."

128

"My son, I must tell you, please be careful. If someone wanted you to die, you would be dead already. Yes, you are correct, you are on a journey. The problem is someone else knows where you are going, and you do not. I will pray for you."

Rafe thanked the priest, left the cave, and continued the trek to the entrance to the monastery. He turned to leave and faced the priest one last time. "Thank you."

"As I said, my son, I will pray for you and your daughter."

Chapter Twelve

Rafe sat at the table in the corner of the library, a stack of books in front of him detailing the history of coinage in Russia, Ukraine, and the general Slavic territories. The small, silver coin he had found at the monastery was safely in his pocket, yet he remembered the imprint vividly. From time to time he would take it out and compare it to the pictures of specimens he found in the books. So far, he had not found a resemblance. He was frustrated.

The Vernadsky National Library of Ukraine was located in central Kiev and was a modern architectural structure filled to the brim with over fifteen million items. It was a virtual treasure trove of Slavic civilization, containing historical writings, art, manuscripts, musical scores, and other matter. Vernadsky, born in the late eighteen hundreds, was the patriarch of Russian and Ukrainian geochemistry and founded the Ukrainian Academy of Sciences during the Russian Civil War. If Rafe was going to find out information on the coin, it would be here at this library somewhere. The problem was the amount of records here was so large, it could take some time. *Maybe a lot of time. Time which I don't have. Time is running out.*

After leaving the monastery, he had made his way as quickly as possible in the rental car back to Kiev, the potholed roads notwithstanding. The priest could not provide any more information on the visitors or the location of the chamber he had seen the day before. Nor could he comment on the ritual he had seen. Rafe had the sense the priest was not being truthful. *Hard to believe. I think the priest is part of this somehow. He's sending me on my way on purpose. It's like everyone I have met knows more than I do. I'm like a lamb on the way to the slaughter.* He had left early in the morning and arrived back in Kiev before the library closed for the day. He searched for answers until forced to leave. Rafe was waiting the next morning for the facility to open to continue his quest for information. After eight more hours of research, he was growing tired, though the pile of books to go through was still formidable.

He had narrowed down the time period from which the silver piece emanated. It was definitely an early example of Russian coinage from the beginning of the sixteenth century. Ivan the Terrible's mother, Elena Glinskaya, had instituted currency reform before Ivan took the throne. Russia, having united many of the eastern Slavic tribes of the land, began to mint currency for the entire kingdom. Rafe knew the coin fit this period because of the inscription on one side, which matched many of the early coins he had found in his research. He had also studied the imprints on the silver under a magnifying glass used for ancient texts in the historical wing of the library. The face of the coin, however, was like nothing that could be found. It consisted of a center Orthodox Cross surrounded by eight smaller crosses circled around it. Coins in that day were struck by cutting a wire made of silver in equal lengths, therefore providing an equal amount of metal for each article. The silver was then hammered between an upper and lower die to create the images. This is what gave the coin its oval shape.

Rafe was stumped. And he was really getting sick to death about his daughter. The image of the man plunging the knife downwards toward Cecilia tormented him. He tried not to think of her and kept looking through book after book until his eyes were red and stinging with pain.

After another hour with no success, Rafe slammed his current book shut, to the annoyance of several nearby library patrons. They looked at him with angry faces. He was not following the rules, and in former Soviet republics, the rules were paramount. He was getting nowhere. *Why am I on this wild goose chase? Where the hell is my daughter? I don't have time to keep looking at books!* Rafe stood up to stretch his legs and walked to the library exit and into the late afternoon sun. The library would be closing soon. He pulled out his phone and called Neal to ask if there was any news about Clare. There was nothing additional Neal could report. Rafe was at a dead end and in danger of losing his daughter. Then he had an idea. He took his phone back out and dialed the number of a Ukrainian friend from years ago who now taught at KNU, or the National University of Kiev.

After the phone call, Rafe was on his way. Since the library and the university were fairly close together in Kiev, Rafe and his friend Maxim had agreed to meet at a restaurant for dinner that was located approximately equidistant between them. The place was a Georgian establishment which served a style of food that Rafe loved. The Georgian cuisine developed over time as the trade routes between East and West crossed the Georgian territory in central Asia for centuries. The food was a blend of many cultures and tended to be spicy and exotic. The style of food permeated all the countries of the former Soviet Union, as Stalin himself was a Georgian and encouraged the cuisine to be prepared wherever he traveled within the Soviet republics.

Rafe entered the establishment after driving the short distance required. The mild smoke from the hookah pipes hit him in the face as he walked in. Smoking the hookah or kalyan had made its way up to the Ukraine from the Levant over the centuries. It was the custom of smoking a device that forced the smoke through water before being inhaled. Westerners would know it as a form of a bong. A myriad of tobacco flavors were available, and the practice was quite fashionable during a long meal with friends. Georgian meals tended to be long. Every table was adorned with colorful, ornate pipes set to one side.

Rafe and Maxim enjoyed a nice meal complete with wine and enjoyed catching up with each other and discussing the current events in Ukraine. This had been Rafe's task in the past to stay up to speed on the happening in Kiev, so Maxim expected the same at this meeting. After some time, Rafe changed the direction of the conversation.

"I need your help, my friend."

133

Maxim said nothing for a moment and then replied. "Tell me what you need and it will be done."

Rafe reached into his pocket, pulled out the coin, and handed it to him. Maxim's eyes widened as he visualized the imprints on the silver.

"Where did you get this?" he said excitedly.

Maxim had built his reputation at the university as being an expert in Ukrainian, Russian, and general Slavic history. That is why Rafe had cultivated a friendship with him over the years while working to provide Neal information on what was happening in Ukraine.

"It's not important where I got it. What I need to know is what it represents. I need to know anything you know about this coin. It's a long story, but my daughter's life depends on it."

"Your daughter's life? I don't understand."

"And you won't understand. I just need to comprehend completely everything you know about the period and what this could represent. What it could be telling me."

Maxim thought for a few moments and then began speaking. "Ivan the Terrible had these struck in the mid sixteenth century. After Russia captured Kazan, he commissioned a cathedral to be built near the Kremlin in Moscow to commemorate the event. The cathedral consisted of a central church surrounded by eight smaller churches. There were one hundred coins struck to celebrate the cathedral being finished. See the central cross surrounded by the smaller images? These represent the central and surrounding churches of the cathedral. It is said that Ivan thought the structure was so beautiful that he had the eyes put out of the architect to prevent anything so beautiful from being built again. Although, that probably is not true but we will never know."

"You mean this coin was struck to commemorate the completion of St. Basil's Cathedral on Red Square?"

"Yes. And there are only a couple known to be in existence, and they are in museums. Where did you get this again?"

"Like I said, that's not important. I appreciate your expertise. This has been very helpful."

"This belongs in a museum."

"Once I find my daughter, I give you my word, I will put it in the museum of your choice." Rafe and Maxim finished their meal, parted, and Rafe was once again on his own in Kiev.

Rafe again sat alone in a bar in Kiev, surfing the net on his laptop and trying to make sense of his whole situation. *Why does someone want me to go to Moscow?* The questions were too numerous to make sense of anything. *I guess I have to go. Luckily my visa is still valid. Whatever rollercoaster ride I'm on, I hope I get off soon.*

He pulled up information on St. Basil's Basilica. The onion-domed church was a historical symbol of Russia and Moscow in particular. The architecture was unique among Russian work and was not replicated anywhere else during the tsar's reign. The multiple domes were meant to portray a flame flickering towards the heavens. Rafe had visited the structure, now a state museum

135

since being secularized almost a century before by the Soviets, years before on a trip to the Russian capital. He tried to remember the layout, but the details were fuzzy in his mind. He studied the web page which described the cathedral in depth. *What is the relation to me?* Nothing was clear.

Rafe ordered another drink and tried to reorient his thinking. *Maybe I am thinking about this the wrong way? How is all of this connected? Ancient Rome, Mythraism, Kiev, the monastery, Vladimir the Great, Ivan the Terrible, now Moscow? And the rituals? Clare's disappearance? Cecilia's death?* The thought of Cecilia being gone chilled his soul, and he felt a numbness from his body's natural reaction to the psychological pain.

Rafe was tired and the alcohol was clouding his thinking. He couldn't put the pieces together. Nothing made sense. *Someone is taking me on a tour through history. But what history? What is the significance?* Rafe went over his words again in his mind.

Suddenly he sat upright in his chair and started typing on his electronic notepad while the thoughts were clear in his mind. *All of these things are connected! When western Rome fell, all that was left was the Byzantine Orthodox Christian Empire. When they were overrun by the Ottomans, Vladimir the Great had turned Kievan Rus' into a Christian kingdom. Kiev was also overrun by the Mongolian hordes and destroyed! Then Moscow attempted to become the third Holy Roman Empire, taking the mantle from the kingdom of Kievan Rus'. Ivan the Terrible tried to make this happen! Is that the connection? The fortunes of these great civilizations?* Suddenly Rafe had energy. He redoubled his efforts to study the layout of St.

136

Basil's Cathedral. *The answer is here somewhere! I can feel it! I'm coming Clare! Daddy's coming! Hold on, my love, I'm getting closer!*

Rafe poured over the diagrams of the cathedral. There had been many changes and additions over the centuries. There were countless nooks and crannies, as the nine different churches were designed to all fit together. There was a crypt located below the entire structure with secret entrances. A tenth church was added after Ivan's death and was built upon the grave of the famous St. Vasily; hence the cathedral's name was changed in his honor. There were thousands of places inside the structure where clues could lie. Rafe decided he could not figure out the answer by looking at the cathedral online. *I have to go there. I have to go to Moscow.*

Chapter Thirteen

The Aeroflot jet descended towards Sheremetyevo Airport in Moscow, the capital of the Russian Federation. The flight had been a pleasant one, the Russian female flight attendants taking good care of him. Aeroflot had changed dramatically since the Soviet days, now flying state of the art aircraft and staffed with professional crews schooled in customer service. However, Rafe missed having Cecilia next to him, and the loss was unbearable. *I'm going to make whoever did this to her pay!* he thought murderously to himself. The flight had been delayed on the runway for some time due to unknown reasons, but the delay had given Rafe a lot of time to think. He had tried to draw out a diagram of everything he knew was going on and put the pieces together. Luckily the flight was not full, and he could spread out with his hastily jotted notes on the seat next to him. He was no closer to enlightenment, but he could feel the answer somewhere in the back of his brain. It just wasn't part of his consciousness yet. The thought of this was maddening all the same. It was like waking from a vivid dream and trying in vain to remember what his mind had told him while asleep.

The monk's comments about the visitors kept creeping back into his mind. *Who are these people? Why did they want to come to a monastery in Ukraine? How can I find out more about them? Do they have Clare?* He was being swept up by something that had been going on for a thousand years. *Or longer? But why me?* The questions kept coming that he couldn't answer. *Are they in Moscow as well? I guess I'm going to find out one way or the other.*

Upon landing, the plane taxied for a long time. Eventually Rafe looked out the portal near his seat to find out what was going on. They had parked at the Aeroflot terminal, which was currently not being used and located across the airfield. There had been some type of fire on one of the parked commercial airliners. The top of the plane was burnt, and fire trucks and crews were all around it. This was the reason for the delay. Soon, his aircraft was parked and then began to exit onto the tarmac. Buses were waiting to take them to the main Aeroflot concourse. A long drive and forty-five minutes later, Rafe was waiting at immigration for entrance into Russia.

He processed through customs and immigration quickly, as his bag was spit out immediately on the baggage claim conveyer belt. He had taken a chance, and he felt the outside pocket of his sutcase. His pistol grip was safely inside. The remaining pieces were spread throughout the bag.

The first thing he noticed about Russia was the plethora of young, beautiful women in high heels strutting around the different boutiques. Rafe resisted the urge to have a coffee and people watch at one of the many small cafes sprinkled among the high-end retail shops dominating the airport interior. Multiple stores with a myriad of matryoshkas of all shapes and sizes on display were also prevalent. The nesting dolls were an old Russian village craft, which was said to represent the generations of mothers in Russia, taking care of their young and passing on the ancient traditions of the Motherland.

Instead, Rafe bought a ticket at the kiosk and boarded the Aeroexpress train into the city from Sheremetyevo. Soon he was staring out the window of the train. Forests of white birch trees lined the sides of the railway tracks as he endured the forty-five minute ride. The cabins of the train were spacious and modern and filled with travelers. Rafe understood most of the Russian language being spoken, as it was similar to Ukrainian. His Russian was somewhat out of practice. The passengers left him alone. *I must look like I fit in.* He closed his eyes to rest as the train rolled on, rocking him back and forth.

The cabin was equipped with a thin-screen television mounted over the entrance to the car. The channel was tuned to some kind of state media, and Rafe did his best to ignore the talking heads as he tried to sleep away the ride. It was then that he had a flash of insight. Rafe opened his eyes and stared at the screen. Some type of business investment show was airing. *The face I saw before at the underground ritual. I remember it now. He's a former politician. Now he is some type of political operative. A talking head on the Sunday shows. Yes, I remember him now. But how does he connect to the woman I saw before?* Rafe was no closer to an answer. Fully awake now, he pulled out his phone and called Neal.

"Yes?" Neal answered.

"Have you found any more information on people from the UK traveling to Ukraine, specifically Kiev?"

"No, not from the UK. But we have done similar runs with our friends across the pond. And yes, there are many. All very high-profile people. Why?"

"Because I've seen one of them." Rafe recounted the incident at the monastery to Neal, including his assumption that Cecilia was dead. He also mentioned his discovery regarding the coin the priest had given him. *Did the priest really find it next to me, or was he instructed to give it to me?* "I again recognized one of the participants. His name is Roger Badson. He's all over the Sunday talk shows talking about domestic policy. I think he was in a previous administration in the U.S. as an undersecretary or something. I never really listened to him, so I'm not positive on his background. Check him out for me, okay? He's in up to his eyeballs in whatever is going on, and I want to know what he knows."

"Got it, will do. I'm sorry about Cecilia, Rafe, but let's concentrate on finding your daughter," replied Neal. "Where are you?"

"I'm in Moscow. I'm going to find out what the hell is going on no matter where it takes me. Someone wants me here. St. Basil's Basilica is next on my must-see list."

"Be careful. Call if you need help."

"Will do, thanks." Rafe hung up the phone.

No longer able to sleep, Rafe soon arrived at Belorusskaya metro station in Moscow. The station was on the outer ring of the subway and was packed. He had difficulty getting to the other line on the perpendicular track. Finally, he changed trains and took the line into the center of the city. The passengers on the subway were more finely dressed than in Kiev and carried themselves in a different manner. There was much more wealth in Moscow. The people emanated a more obvious self-confidence. The confidence of a people used to ruling others.

He emerged into the terrazzo area outside the Kremlin near Red Square thirty minutes later. The area was full of tourists and groups of Russian schoolchildren taking tours of Russian history. Laughter and the excitement of being let out of school filled the air. The center of Moscow gave a visitor a feeling of power, which was the original architect's intention. The massive, deep red walls of the Kremlin, which means fortress in Russian, stood menacingly, surrounding the interior, where the heart of the Russian government was located.

The site where the Kremlin stood, overlooking the Moscow River, was initially inhabited at the end of the first millennium by Slavic tribes using the river for trade. As the seat of Slavic civilization moved north to Moscow after the Mongol invasions, slowly a fortress city took shape on the historical trading route. In the fifteenth century, Italian master craftsmen, fresh from the Renaissance, were hired to build the Kremlin walls that exist today. The Italian style of design can be seen in the architectural flourishes that adorn the towers.

The interior of the citadel initially held multiple cathedrals, palaces, and churches and had changed drastically over the centuries as each successive government made its mark on the area. Many of the structures had been demolished and others rebuilt. Invaders such as Napoleon also destroyed many of the relics. Stalin and the Soviets tore down many buildings as well. Currently, the Russian government was slowly restoring what remained to its former glory. The residence of the Russian president was also located inside the Kremlin walls, curiously accessible to the wandering tourist.

Rafe made his way from the metro towards Alexander Garden on the west side of the citadel. He passed the Tomb of the Unknown Soldier, a reminder of the Great Patriotic War, the Russian name for World War II. After almost being defeated by Hitler, the Soviets repelled the Nazi invasion of Moscow early on in the war in a cataclysmic battle and pushed the Germans back towards Eastern Europe. They lost twenty million men to the Axis powers during the war, a scale of loss that most Westerners can't comprehend. The victory was a great source of pride for the Russian people.

Rafe crossed the garden to the ticket office for entrance to the Kremlin. After paying the fee, he crossed through Kutafya Tower, a medieval outer defense perimeter, and walked the causeway towards the open gates of the Trinity Tower and soon was crossing the cobblestone road near the president's residence. However, Rafe did not notice his surroundings; his eyes were focused across the Cathedral Square, towards a single golden-domed structure on the

143

eastern corner of the area. He was headed towards the Archangel Cathedral. There was something located inside he wanted to see.

Rafe passed the Tsar Bell and Tsar Cannon and found himself staring up at a single golden onion dome surrounded by three blue, circular, smaller domes. The cathedral was made of white stone and had many frescoes adorning the sides of the structure, mainly ordered by Ivan the Terrible in 1564. He walked to the southwestern wall of the building and entered through the main entrance. The first things he saw were the icons, hundreds of them, large and small, decorating the interior walls of the cathedral and filling the air with glittering gold masterpieces. Then he saw the tombs, which lined the floor of the cathedral near the columns; for the Archangel Cathedral was the royal necropolis. More than fifty members of the royal dynasty were buried here. The bodies were entombed under the floor beneath white stone grave monuments covered with polished brass. Rafe looked skyward inside the structure and saw the walls and columns were decorated with elaborate murals depicting religious scenes and ancient Russian saints, their lives playing out across the ages through art. However, Rafe was not here to look at icons or graves of unremarkable tsars. He moved through the crowd towards the eastern corner of the church where a special vault was located on the altar. There were three graves. Rafe patiently waited his turn to look, as this was the most popular part of the cathedral, and there was a small line. Rafe finally arrived in front of the vault a few minutes later. There he saw three graves

144

with ornate, polished-stone monuments above. There lay Ivan the Terrible and his two sons, Ivan and Feodor.

Ivan Grozny, or Ivan the Terrible in English, was the first tsar to reign over all of what we consider modern-day Russia. He was a tortured soul after the death of his beloved wife Anastasia, who was thought to have been poisoned. It is said after this event, he was prone to fits of rage and mental illness. In fact he beat his daughter-in-law, who was married to his groomed heir, Ivan, and caused her to have a miscarriage. Upon confronting his father, the younger Ivan himself was struck in the head by his father and died shortly thereafter. The loss of his son threw Ivan Grozny into further fits of depression and terrible rage. The death of the younger Ivan left Ivan Grozny and the Rurik dynasty heirless. His weak son, Feodor, took the throne upon Ivan's death, and when Feodor died, he ushered in the Time of Troubles as Russia looked for a leader. Ivan Grozny also greatly centralized power in the hands of the Kremlin, which still can be seen in Russian society to this day.

Rafe pulled the small, silver coin Ivan had struck out of his pocket and looked at the imprint of the nine crosses. He then looked up and right to the icon of Archangel Michael, who stood guarding the remains of the tsars. The royal Russians believed the archangel would protect them in battle and guarded the bloodline of the tsars. A narrative was starting to shape in Rafe's mind. Slowly he thought maybe he was starting to figure out what was going on. *But it's not clear yet. Not yet.*

Rafe left the cathedral and reversed his course back out of the Kremlin gates. Soon he was walking towards the tourist center on the northern wall of the fortress. There he paid for another ticket for entrance into St. Basil's Basilica. Then he walked through the Iberian Gate onto the paved Red Square. The Kremlin Walls to the right were the highest here, as this side of the fortress was the most prone to invasion, because it was not protected by natural barriers such as the Moscow River on the opposite side. To the left was the famous GUM department store, which began its existence as a trading center centuries ago. Today it was filled with high-end boutiques and designer goods for the wealthy Muscovites to enjoy. No longer was it a drab, communist magazine adorned with empty shelves and inferior products. In front of him, across the massive expanse of cobblestone pavement, rising from the earth like a flame to the heavens, was St. Basil's Basilica. *Well, this is what I came for. Let's see what it has in store for me.* Rafe kept walking towards the cathedral.

The light darkened as Rafe stepped into the ancient structure. Hushed tourist voices could be heard throughout the catacomb passageways. Directly in front of him was a small, circular church with a glittering altar. Icons and murals adorned the walls, similar to the other religious buildings he had seen earlier in the day. To his right was a small museum room with examples of the different types of construction techniques and materials that were discovered at the cathedral over the centuries. As Rafe walked around the first church and into the passageway towards the interior,

146

the displays continued with works of art and examples of life years ago. He stopped to inspect a display of ancient Russian coinage. There among the small pieces of silver under the glass casing was a replica of the coin the priest had given him at the monastery. *At least I know I'm at the right place,* Rafe thought to himself.

Soon he was faced with a multitude of choices of direction to continue. He chose a small doorway to the left and found himself in the entrance to the crypt below. It was walled off but explained what existed below the floors of the basilica. Rafe could not find a way to sneak into the underground vault. *Dead end,* he thought.

Making his way back to the center, he encountered a sliver of an ancient stairway winding its way to the second floor. He took the bait and soon found himself struggling to maintain balance on the warped and sinking stairs. He emerged from the steps into one of the small churches surrounding the main hall of the basilica. The tourists were whispering in soft tones as they examined the old relics and icons adorning the stone walls. Light shone in from windows above designed to highlight certain areas of the church. *What am I supposed to find here?*

Rafe made his way around the circular passageways that connected the eight unique, smaller churches and surrounded the interior. Each of the smaller altars was similar but with different icons and saints staring down from above the entrance. Open-air, covered stairways exited from different points to the cobblestone square below. Rafe checked each small church, looking for clues or something that would explain why he had been drawn to this location. *Maybe I'm mistaken. I don't even know what I am looking for!* His frustration was building.

He rounded a corner towards the next church and noticed that there was a metal grate embedded in the wall on the other side of the passageway, which gave a view into one of the earlier churches he had inspected. The entrance to the small cathedral he had ventured into earlier, however, was far around the corridor on the other side of the basilica. Rafe froze in his tracks as he peered through the metal grating. There, sitting on the floor alone and staring at the ground, was his daughter.

"Clare!" he shouted.

She looked up and saw him but did not seem to recognize him. She looked scared and unsure of what to do. He ran to the grate and spoke to her.

"Clare, it's Daddy, come here, my love!"

Clare stood and seemed to hesitate, saying nothing. Then she turned and ran out of the church into the far alleyway of the cathedral, disappearing into the crowd of tourists.

"Clare!" Rafe yelled again. "Please, someone, that's my daughter. Stop her!" he screamed. The people around him, not understanding English, only stared.

Rafe bolted from his position and sprinted around the circular passageway, trying to make it back to the entrance to the church opposite the circular basilica where she had exited, knocking into several tourists as he did so. He didn't care. He arrived about a

148

minute later. He searched everywhere in the area to no avail. She was gone.

Rafe had searched the entire cathedral twice. He had even enlisted the help of the local policeman who was guarding the entrance, and tried to explain his story to him. The policeman did not seem to be of much help. In fact, he started asking questions of his own, demanding Rafe's passport, which he showed him. This threatened Rafe, so he left it alone and wandered off. *Nothing.* He was eaten alive with anxiety and worry. *She couldn't just vanish into thin air!* He left St. Basil's and walked out onto Red Square, as if he would find something there. The sky was slowly darkening, and the frustration was maddening. He walked toward Lenin's tomb, stood in front of the Kremlin wall, and just stared, lost in thought and sadness. *I don't know where to go from here. I almost had her back.*

"I think they should bury him, don't you?" a man asked behind him. Rafe turned. There standing in front of him was the man he had seen in Barcelona and on the train. Rafe's fists clenched with fury. The bulge of the 9mm felt reassuring, tucked into his belt under his sport jacket. Rafe debated grabbing it. The man sensed his anger.

"Your anger will do you no good. Especially here." He motioned with his eyes towards the Russian policeman standing guard towards the tomb's entrance.

"Where is she, you son of a bitch?" Rafe said angrily, his mouth full of grit.

"She's safe. I just wanted you to see that. Really, she's just fine. She rather likes her new set of parents."

"What the hell do you mean by that?"

"Don't worry, just a joke. I know I've put you through a rough time, Rafe, but I have a favor to ask. I want you to listen to me, right here for a bit. Okay?"

"Doesn't seem like I have a choice."

"No, you really don't. I planned it this way. It worked out well, didn't it?"

"I guess it did. What the fuck do you want?"

"I want you to join my little merry band of men. And women, for that matter."

"Why would you want me to do that?"

"That I cannot tell you, not yet. However, I do want you to meet me tonight. We are having another one of our little gatherings. Can you be there, say at 2:00 a.m.? Then we can have a little discussion. Does that work for you?" the man said in a gentlemanly voice.

Rafe stared at the man intensely. If he didn't know the man was a vile kidnapper who held his four-year-old daughter, Rafe would have considered him quite charming. He was smartly dressed and obviously very confident. He decided to play along with whatever game the man was playing.

150

"Again, I don't think I have a choice. Will my daughter be there?"

"Oh, she most certainly will be."

"Where?"

"Do you know of the Tsaritsyno Estate south of Moscow?"

"Yes, I have been there before some time ago."

"Good, meet us there."

"Where? That reserve is over five hundred hectares."

"I think you will find us." With that, the man turned and slowly walked away.

Chapter Fourteen

Rafe held on to the metal, horizontal pole running the length of the cabin on the metro as the train decelerated, violently coming to a stop and throwing him forward against fellow travelers. A teenage girl was taking advantage of the free WIFI on the train, and he almost knocked the iPad out of her hand. "Izvenetia (sorry)," he muttered. She turned away with an annoyed look on her face.

He was so lost in thought, he almost didn't make it out of the car before the doors closed. The doors on trains and elevators in Russia were not so forgiving as those in the West; one could lose an arm trying to stop them from closing. He exited the train car just as they shut behind him. *Get hold of yourself! Concentrate!* He was standing in the middle of Tsaritsyno station. The complex, opening on a subway extension in the early eighties, was not an artistic masterpiece like the interior metro stations of Moscow. However, it was clean, modern, and safe. He followed the commuters and found the way to the vyhod v gorod, or exit to the city. The traffic was heavy at this time of the day, as people were heading home from work.

Rafe was no longer frightened or worried about what was happening. No, he was just angry, murderously angry. He would make this man and this group, whoever they were, pay and pay

152

dearly. Those around him in the station could tell he was a man with a purpose. He noticed no one. The Beretta was lodged in the back of his belt, under his shirt. Seeing the look on his face, people avoided him as they went about their business. They were used to the angry gangster type in Moscow and knew to stay clear.

He left the metro station as night was falling and began walking toward the large, metal gates to the estate. Tsaritsyno was a four-hundred-year-old royal retreat southwest of Moscow. The five-hundred-hectare reserve was originally owned by aristocratic families in the seventeenth century. However, Catherine the Great was riding through the countryside around Moscow in the seventeen hundreds and fell in love with the idyllic surroundings of rolling grass, sparkling lakes, and carved canyons. She immediately commissioned a summer home to be built on the site. Several years later, upon visiting the construction for the first time, she hated what had been built. She considered the rooms cramped and dark, so she gave instructions for the stone structure to be torn down. The empress commissioned another architect, and a larger, more grand retreat was initiated. However, she died before the estate was completed, and it sat abandoned for two hundred years, used for rock climbing, among other things. After the fall of the Soviet Union, the new Moscow government restored the site to its former glory and finished the structure. It was now a sprawling estate and park and a heavy favorite of Muscovites to relax in any season. In addition to the plethora of museums located in the original residence and beyond, there were a myriad of cultural activities offered, along with restaurants, nature walks, and other public activities.

Rafe made it into the reserve right before it closed for the evening, as he had planned. While he walked towards the initial opulent fountain, placed squarely in the middle of one of the large ponds via the causeway, the shadows from the spiraling water were making shapes on the grassy hill on the other side. Mothers were pushing their tired children in strollers to the exit after a fun, adventure-filled day in the park. He strolled quickly, as he endeavored to make it to the edge of the woods with plenty of time to spare. He wanted a place to be secluded and did not want the security guards to see him enter the forest surrounding the estate. The throng of people exiting the park gave him cover. Rafe briefly stopped on the ornate bridge, lined with large, opulent, stone chess figures. The white and red statues gave the walkway a childish, magical feel. He gazed at the entire structure rising in front of him. It was magnificent. *No wonder the Russians were so angry at the Romanovs.* The main residence was a splendid, gargantuan specimen of neo-Gothic architecture, a stunning masterpiece. Various outbuildings complemented the main structures. Soon he was walking again. He was not here to see the historical buildings. He was here to find a ritual. And, he thought he knew just where that would be.

Rafe purposefully bypassed the residence towering to the right of him, following the paved walkway. He passed through the ornate gate that led to the inner grounds and entered a courtyard centered on a large statue of the architects who designed and built the compound. On the opposite side of the terrace, multiple pathways extended into the forest, which protected the rear of the residential area. Far to the right, Rafe saw a continuation of the ponds that had adorned the front of the estate. He chose the path in that direction and eventually passed by gardens that had been cleared and created in the forest. He soon found himself walking along the shore of the water. Ducks and other birds dove into the water, feeding on the plethora of small creatures abundant in the ponds. Eventually he turned left up the embankment on another path, which led deep into the woods. He was following the signs to the amphitheater. *If there is anywhere there will be a ritual, it will be there,* he thought to himself. Soon Rafe was surrounded by white birch trees, which seemed to draw him deeper and deeper into the abyss, their leaves further darkening the light. Twenty minutes later, the quiet was deafening as he walked slowly. The forest seemed magical as the red squirrels danced around him, occasionally standing to beg him for a morsel of food. They were used to the humans in the park offering treats for free. The birds occasionally chirped their ancient hymns. The sun would be setting within thirty minutes or so. There was no one around.

He crested a small hill, and the amphitheater opened up in front of him. *Perfect. Yes, this has to be it. The scene is exactly what they would want.* Rafe studied the area for five minutes, walking around and checking all the entrances and exits so they would be fresh in his mind. Then he decided to walk up into the forest and wait, somewhere where he could see what was happening below in the general area of the theater. He wanted to be in control, to dictate the events to come. He was tired of being caught off guard. It was time to change the momentum of this game and find his daughter. Rafe was happy with his plan. He walked from the stage back to the crest of the structure and continued up the hill into the woods.

He had gone about fifty yards when a man walked out of the trees onto the path ahead, startling him. The man held out a small glass towards Rafe. It contained a liquid.

"Drink this," the man said.

"Yeah right, like I'm going to do that," Rafe replied angrily after regaining his composure and feeling for his pistol.

"I think you will, and if you ever want to see your daughter again, you'll put your hands by your side. I know you have a weapon. But it will do you no good here, especially if you want to see Clare."

Rafe said nothing for thirty seconds. "Fine," he replied. *What choice do I have?*

"I knew you would come to your senses. You're not a stupid guy."

"Hey, I know you," Rafe said.

"You know nothing."

"Yes, I know you. I've seen you on TV. You're some congressman or something."

"Drink," the man said coldly.

"Tell me what's going on here."

"This is your last chance. Drink."

Rafe walked forward, took the glass, and drank the liquid. Then the world went black.

The first thing he saw were the flames licking the dark night all around him, again like orange northern lights. He felt as if he was in the middle of a giant fireplace but not burning. Then he realized the flames were coming from the torches. They encircled him. In the fog that was his mind, Rafe heard the chanting. Then he was scared. And even though it was a warm night, he felt cold, like he was shivering in the fires of hell.

As the drug wore off, Rafe realized he was lying down. He was lying down on something hard. It hurt his hip bone but he couldn't move, couldn't shift to relieve the pain. It felt like stone. It was stone. He was lying on an altar in the middle of the amphitheater. He was restrained by some type of straps. He couldn't even move his hands. His weapon was gone. He tried to resist but couldn't, so instead, he relaxed.

"Don't fight it," a voice said, a voice he recognized.

Rafe fought to speak. "Where's my daughter?"

"She's safe as I told you."

"I want to see her."

"That's not possible. Not now. You've seen her once today; that's enough."

Rafe slowly started to realize where he was and looked at his surroundings. He turned his head left and saw dozens of white, hooded figures chanting softly towards the altar. The sight frightened him. *I'm going to die.* Somehow the thought calmed him, and he turned his head to the right. There on the stage stood the man from Barcelona. He was clothed in a black robe. To his side was another black-robed figure. It was the congressman and he held a long blade. Its steel sparkled in the dancing light of the torches. The American walked over to Rafe, smiling an evil expression. The other man from Barcelona, the European he had met on Red Square didn't move; he just looked at Rafe from his black covering.

"What do you want from me?" asked Rafe with anger in his voice.

"I want you to find something for me," the dark man answered, again with an accent Rafe couldn't quite place.

"And we want you to join us," the congressman added.

"And if I don't agree to do this?"

"Then you will die right now, along with your daughter." The American came closer with the knife, his smile widening, happy at the thought of slicing open Rafe's gut, although he said nothing.

"What is it you want me to find?"

"You will have to figure that out for yourself."

"That's ridiculous. How can I find it if I don't know what I am looking for?"

"You will know, eventually. You will understand at the right time. Now is not that time yet."

158

"Where do I look for it? And why me?"

"That will come in time as well. Do we have an agreement?"

"I don't have a choice," said Rafe. "Yes. Now when do I get to see my daughter as you promised?"

"Your daughter will be returned to you in due time, when you have completed what I ask."

"Who are you and these people? Are you the visitors the priest spoke of? Why do you go to Kiev? Why to Moscow?" Rafe motioned with his face towards the robed figures, who were chanting quietly.

"You will come to know who I am and who we all are. And you will become one of us. In due time."

"I will never become one of whatever you are!"

"We will see about that."

It was then Rafe realized there was another altar next to him, at his feet. There was a bound animal on the stone table. The American raised the knife high above what looked like a goat thrashing in the night. The crowd's chanting became louder. The poor animal was wailing loudly, obviously terrified. Rafe glanced around again; there were other symbols painted on cloth banners held up by pikes. Impaled on these pikes were the bodies of animals recently slain. Rafe tried to make sense of the symbols, but alas, his mind was still groggy from the effects of whatever drug they had given him. Someone put a cloth over Rafe's face, and he tasted metal before he blacked out yet again.

Chapter Fifteen

Rafe opened his eyes but quickly closed them as the blinding sun crashed through his pupils. His head hurt, really bad. The sunlight wasn't helping. The straps were gone and he tried to sit up. The pounding in his head was like a jackhammer, and his back ached. Slowly he rose from the stone altar in the amphitheater to the sound of birds chirping in the nearby forest. He tried to regain his composure. The grogginess withdrew from his mind, ever so faintly. I have to stop waking up in these strange places, he thought as he struggled to become completely lucid.

The conversation from the night before with the leader of the visitors came back to him in bits and pieces, like an amnesia victim. The piecemeal recollections hit him like a brick. Clare! Rafe was jerked back to reality when he thought of his daughter. He jumped off the altar and then surveyed the area around him. There was no trace of the sacrifice from the night before, not even a drop of blood on the ground. Any evidence had been wiped completely clean, like it had never happened. He was alone and felt it. The aching for his Clare was more pronounced, like a deep hunger pain that wouldn't be satisfied, coupled with nausea by the thought of her predicament.

What do I do now? Rafe tried to make sense of the previous night's conversation. He needed to find a lead, a way forward. He needed to make something happen. I think it's time I get smarter on my Roman and Russian history. I need to figure out what's happening. He started walking back towards the exit to Moscow. The estate was deserted. With nowhere else to turn, Rafe pulled out his phone and called his MI6 contact once again.

"Hello, it's me," he said into the phone quietly, although he could see no one around him as he walked the long trek back to the entrance to the Tsaritsyno Estate. The gates would not open for several more hours.

"Where are you?" asked Neal.

"I'm leaving Tsaritsyno. Let's just say it has been a long night."

"Really, I guess you will fill me in at some point. What can I do for you?"

"I need a resource. I'm not that connected here and I need to speak to someone. Someone very learned in Russian history. I've got to make some sense if I can with what is going on around me. There is a method to this madness. I just have to find out what it is! Can you do that for me? Somewhere discreet? I'm sure I'm being followed or watched somehow."

"Sure I can do that." Neal was silent for a moment as he thought about the situation. "Head to Gorky Park. There is a parkour arena there with seating around so people can watch. Have a seat and call me when you get there. I'll have someone meet you."

"Thanks, Neal."

"No problem. Also, whatever you are on to, believe me, it's big. There are people all over the country involved in the U.S. It's the same in the UK. People in very high places. It's alarming. It's been happening for quite some time, right under our noses. We appreciate your bringing this to our attention, and please keep me in the freaking loop, okay?"

"Well you should know what happened last night. They have me on a mission now. I just don't know what it is." Rafe told Neal of the prior evening's conversation while he lay prostrate on the altar.

"Interesting. Again, keep me informed. We are not as deep as far as resources as we were during the Cold War, but we do have people there. You will talk to one of them today. Take care."

Rafe hung up the phone and found a place to wait near the gardens behind the estate residence. Two hours later, the huge gates to Tsaritsyno were opened and he exited, making his way to the metro.

Neal hit the red button on his cell phone and terminated the call. However, he did not replace the phone into the pocket of his sport coat, from where he had taken it when Rafe's call came through. Neal had another call to make. He typed the numbers and dialed.

"Yes?" a European male voice answered.

"I've sent him to Gorky Park as you requested. My guy is going to meet him there. I've told him what to say, how to lead him in the right direction. I've done what you asked me to do."

"Thank you, Neal. You have done your job well as always since we concluded our little agreement. Your loyalty and efficiency will be rewarded in due time. Let me know please if he calls again."

"I most certainly will. Do you have any other instructions for me?" Neal asked.

"No, just keep me in the loop if he calls you."

"Done." Neal ended the second call and pulled out a cigarette to light, in spite of the heat of the Mediterranean, which beat down on him from above, to try to quell his uneasiness. He needed to calm his nerves. I hate doing this to Rafe. I hope he's going to be okay. He really is a nice chap. But I really hate talking to this Spanish guy, whoever he is. He gives me the freaking creeps. Neal looked down at his hands and noticed they were shaking. He felt cold.

Rafe left the metro station near Gorky Park after a forty-minute ride. He walked to the entrance, which was guarded by a large triumphal gate, reminiscent of Soviet days gone by. The face of Lenin stared down at him from above as he passed under the ornate structure and entered the plush park. Huge banners for IKEA also billowed down from overhead. Lenin and IKEA, interesting. Rafe smiled to himself. How things change.

Several years back, the Kremlin pressured one of the many extremely wealthy oligarchs in Moscow to pay for refurbishing the park, which was always a favorite destination for Muscovites. Today Park Gorkova, as it was called, was teeming with visitors. The sky was blue, the weather warm, the breeze cool, and it seemed no resident of Moscow was going to miss taking advantage of their new oasis in the city on this beautiful day. Gone was the drab landscaping and rusting benches. The area now boasted restaurants, outdoor theaters, gardens, fountains, bike trails, and other amenities. It was an adult playground now as well as for children. *The more crowded the better. I want to be invisible.*

Rafe stopped at a metal sign that highlighted the attractions of the park and their location. He studied the map intently. The parkour arena was about a quarter mile down on the left, hidden behind a small lake, where one could row two-person rowboats, and a skateboard ramp. He could make out the grinding noise of the skateboard attraction as he approached and bypassed it for the area behind.

Parkour was an urban fad emanating from France and owing its origin to military obstacle course training. It consisted of jumping from site to site throughout an urban environment using a fluidity of movement and a certain grace, using momentum to propel oneself. There were about ten teenage boys and a few younger kids actively jumping, climbing, and rolling around a gauntlet of

164

structures meant to mimic an urban area. Rafe sat down to watch the festivities. It was quite interesting to watch, and he almost lost himself in the spectacle. Soon, however, he gave Neal a call. His English handler informed him someone would be there within the hour. He casually kept an eye on the entrance to the arena for whomever may walk through to meet him. He didn't have to wait long.

A middle-aged, Slavic man dressed in business casual walked into the arena, acting as though he was just there to be amused by the parkour demonstration. A couple minutes later he purposely locked eyes with Rafe then turned and walked out of the arena. Rafe waited about a minute then stood and followed.

He left the arena just in time to see the man enter a small cafe overlooking the pond, where children were laughing while they furiously pedaled white paddleboats around the water. Ducks cautiously kept an eye on the humans and swam opposite their presence while looking for food in the water. On the opposite shore, a bocce tournament raged on the predesigned play area. Rafe casually walked towards the cafe. The tables were spread out under the edge of the forest and were mostly hidden in the shadows. The man had sat at a bistro table on the edge of the cafe's territory, set several meters into the trees and totally secluded.

Good, thought Rafe. He slowly walked to where the man sat and joined him in the opposite chair.

"Who are you?" Rafe asked.

"Call me Leo. I work at the State Historical Museum on Krasnaya Ploshchad, or Red Square. I've helped out my British friends from time to time. I was told you were yearning to discuss Russian history with someone knowledgeable. Am I correct?"

"Yes, you are right. I want to know about Ivan the Terrible."

"Ah, the most influential tsar in all Russian history. Peter the Great is more famous, but Ivan Grozny left his mark upon Russian society and culture like no other. You see he established the concept of a *guard* to enforce the tsar's will and protect his power. They were a group of favored soldiers and were called the oprichnina. You can still see the effects of this invention today in Russian society. The oligarchs cling to power by protecting the status quo, the powers to be, whether they be corrupt or not. And, they are definitely corrupt."

"Why would someone want me to learn about him?"

"Strange question. Someone wants you to learn about him? Perhaps it is because he wanted to establish the third Holy Roman Empire?"

"Yes, I've thought of that. Tell me, in the end, Ivan was responsible for ending the Rurik Dynasty, which eventually installed the Romanovs to power. Why did he kill his own grandson by beating his son's pregnant wife and then killing his only son who could have children, condemning the Russian empire to the rule of his incompetent brother?"

"Ivan had become quite corrupt and quite paranoid. He thought his loving wife, Anastasia, had been poisoned. Ivan was emotionally

166

attached to her. He was never the same after her death. The regime was deep with corruption. That is what destroyed him. Did you know he engineered a campaign of terror against the nobility he perceived were conspiring against him? He used to fry them in giant skillets. It was the corruption that killed the Ruriks. Ivan was just a convenient vehicle to make it happen. That's all. Corruption is a constant in Russian history and still is today. It's in our DNA unfortunately."

"So if Ivan's son Ivan had been allowed to take the throne, Russian history could have turned out much differently."

"Quite likely."

"Tell me about the third Holy Roman Empire," Rafe requested.

"After the fall of the second eastern holy empire in the fifteenth century, Russia saw herself as the natural heir to the title. The monks actively strove to have Russia take the imperial mantle. The concept was based on the Christian religion. After the Ottomans defeated Constantinople, Russia saw herself as the last stand of Christianity. But Ivan the Terrible's son was the end of the Rurik bloodline. Upon coming to power after a short struggle, the Romanovs over time strove to weaken the influence of the church. The rest is history."

Leo leaned forward in his seat and looked Rafe in the eye. "Rafe," Leo said softly, "you didn't hear this from me, but I know what you are up against. It has been going on for centuries here. It is very dangerous. You don't know what you are dealing with. People have tried to fight it in the past. You need to be very careful. Heed my warning!"

"That's not an option. They have my daughter."

"Then I feel you are doomed. I don't know what to tell you. You can't win against these people. I shouldn't even be telling you this!"

The two of them sat silently for a moment then Rafe spoke again. "How do I find out more?"

Leo looked around hesitantly. "If you want to know how it started, you need to talk to the Old Believers." Leo suddenly looked very frightened, like a switch had been flicked in his brain. "I've said enough. I've said too much," he stated tersely and got up from the table. The conversation was over.

He started walking back to the entrance to the park. Rafe followed some distance behind as they made their way through the myriad of gardened walkways, wondering where Leo was going and who he was going to talk to next. Soon Leo reached the gate. The metro station was across a six-lane thoroughfare in the middle of the city. Unlike in the West where there were overhead walkways, in Moscow, crosswalks were constructed across these roads, and it was an understatement to say the signage and safety of these crossings were not vivid enough. A pedestrian may make it across a couple lanes and then step out in front of a speeding vehicle to his death. If the visibility was low, the danger was even more acute, as the driver usually had no idea the person was coming. It happened frequently, especially to old women.

168

DELTA

Leo made it across four lanes before a large delivery truck slammed into him as he walked from the secluded view of a stopped car at the crosswalk, knocking him across the other two lanes. His body was thrown like a rag doll. Leo soon lay lifeless in the gutter. The truck never stopped.

Chapter Sixteen

Rafe stared in horror as Leo's body was catapulted across the busy thoroughfare. Multiple cars heading the opposite direction could not stop, and Leo was pummeled under several automobiles as they repeatedly drove over his mutilated corpse. Many of the follow-on cars that hit him didn't bother to stop. There was much more grief if one faced the police for hitting a pedestrian; the risk of a hit-and-run charge was worth taking. Rafe looked into the eyes of the driver of the truck that first struck him as he fled the scene. The man stared directly at Rafe and then he was gone; his eyes were wide but filled with hatred. He meant to hit him. Am I next? thought Rafe to himself, and he blended back into the crowd of onlookers, frantically trying to get away from the scene. Someone called the emergency services, and the wail of sirens could be heard in the distance. I need to get out of here!

Why was he killed? Rafe asked himself. Because he told me to be careful? That I had no idea what I was dealing with? What was it he said? I need to talk to the Old Believers? This is getting crazier by the minute. Rafe keep walking and walking, with no specific destination in mind. He just wanted to get away.

170

He eventually found himself on the metro, just riding, going nowhere in particular. The doors opened and closed at station after station. No one paid attention to him. *I'm safe here I think.* He had to clear his head and make a plan. He had been one step behind in this whole episode or journey or whatever it was. He had to get ahead of things. He had to figure out a way to get a grip on what was happening to him and the people he loved. The train slowed to a stop and the doors opened once again. Rafe made a snap decision and decided to exit the subway, following the crowd to the passageway to the city. He looked at the sign upon exiting the fairly new metro station. He was at Preobrazhenskaya Ploshchad, or square. Upon climbing to the street level and walking out into the open, Rafe took in the area. He was in a nondescript but bustling area of the city. Large, Soviet-era apartment buildings surrounded him as he viewed the busy thoroughfare, which split the group of buildings down the middle. *To live here was a drab, dull existence*, he thought to himself. The people here on the outskirts of Moscow were not fashionable and beautiful as they were in the center of the city; they were just ordinary. A bevy of workmen were hurriedly laboring to remove the dirty effects of winter. They were cleaning the sidewalks, painting the small, metal barriers that surrounded the landscaping beds, removing the dead plants, and injecting new bulbs into the ground. In a few months, Old Man Winter would destroy their efforts all over again.

171

Something was driving him here. That he knew. He just didn't know why. The reason was in the back of his mind somewhere, but it wouldn't surface. *I've been here before. I know where I am going.*

In 1652, Patriarch Nikon of the Russian Orthodox Church in Moscow made a series of changes in liturgy and practices to greater align the Russian Church with the Greek Orthodox, or Byzantine, Church. The changes were made unilaterally without consultation of the church leadership across Russia. This caused a great schism within Russian society. Many believers could not understand why Russians should copy practices of the Greeks when the Greek Church was now controlled by the Ottomans. Even though the Muslims allowed the Orthodox Church to survive and even thrive, as they considered the Orthodox another people of the book, the church was not free and was subject to Ottoman corruption and domination.

The changes made by the Russian patriarch were relatively minor. They included making the sign of the cross with three fingers instead of the Russian two fingers. They spelled the name of Jesus in a different way. They made changes to the liturgical texts to make them more in-line with the Greek practices. However, these changes were enough to cause a cleavage among the faithful. Many believers of the old Russian Church refused to take part in these new ways and proceeded to form their own ecclesiastical orders away from the Patriarch of Moscow. They were hounded by imperial Russia as well as by the Soviets. They were called the Raskolniki, derived from the

Slavic word raskol, meaning to split with a sharp object. Many were executed, but many escaped and formed communities in Siberia, other parts of Europe, and beyond. There were communities started in the United States and Latin America, even Mongolia. They still existed in modern day. This group of people came to be called the Old Believers. Rafe knew about the Old Believers, from a historical frame of reference. Naturally, being from Ukraine, he had heard of them before, but he understood only from a very limited viewpoint and was not a scholar on the subject.

Rafe crossed under the busy road via the tunnel connected to the metro station. The underground channel was filled with merchants hawking their wares. Flowers, figurines, and magazines lined the passageway. Two men played the violin with a case open for money in front of them. *No break dancing here,* thought Rafe. He exited the metro area and started walking slowly down Preobrazhenskaya Ulitza, or street. A quarter mile down the road, he ventured left into a wooded area; the trees were overgrown and reaching into the sidewalk, grabbing at passersby. *Something is here, I can feel it.* Something shiny glinted high between the tree limbs as the sunlight bounced off the object. It was gold. Soon Rafe came upon an ancient, brick wall, which was crumbling from disrepair. An ornate, octagon tower loomed to the right, its apex decorated by eighteenth-century Russian architecture. The gold above him was from the sculpted onion dome that sat atop one of the interior structures. *This is it.* In the distance, he could see religious buildings and rows upon rows of gravestones, their Russian Orthodox crosses reaching above them in various sizes and colors. Rafe followed the wall back to the right and soon entered the compound through the main entrance near the street. He had entered the Preobrazhenskoye Cemetery and monastery on the western side of Moscow, right outside the old city limits.

The group of buildings that unfolded in front of him were built in disguise in the eighteenth century. The tsar and the Moscow Patriarchy thought they were a plague quarantine area, but in reality they were the spiritual center of one sect of the Old Believers, or Bespopovtsy, meaning without priests. They practiced minimalism and led a cloistered life.

The site consisted of two monasteries, one female and one male, divided by a road that led to the cemetery. For some reason, Rafe felt like he knew where to go and soon was entering the chapel, which was called the Church of the Exaltation of the Holy Cross and located on the grounds. Although there were several denominations, this group of Old Believers never had priests, as their bishops were executed centuries before. So, there were none to ordain new priests. Therefore, they only had chapels, not cathedrals with altars. Many also did not marry or perform other sacraments that a priest had to perform.

It seemed surreal. The surroundings were familiar. *I've seen this compound and the grounds before!* Rafe shook his head to try to clear his thoughts and make sense of the feelings that were coming over him. *What am I supposed to find? I don't understand what is happening!* He continued into the building and stood, taking in all of the art and
174

golden icons adorning the walls. The church was empty, as it was during the week and most of the parishioners were at work.

"Can I help you?" a deep, male voice said from behind him. Rafe turned quickly to face the person speaking to him. He was an elderly man in his eighties with a long, gray beard. He was dressed in religious clothing and seemed to be some kind of religious leader.

"I, I'm not sure...," Rafe stammered. "I felt drawn to come here. Like I had some familiarity with place. It's there, I know it but I can't place it. It won't surface in my memory. I think I'm going crazy."

"My name is Roman. I am one of the spiritual leaders here in our community. I don't believe I have seen you before. Are you a believer? Are you one of us?"

"I really don't go to church. I...I know I should but I don't. I think I did when I was a child."

"Perhaps someone is trying to tell you you should?" the man laughed heartily. "Have you eaten? I was about to have a late lunch. Would you care to join me?"

"I'd love to! I'm starving!"

Rafe followed the man out of the chapel and the short distance to a small room in the monastery. There was a miniscule, wooden table by a single cot. The man proceeded to take food from a small kitchenette and place it on the table. There was smoked fish, olives, black bread, and cheese. "Help yourself," the man said as he sat down across from Rafe. The two of them ate silently for several minutes. "You didn't tell me your name," said the man.

"Well people call me Rafe, but it's not my real name. My family was from Ukraine. We immigrated to the West during the Soviet times, and my parents gave me a more acceptable name for the U.S."

The older man stared at him for a long time, seeming to study his face intently. "So what do you think your name is?"

"My real name is Alexander." The man dropped the food he was bringing to his mouth. It spilled down the front of his garment, but he didn't care. His eyes grew wide. He said nothing for some time.

"What?" asked Rafe.

"I used to call you Sasha," the old man finally replied. 'I cannot believe you are here. You see, Sasha, I am your father's brother. I am your uncle."

Rafe looked at him incredulously. Then it all came back to him, even the room they were eating in. He remembered the chipped paint on the ceiling, the bars on the windows. He even thought he remembered the old man's face.

"I used to live here," Rafe said unequivocally. "I had forgotten everything. How long ago was it?" he asked.

"You left with your parents when you were three years old. In those days, the Old Believers, and especially our denomination, were being persecuted greatly by the Soviets. We smuggled you all out one evening. You went south through the Caucasus and eventually to the Black Sea, where you were smuggled onto a ship in Crimea. Your parents were going to start a new community in the United States. However, they left you with a friend in America and came back to Russia. You see, they wanted to also bring over Vladimir. But they never made it back out and were arrested and disappeared. I am sure they are dead now. You see, Sasha, you have a brother."

"A brother? I never knew." However, suddenly long-forgotten images came back to Rafe. Wisps of an image of a face, younger than him by a year, crawling toward him on the wooden floor, dressed in a white garment. A flood of memories washed over him. He felt dizzy. *This is why I was drawn here, to this place.*

"I remember now. But I always thought I was from Ukraine!"

"Yes, you grew up with a Ukrainian family. However, they were not your parents. But they did teach you Ukrainian and Russian. Your real parents were not married, per our tradition and beliefs, but they did love you very much."

Rafe looked again around the small room in wonder. "Why am I here?" he said softly so the man could barely hear.

"That is a very good question. I never thought I would see you again."

"My daughter has been kidnapped."

"My God! We will help you all we can! You are safe here. How did this happen?"

Rafe told Roman the entire story, from Venice to the present. He listened intently with surreal understanding. Rafe felt as if he could trust the man, even though he hadn't seen him in over forty years and really didn't know him. But he felt a connection. He knew

177

what he was telling him was true. He had the flashes of memories that told him so, and he had no choice, he had to trust someone.

The old man looked off into space for some time, lost in thought. Then he spoke. "I know who you need to talk to, in addition to your brother. But you have to hurry, he is not well and is very old. He can help you I am sure. He has had experience with these things, and the stories of the past have been passed down to him. He is now passing them on to your brother, in order to preserve our beliefs and our heritage. For you see, I don't think this man has much time left on this earth."

"Of course!" replied Rafe excitedly. "When can I meet them?"

"It will be some time, Sasha, as you have to travel. You see, when the persecutions started getting worse under the Soviets, we Raskolniki dispersed to the far corners of the earth. Your brother and the man I speak of live in the far regions of Siberia and have for decades. I have not seen them in forty years."

Rafe thought of Clare through the onrush of distant memories from his past. He could see her running toward him, her arms wide open. "Daddee!" she would scream. A tear rolled down his face. "I will go to Siberia then. I have no choice. I have to find my daughter. And now I guess I have to meet my brother."

The old man smiled. "I will go with you. I have always wanted to see Siberia. You see, the old dying man is my brother." Rafe and Roman laughed heartily together as the sun began to set in Moscow.

Chapter Seventeen

Rafe and Roman sat in the dining car of the old passenger train as it moved swiftly eastward, baking under the overhead sun, which burned brightly through the windows. It was lunchtime, and they were enjoying a fine Russian meal of borsch, grechka (buckwheat), and black bread. They had become fast friends during the eight-hour plane ride and the subsequent four hours they were on the train. In another hour, they would be getting off the railway and traveling the rest of the distance by truck, another five hours. They were tired but in good spirits. A bottle of cheap vodka sat on the table between them, almost empty. The alcohol had enshrined their friendship and familial ties during the long lunch.

"Tell me about my parents, the Old Believers," said Rafe, once they had finished half the bottle.

"Your mother was a very kind woman. She loved you very much. It broke her heart to leave your brother behind and then you in America. However, she took solace in the fact that at least you were safe. She came back for Vladimir. But then, as I said, your mother and father were arrested. I have been told they were tortured and killed in Lubyanka."

"Why didn't she take him when she left with me?"

"It was considered too dangerous to have such a young baby, who could cry at any moment. So, she let him grow for a year and then returned, never to be heard from again."

"So how did Vladimir get to Siberia?"

"When the persecution became too intense, a large part of our community decided to move to exile on the eastern Siberian coast. They left one Sunday afternoon and I never saw them again. I have heard that they are happy there. There are not many people in the region, and that is exquisite for an Old Believer. The less people the better. However, their lives are very harsh. The climate is unforgivable. You cannot make a mistake in the winter. It will be your last. Since the Soviet Union is no more, the government has been paying the expenses for expatriates overseas who fled the persecutions to return to Russia and settle in Siberia. It's a match made in heaven and has been very successful. Tens of thousands of Old Believers have returned to Mother Russia."

"Does my brother know I exist?"

"Yes, he knows. However, he put that hope to the ground decades ago. It will be very interesting to see the two of you together." Rafe turned to stare out the window of the train, the taiga passing by in a never-ending, formless shape. The train rumbled on.

An hour later, Rafe and Roman left the railway to join a two-car convoy to make the final five-hour drive to Dersu, Siberia. The community was located on a small spit of land that reached its way as far as it could down the Chinese border with Russia, almost to North Korea, a few hundred miles north of Vladivostock. This was where the community of Old Believers had made their homestead. China was only ninety miles to the west. To the east lay the Sea of Japan. Around their compound, there was nothing but winter and the bush.

Dersu was named after the legendary Siberian hunter who was profiled in the book *Dersu Uzala* by Russian explorer Vladimir Arsenyev. Dersu was so in touch with nature that he saw plants and animals as equal to humans. He saved the lives of Arsenyev and his crew during a difficult expedition in the early twentieth century in Siberia and is immortalized in Russian folklore.

Rafe and Roman forded several rivers during the journey. Some they drove through with the vehicles, others they had to cross via a rusting barge. However, despite the rough terrain, five and a half hours later, the vehicles lumbered into Dersu.

The first thing Rafe noticed was the silence. The village was a collection of dark gray structures made of wood and other natural materials. Stove pipes belched white smoke and surrounded the compound in a strange mist. It was as if the houses weren't really there but hiding behind the gray, moist air. The only sound was the wind rustling through the upturned leaves in the trees. He got out of the truck.

Peering through the overturned snow fences, Rafe could see no sign of life. "Where are they?" he said to Roman as he turned back to face the truck.

Roman shrugged his shoulders but then shouted, "There!"

He pointed down the makeshift road to a lone figure riding a bicycle out of the woods towards the compound. He had a long, gray beard and wore a Russian cap. His hand was raised in friendship. Rafe watched him approach.

"Is that Vladimir?" he asked Roman.

"I believe so but I am not sure," Roman replied. Rafe walked forward and waved. The man waved back.

The reunion was somewhat awkward, although happy. Roman felt more emotion than anyone, as he had known the two brothers when they were young. Vladimir had no memory of his distant family. They slowly began to get to know each other as the time wore on.

An few hours later, they sat inside one of the ramshackle huts that comprised the small community, around an old, scarred, wooden table. Deep grooves from large knives cleaning fish crisscrossed the surface. Rafe and Roman sat across from Vladimir and another man from the village. The two men from Dersu were pensive, and foreboding washed across their faces. The mood had changed and there was no happiness, only tension and fear.

"Why are you here?" Vladimir asked. Rafe was somewhat taken aback. He had just found his long-lost brother, who he didn't even know he had, and the man was not happy.

"I'm here to find you and to meet you," replied Rafe.

182

"No, you are not," said Vladimir and stared into Rafe's eyes for the truth. "Tell us why you are here."

Rafe didn't reply for a long while, staring into Vladimir's eyes. "They have my daughter," Rafe finally responded after a period of silence. He saw fear and anxiety cross the Old Believers' faces. Vladimir turned to Roman.

"And you brought him here? Do you know what you have done to us?"

"It was the right thing to do!" replied Roman.

"He is right," said the other man. "We are family." That seemed to calm Vladimir down somewhat.

"We should show him," Vladimir said.

"Yes, I agree we should show him," said the other man.

"And what he is up against," added Vladimir. "Yes, he should know. It is time." Vladimir stood and turned to Rafe. He spoke quietly. "Come with us," he said authoritatively.

Rafe, Roman, and Vladimir walked out into the evening night. Without any competition, the millions of stars formed a blanket of light above them, twinkling like diamonds raining down from the heavens. The night was warm and the air was still as death. Rafe marveled at the peace these people had found, so many miles from the rest of human civilization. *There is a comfort here, a freedom that is pleasant, even though they don't have material things. They are free, free to be who they want to be, which is all they have ever wanted.*

183

Night was fully developed now. They walked away from the small community of houses and went into the forest. Each of them carried a large flashlight that now burned bright. The darkness enveloped them as they penetrated the tree line. *This is scary,* thought Rafe.

Seemingly reading his mind, Vladimir spoke. "Don't worry, my brother, I've been in these woods at night for decades. There is nothing here that will hurt us, especially with the torches. All of the predators are long gone, since we have announced ourselves to the wilderness. They are more afraid of us than we are of them!" The three men walked on and on for an hour it seemed, the tree canopy growing thicker overhead.

Suddenly, the stars reappeared as they entered a large, cleared area, which had been hewn from the forest by human hands long ago. Trees now dotted the landscape, which obviously had not been inhabited for some time, decades at least. The forest was reclaiming its ownership. Wooden structures were sprinkled around the open area, their roofs slowly falling in and their walls buckling. Soon Rafe spotted a barbed wire fence, which ran the perimeter of the compound. It too was torn down in spots; only the outline of its maliciousness remained for the astute observer.

"What is this place?" asked Rafe incredulously.

"It's one of the old labor camps built by Stalin. It's a gulag," responded Vladimir. "Thousands of our Russian brothers and sisters died here, a long time ago."

"Really? It's amazing, but why are you bringing me here in the dead of night? I don't get it."

"You will see," responded Roman. They kept walking and Rafe followed. They entered the old prison camp and soon were headed toward one of the main buildings. It looked like it had at one time been the commandant's residence. The main door had been broken in at some point long ago. The structure still seemed sturdy enough, and soon they were inside. Vladimir eventually found a doorway that led to a cellar of some type. Vladimir opened the door. There was a flight of stairs leading down into the darkness. Rafe followed the other two men as he started downwards, the boards creaking dangerously under their feet. Soon they were standing on a dirt floor in a small room. Stone bricks lined the walls, cut by slave hands years before. *How many died to build this place?* Rafe wondered. Vladimir was shining the light on the far wall, seemingly trying to find something.

"It's been a long time since I have been here. It is here somewhere."

"What?" asked Rafe.

"The door," he replied.

The door to what?

"Ah, here it is." Vladimir pulled on one of the edges of a line of bricks in the wall. Part of the wall began to move. Rafe glanced at Roman and saw that his eyes were wide. He obviously had never been here before. Vladimir pulled harder, but he was having trouble with the opening in the wall. "Help me!" he said demandingly. "Don't just stand there!" Rafe and Roman moved

185

to apply force to the edge of bricks as well. Slowly the outline of a stone door emerged in the wall as they pulled it towards them. A few minutes later, a dark outline of a tunnel became clear to Rafe as his eyes adjusted to peering into the darkness.

Vladimir spoke to both of them. "Don't be afraid, follow me." Rafe and Roman did as requested. They went about ten meters into the earthen tunnel, and then Vladimir stopped. He turned to his right and held up the lantern to another opening. They stepped inside the cavern hewn into the earth and supported with wooden beams. It was a Mythraic temple.

The design was the same. There were two long, stone slabs running down each wall with a long, stone bench connected to each one. There was old tableware strewn atop the tables, as if long ago there had been a feast. Across from the entrance was an altar. Above the altar was the image of a soldier atop a massive bull, stabbing a spear into the animal's side.

"I'll be damned!" exclaimed Rafe. "I don't understand. What is this doing here?"

Roman spoke up this time. "Our people have been fighting this evil for centuries, Sasha. It has been around a long time. It is an evil cult. A cult of destruction. A group of people who try to stop the advancement of civilization. As far as I know, they have been around throughout the ages, since the beginning of time. They worship in these temples. This is where they plan their evil activities."

"This is exactly the type of temple I have seen in Spain, Rome, all over Europe. Are you saying they had a part in the fall of the Roman Empire?"

"Yes," said Vladimir. "And many others, including our own. We moved our families here decades ago to get away from them. To get away from the persecution. But as you can see, we were not so lucky."

"But why would they want to persecute you? The Old Believers?"

Roman responded, "Because we represent order, civilization, religion, you name it. The cult influenced the tsars throughout history. And the Caesars before that. Tsar is the Russian word for Caesar, you understand. They influenced Peter the Great to distance Russia from the church, to distance Russia from her past, from Christianity and the idea of the third Holy Roman Empire."

"Yes, I am aware of that history," replied Rafe.

"And then the final coup de grace," replied Vladimir. "They got rid of the influence of the church altogether by encouraging the Soviet Revolution. The USSR was an evil empire, dedicated to destroying the church, the great Russian people, and the human spirit. The cult was at the apex of their power during those times. Look around you, this entire camp was built by thousands of slaves who came here to die. Their only crime was being an intellectual or having been denounced by some other citizen or even by their own children. Tell me that is not evil."

"So they were worshiping here in the gulag?"

"Yes, all over the Soviet Union. We were one small thing that was standing in their way. We were reminding Russia of her history. A history that was intertwined with the church, and Russia was on her way to greatness. The cult destroyed her and she has struggled to recover."

"It makes sense now. The temples, the rituals. But what do they want with me? Why do they have my daughter? I don't understand what they want from me!"

"Neither do I. However, we are worried. We are worried you have brought them here. We are worried they will come and destroy us and our community. They will destroy what we have built."

"We have to leave, Sasha," added Roman. "We are going to depart the day after tomorrow. After you've had a day to get to know your family. At least what's left of it. We will go back to Moscow. Then we will decide how to best find your daughter."

Rafe replied, "I thought you mentioned there was a patriarch here, instructing Vladimir on your traditions and history. I have not seen him."

"My teacher has moved on to another community. An Old Believer group in Alaska actually, which was part of Russia at one time you know. He is passing on the torch there. His work here is done. I am the patriarch now. I am leading my people," Vladimir announced.

"I look forward to getting to know you and my history, Brother, but as I'm sure you can understand, I first must find my daughter."

188

"Yes, I understand. Let us go now back to the compound." Vladimir moved towards the stairs and began climbing.

Rafe lay sleeping in the comfortable bed, oblivious to the world around him. The sheets and blankets had a country, soft feel to them that brought more memories back of his childhood. It had been a long several days traveling to the Siberian village. His body needed the sleep badly, and he was in a deep REM state.

The bedroom he occupied was in Vladimir's rustic home. He had spent the day and dined with his family, getting to know them. They were a simple group of people but very kind and gracious. They had given him access to everything they had, and he was grateful. Vladimir's wife was young and attractive, even beneath her religious garments, as Russian girls tended to be. Her five-year-old daughter, Ksyusha, reminded him very much of Clare. She had jumped in his lap when he sat down earlier in the evening, and they had become fast friends. She was enjoying having her Uncle Sasha around the house. Rafe slept happily and contently for the first time in weeks.

The first scream sounded like the wail of a mother cow who was bleating in sorrow. It was a deep, gurgling howl of a mother's emotional pain. The sound woke Rafe in an instant, but he was not sure what he had heard, or hadn't heard. The second scream was that of a small child. Rafe immediately sat up in bed and then

189

dashed for his clothes. He ran out of the house into the night, now awash with sounds of horror.

He saw a hundred horsemen, dressed in white, hooded robes and carrying bright torches galloping through the compound. Many of them were armed with swords. They were dismounting in front of the cabins and pulling all of the residents out into the dark night. Then they torched the houses. Several of the men tried to stop them but were cut down by the sword, never to rise again. The women wailed and the children cried. Rafe wondered if he was living a nightmare. The scene was medieval, from the Dark Ages.

He caught a glimpse of the leader of the mounted marauders. It was the man he had met in Red Square. There was an evil grin on his face as he murdered men, women, and children alike, slashing them like stalks of corn at harvest. The flames licked into the black sky like Hell itself. They were killing all of them, all of the Old Believers.

Suddenly Rafe saw baby Ksyusha running out of her home toward him. Her parents lay dead on the ground behind her. Rafe ran to meet her; he wanted to scoop her into his arms and get her away from this evil. He desperately wanted to protect her, as he had not protected his own daughter. He was about halfway to her when the leader bore down on her with his horse. Before Rafe could catch her, the little girl was trampled by the giant steed. Rafe screamed in horror and grabbed a nearby post on the ground and swung at the man. Suddenly another rider jumped down behind him and hit him from behind with some type of weapon he was carrying. Rafe crumpled in blinding pain.

190

He awoke again to the flickering of fire, except this time he was standing. His arms and shoulders screamed for relief. His legs ached from the blow he had received to the back of the knees. He noticed ropes were wrapped around him. There was a foul stench in the air. Dawn was breaking over the horizon.

"You are awake! Good," he heard the man say behind him. Rafe looked around. The horsemen had dismounted and were piling the bodies of the Old Believers into a mound, which had been doused with gasoline and lit. The funeral pyre burned high and emitted an ungodly odor. Rafe saw his brother and his wife thrown onto the burning mound. His mind refused to accept what he was witnessing. Roman was nowhere to be seen, but Rafe was sure he was dead. Rafe realize he was tied to a fence pole that surrounded what was left of the community. The houses were all gone, mostly burnt to the ground. There was no one else alive.

Suddenly, the man from Red Square walked in front of him and stared him in the face, a few feet away. "You disappoint me. You have been trying to find out how to deceive me, trying to get the best of me." Rafe tried to talk but couldn't. His mind was still foggy, and his speech was not coming out right. "Don't worry, you will recover. Tomorrow you will be as good as new! Nothing is broken," the man said laughingly. "I can't say the same for the rest of these animals!" He pointed to the burning bodies. He turned back to Rafe and his voice became harsh, evil if you will. "You listen to me! You have thirty days to complete our bargain, or your daughter will meet the same fate as little Ksyusha! Do you understand me?"

"Yes," Rafe whispered.

"Good. I'm glad we have an understanding. You will continue to look for what I want you to find. Then we will talk again. At my discretion. And just so you have a good idea of what lies in wait for Clare, here is a reminder."

One of the white-robed horsemen walked in front of Rafe, carrying little Ksyusha's broken and bloodied body. He threw it onto the burning pile of flesh.

Rafe closed his eyes in horror, but not before looking into the horseman's eyes and realizing that this man too he recognized. Perhaps from where would come to him later. He passed out from pain, emotional and physical.

Chapter Eighteen

When Rafe awoke, he was still tied to the pole. It took him some time before he could wriggle his hands free from the ropes, which tied them behind his back. As soon as the knot was released, he collapsed to the ground. He lay there for several moments as the sun rose in the sky. The mosquitoes, as big as small birds and so common to this area, had been feeding on his exposed skin. He was empty inside, physically and emotionally. He didn't know if he could recover. However, ever so slowly, his strength started to return, and eventually he rose to a sitting position against the wooden pole.

The first thing he noticed were the pikes, which held the cloth banners with symbols on them. Instantly he remembered the night at the amphitheater at Tsaritsyno. The symbols were the same. There was again the man with the lion head, holding two keys, wrapped by a snake. There was the soldier slaying the dark bull, and there was the triangle with a human eye in the center. The pikes were placed randomly about the compound, for all to see, their banners fluttering in the wind. He made a mental note to research the later symbology more thoroughly the first chance he got when he made it back to some form of civilization.

The horrors of the night slowly came back to him, and he glanced at the now smoldering pile of ashes, which used to contain his family and newfound friends. He became physically ill, emptying what was left in his stomach. The sorrow washed over him. He again crumpled to the ground. His mind fought for control, fought to move forward. *Let it turn to something else,* Rafe told himself. *You still can save your daughter. Clare is still out there somewhere, and you have to find her and save her from this evil. You now have no other purpose in life.* Rafe stood and attempted to restrain the feeling of helplessness, the feeling of approaching doom.

His thoughts now slowly turned to how to survive this situation, for he was alone in Siberia with no food or water. The majority of the homes were burned to the ground. He slowly stood and walked among the still smoking ruins, looking for anything of value he could use to stay alive. He was so far from anywhere, so far from civilization, anything could make a difference. There literally was nothing. Everything was burned. When a structure wasn't totally destroyed, there was nothing of value inside to suit his purpose. Rafe became distraught and found himself fighting again to control his emotions. *Stay calm and think!* he told himself. He then remembered the truck in which he had driven to the community with Roman. It was still parked down near the forest, where Roman had left it, looking for a place to possibly build another home, as he was considering moving to the compound to be with the extended Old

194

Believer family. Rafe started walking in that direction. Thankfully, ever so slowly, the vehicle came into view as he walked down the dirt road in its direction. Fifteen minutes later, he arrived at the truck and walked around it, checking for any damage. There was none. He looked inside. The keys were in the ignition and there was a half tank of fuel. *That will get me somewhere I guess. I might as well get going, there is nothing left for me here.*

"You are still alive?" a familiar voice said from behind him.

He turned quickly to see Roman walking out of the woods. Rafe was overjoyed and ran to him, embracing him in a bear hug.

"How did you survive?" Rafe asked.

"I was out here sitting under the trees as evening set in, thinking of making this my new home when the raid happened. I saw the whole thing but was too scared and ashamed to do anything about it. My concern for my own personal safety stopped me from confronting those people. I feel I am to blame for what happened. My god, what is the world coming to?"

"You would have only been killed as well," added Rafe.

"I…I did nothing to save my own family. But they let you live!" said Roman forcefully. "That means they want something from you."

"Yes, I was told again as much, but I have no idea what that is."

"We need to leave this place. It is evil. I did not know there was a temple close by. I did not know the history of this place, all of the people who died here. My brother and his father discovered the gulag after they had settled here. Then they found the temple.

195

They really did not know what it was. They did not know about the visitors being here. They thought they had found paradise, free of these marauders. They have been telling me all of these strange things for years, but I never understood the danger, until now. These people had to destroy our family. Our brothers and sisters stood in the way of their agenda, as they have for centuries."

"Yes, let's leave. We can find our way to the coast and to civilization."

"Then what will you do?"

"I need to find my daughter. The only person I can think of who can shed some light on the entire situation is your brother, and he's now in Alaska."

"Yes, he will help you. I'm going with you."

"You don't have an American visa."

"I don't think that will matter. We will get in through the docks. I know people who will help us. I don't plan on going through your immigration."

"I guess that sounds like a plan. At least we now know where we are going." Rafe and Roman got in the truck, started the engine, and drove away from the still smoldering compound, never looking back.

The boat lunged to one side, and both Roman and Rafe were thrown against the portal, the water crashing into the glass, trying desperately to enter the hull of the ship. But the ship held and the water retreated. They were safe for the time being.

"I can't take much more of this," Rafe complained.

"You have no choice. It's not as bad as it could be," replied Roman.

"How much longer do you think?"

"I think we have another day and we will be in Alaska."

"I' hope you're right." Rafe tried to buttress himself against the hull to try to get some sleep. It was no use. The storm was too strong, and his head banged against the bulkhead with the next surge. He put his jacket, balled up into a wad, under his head and held on for dear life.

The two of them had taken the truck as far as they could on the fuel that remained. They made it to another village one hundred and fifty miles away, towards the coast. There, they bought a ride on a truck headed for Vladivostok. In the port city, it did not take them long to find a captain that was headed north and would be willing to deposit them in an Alaskan port. Rafe had paid for this privilege with hard currency he had withdrawn via a bank downtown. That was days ago, and the experience of being hidden down below was not a pleasant one.

Vladivostok was closed to outsiders during the Soviet years, as it was the home of the Soviet Pacific fleet. Upon the fall of the communist system in the early nineties, the city was opened to the world and its infrastructure upgraded. Currently it was a major tourist, conference, and trading center for the eastern half of the Russian Federation and a major shipping port as well.

Occasionally when there was no chance of being close to any other ocean traffic or being spotted by satellite, Rafe and Roman were allowed some time on the upper deck, usually under an overcast night sky. They had bonded during the time together. However, both of them were very concerned about what their destination would bring. They hoped they could stealthily enter the U.S. and find their way eventually to their extended family's community. The future remained a terrible mystery.

Rafe had had enough. Angrily, he sat up and considered puking again. He decided to try to tough it out a little longer and started up a conversation with Roman to block out the misery.

"So what do you think we are up against? Why have they taken my daughter? What do they want?"

Roman stared at the ocean out the small, round window for a while and then spoke. "This group of people have been around a long time, for centuries in Russia anyway. Before that they were involved in other empires, Rome, et cetera. I think it's safe to say their agenda is not a good one. I don't pretend to understand their motivation or where they are from, how they originated, but they have fought to keep Russia a backwards state. They have fought progress. They have fought morality and religion. They have fought success and enlightenment. And they helped the Mongol invaders centuries ago. They were instrumental in the fall of Byzantium

198

against the Ottomans. They helped form the Soviet Union for God's sake. They nurtured the communist, totalitarian evil. They don't like us because we represent something in their way. We represent the opposite of everything they stand for."

"What do they stand for?"

"Evil, misery, pain, sloth, you name it."

"Why would they want Clare? Why would they want me?"

"I think it is obvious they wanted Clare to control you for some reason. You are valuable to them. They want something important from you. You have to figure out what that is. I cannot do that for you."

"I don't understand."

"I don't think you are meant to yet. I have a foreboding feeling that everything will become crystal clear to you in due time and not in a good way. Rafe, that is a scary thought."

"Aren't we endangering the Old Believers in Alaska by coming to them for help?"

"Well, I know that my brother would want to help us no matter what, and there is no one else who can help us understand what is going on. We are in a bigger struggle than for just the safety of a few old religious families. But yes, we are endangering them. I have not heard of a temple near their community. So possibly the circumstances will be different. But we have to be aware and be careful. I do not care about my own life. I care about you and the other younger members of our family. My brother's life is almost over as well. We will meet him away from the others and see what light he can shed. We will see what he can tell us, and then we will take what life gives us and be thankful."

"Such wisdom. I for one will carry the guilt to my grave for what happened to these people. I came here and this happened to them. I suppose I can learn a lot from you, Uncle," said Rafe. "I can feel my life changing. I will never be the same again after all of this is over. *If* it is ever over."

"Try again to get some sleep," said Roman. "We may not have much time for it soon." Rafe lay down again against the hull, as the sea had quieted somewhat. Roman sat watching out the window, worry etched into deep caverns across his ancient face.

The sun broke over the horizon, streaming its bright rays across the green landscape of Alaska in the distance. There was something different about this country, something special. It was the last frontier. The colors of Alaska were more vibrant, the smells more sweet, and the weather more dangerous than the boring states of the Lower Forty-eight. If Alaska was stretched from the bottom of the Aleutian Chain to the North Slope, it would be the same distance as from Los Angeles to New York. And there were less than a million people living in the state. The bush was overrun with wildlife and blessed with magical scenery. Alaska was a land like no other.

Slowly the land came into view. Roman and Rafe were on the bridge, searching with the rest of the crew for the first glimpse of terra firma, although they had passed Kodiak Island some time before. Rafe had seen several grizzlies on the Kodiak shoreline, pawing for fish at a river emptying into the ocean. Kodiak bears were famous for their size as well as their numbers on the island.

"Land ho!" the captain shouted. "Time for you comrades to go below decks and to your respective containers to sneak ashore." Roman and Rafe nodded, thanked the captain, and followed a sailor who led them down to ensure their concealment. Soon they were ensconced within separate containers, hidden behind spare parts for a Russian helicopter being legally imported into the U.S. The large aircraft were used in certain situations in Alaska, primarily for heavy lift in the oilfields. Helicopters were a bright spot for Russian exports. They had captured a large market share, as they were known for their simplicity of design.

The Russian freighter had traveled up the Gulf of Alaska and was now making her way up the Cook Inlet towards Anchorage, a natural, sheltered harbor and the largest city of the state. Anchorage sat nestled against the Chugach Mountains and was therefore protected from most of the severe weather of the interior. Fairbanks, many hours' drive to the north, was not so lucky. The city was annually buffeted by horrendous winter conditions and frigid temperatures.

Hours later, both emerged into the night air as they unhooked the container locking mechanism, which had been rigged for access from the inside. They met towards the south end of the shipyard, which was blackened due to lack of lighting. Soon, they had hopped the fence and were now safely, and illegally, in the United States.

201

They quickly made their way to a local hotel, where Rafe paid cash for a room with two double beds, avoiding any contact with law enforcement. Roman had never been in the United States and was nervous but fascinated at the same time. "Alaska reminds me of Siberia. Possibly because it used to be Russian," he said with a smile on his face.

After ravenously eating a hurried dinner at the local family restaurant, they slept soundly, unafraid of being molested by the police or other dangerous groups. The morning came quickly.

The route to the village near Homer, Alaska, on the southern tip of the Kenai Peninsula, was arduous and took several days. Unwilling to expose themselves to the mainstream population, if there is was such a thing in Alaska, the two chose to travel at night and primarily with truckers making their way across the state during the warm summer. Their beards long and their clothes soiled, they fit right in with the local culture of the working man and the loner, living his days in the northern frontier. People didn't ask questions in Alaska; they lived and let live. That attitude sat well with Roman and Rafe, as the less people that knew they were here the better.

Extending down from Anchorage, the Kenai was a large peninsula that punched directly into the Gulf of Alaska. It was famous for its fishing and beauty, as well as its hardy residents. When the salmon were running, combat fishing was the norm. Anglers lined the banks of the Russian River, named for its use by the early Russian settlers, and other waterways by the thousands. Fishermen

202

tried to entice one of the running silver or king salmon to bite. It was easy to snag one of the large fish with a hook and yank it out of the water, but the technique was highly illegal. The park rangers regularly would fish along the banks in disguise, waiting to catch someone snagging a fish. One could lose his fishing gear, pay a large fine, and even lose his car for the offense.

People also had to watch out for the bears during fishing season. The main threat was brown bears, and there were lots of them, looking to fatten up for the winter on the running fish. If a brown bear made its habitat along the coast, he was called a grizzly. If he lived in the interior, he was just a brown bear. The best way to avoid a bear encounter was to let them know someone was coming. Hikers and campers wore bells on their packs to make noise as they walked. The worst thing a person could do upon confronting a bear was to run. The bear then would see him as prey and literally try to eat him. Weapons, unless extremely powerful, were of little use as well. Even if a bear's heart as stopped, he still could run for another ten to twenty seconds, enough time to close the distance with a human and do real damage. And bears were fast, known to run at upwards of forty miles per hour. Experienced people in the bush usually carried pistol grip shotguns, loaded with alternating buck and slug shells. If a man was lucky, he could put a slug in a bear's shoulder to cripple him, or a load of buckshot to his face, hopefully blinding him if he charged. If no weapon was available during a bear attack, the best thing for a man to do was to ball up into the fetal position with his hands interlocked behind his neck and let the bear chew on you for a bit. If he didn't move, the bear might lose interest and leave him alone.

The eighteen-wheeler slowed and stopped with a loud squeal and a blast of air at the outskirts of the village. The onion-domed church could be seen in the distance, announcing to the world the Old Believers were still around. Roman and Rafe opened the door of the cab and jumped to the ground. It was warm, and the sun was moving towards its peak for the day in the sky. They said their good-byes and thanked the driver.

Once the truck had left, Rafe took out his phone to call Neal. He had not spoken to him in some time, as the shock from the attack on the Old Believer community, combined with the lack of signal on the freighter, prevented him from communicating. However, they had a plan now, and he wanted to let Neal in on their way forward.

"Where in the hell have you been?" Neal screamed into the phone when he realized it was Rafe on the other end.

"I've been quite occupied with events, and you frankly were not my priority," responded Rafe.

"Well, I should be your priority! I've got a lot invested in you, Rafe. So why don't you tell me what the fuck is going on?"

"Let's just say I'm in no mood to take it anymore." Rafe recounted the last few weeks to Neal, including the murders in Siberia and the continuing danger to his daughter from the visitors. Neal listened in shocked silence.

"I can't begin to offer any words that would be helpful or healing in regards to the losses you have suffered," Neal responded.

204

"I can, however, tell you I am still here to help you, and we have more and more information coming in that may help you in your quest."

"Go on," added Rafe dryly.

"The visitors, as you call them, at least the ones that are frequently traveling to the areas we have identified, are primarily made up of media and academic circles. And the number of people we have confirmed on the list is growing, slowly but surely. That being said, are you safe now? Do you have any protection?"

"From what I have seen, my English friend, there can be no protection." Rafe told Neal his plans, to visit the village and learn all he could from the elders. He promised he would report back in with his future decisions on how to move forward.

Neal hit the red button on his device and terminated the call. For some reason, he was reminded of a line from an old rock and roll song from the seventies, "Oh, and it's a hollow feelin', when it comes down to dealin' friends. It never ends." *Murder, and children at that. I didn't sign up for this. This is spinning out of control.*

Roman and Rafe watched their latest hitchhiking benefactor disappear into the distance. The wheels on the large truck generated clouds of dust that rose into the sky like small tornadoes. There were no other vehicles around that they could see. Soon they could no longer even hear the eighteen-wheeler. The two men turned and set off towards the village of Nikolaevsk. As they walked, a bevy of vultures circled overhead, scanning for prey.

Chapter Nineteen

The two of them opened the door to the small church in the village and walked in. The building was simple. It was a rather tiny place of worship and resembled a church in the southern United States, except the steeples were replaced with onion domes, two of them. The exterior of the wooden building was bathed in a light blue color. The altar and vestments highlighted the front of the church, and a small number of tapestries were aligned towards the head of the space. There were icons adorning the walls, and gold-leafed religious instruments were everywhere to be seen. Highlighted by the light streaming through the windows was a single elderly man on his knees in prayer at the head of the church. He said nothing nor did he move as they entered and the door slammed shut with a bang. A few minutes later, he spoke without turning to look at them. "I knew you were coming. It is nice to have you here," the old man said.

"Thank you, Brother, it is nice to be here," responded Roman. The man stood and turned to meet the strangers. He walked the short distance that separated them and embraced them

206

both, kissing three times as per the Russian tradition of the Father, Son, and the Holy Ghost.

"I have felt you were on your way. I have felt what you have been through. We are all in God's hands now."

"Yes, I feel the same way. This is your nephew Sasha." The old man gave Rafe a hug. "I was very close to your father, and forgive me for saying I was in love with your mother. She was very beautiful Welcome. I am Mikhail."

"Thank you, Uncle," responded Rafe, respectfully. "I barely remember them."

"Come, let us join the others and eat. Have no fear, you are home. I am the priest here now. The village reinstituted the priesthood in 1983. We had been without priests for hundreds of years; however, we thought it was time. Although, it did cause a little bit of anxiety within the community. Some thought it was the wrong thing to do." Rafe and Roman followed Mikhail out into the sunshine and towards the homes of the village. The town was not large but seemed to have everything the population needed in terms of what was required to support the small, rural community; the expected businesses dotted the main street, such as a small grocery store, gas station, et cetera. Rafe guessed three hundred plus people lived there. The buildings were spread out over the tundra and of similar construction to keep out the cold, arctic winters and placed between groves of evergreen trees. Many of the town's residents were clothed in traditional Russian garb, especially the women. They wore brightly colored, handmade dresses down to their ankles. The men wore embroidered shirts and belts.

After a nice meal of halibut chowder and beer, where Rafe and Roman got to meet many of the families in the town, Mikhail took them on a walk out into the fields behind the church onto the grounds of the cemetery. They walked leisurely on a small path between the graves as he talked. The white Russian Orthodox crosses dotted the landscape of headstones. Rafe listened intently. He had a hard time fully understanding the old man, as he spoke a kind of Slavonic dialect that had been long lost to the ages, except among the community.

"The visitors, as you call them, have been around since the dawn of time. I know this because my grandparents told me and their parents told them before that. The knowledge has been passed down throughout Russian Orthodox history among the leaders of our church. No one knows where they came from or why they exist, but we do know that they are evil. We know that they helped destroy the first Roman Empire of the East. They fostered corruption, greed, and were active in weakening their defenses. They were instrumental in destroying the pillars of their civilization. People became more interested in stealing from their countrymen than serving their country. The peace that had existed in the Roman lands for a thousand years, or the Pax Romana, was destroyed. War flourished and killed millions. The Dark Ages raged, and the human population still doesn't even know what was forgotten that the

Romans had learned. Construction techniques, science, astrology, et cetera."

The man who called himself Mikhail stopped walking and faced them. His eyes seemed to be on fire as he remembered events of the past and regurgitated what had been passed down to him through the generations of Old Believers. He seemed now to be unaware of his surroundings as he spoke, as if he was in another place in time, translating to them the things that the younger generation should hear. Roman was nodding as if in agreement but Rafe said nothing. He just listened, hoping to find some tidbit of information he could use to save his daughter.

"The second Roman Empire of the East lasted another thousand years. But it too grew weak with corruption, fostered by the visitors. They lost the will to defend themselves, to focus on their society, their civilization. They created groups of favored subjects, who received the gifts of the emperor ahead of the others; their economy and society suffered. In the end, the empire died, and the visitors laughed. The visitors had succeeded in destroying two great civilizations. Who knows how many they had destroyed prior to that throughout the millennia.

"However, a new empire was growing to the north. The kingdom of Kievan Rus' was the first version of this new great civilization. But the visitors worked with the Mongols, the Golden Horde of the East, to completely destroy this kingdom a few years before Byzantium fell to the Ottomans. The princes of Rus' moved farther north to the new city of Moscow. They built a grand empire that ruled from the Black Sea to the Nordic lands. Ivan the Terrible was the first tsar to unite all of the eastern Slavic tribes and defeat the invaders from the steppe, the vast plains of Asia. He grew the empire throughout Eastern Europe and to the eastern coast of Siberia. Pushed on by the Russian Orthodox Church, he strove to create the third Holy Roman Empire. The Christian relics, saved from the Muslim invaders of Byzantium, were held in safekeeping and used to justify this new Christian empire. The visitors could not let this happen, so they found a way to stop him, to stop Ivan, and to stop the human progress. They knew Ivan loved his wife Anastasia very much, so they had her poisoned. This drove Ivan quite crazy, and he killed his son and his son's unborn baby in a fit of rage. So the Rurik Dynasty was ended. The empire would not live. The follow-on tsars weakened the influence of the church and destroyed the 'Russianness' of the new empire. They destroyed what had made her great in order to emulate the West. Peter the Great openly mocked the church and the traditions Russians had developed over the centuries. However, the Old Believers continued on in their traditional beliefs. They continued worshipping in the old ways.

"To put the nail in the coffin of the third Holy Roman Empire, the visitors helped create the Soviet Union, who almost destroyed the church altogether. The greatness of Russian society was destroyed. The intellectuals were killed in order to make everyone the same. People were taught to denounce each other. Children denounced their parents. Friends hurt each other out of fear. The fabric of the society was torn. The human spirit was decimated. The desire to better yourself was killed. Now the visitors are after us, the Old Believers. They know we remember the old ways. We stand in the way of their goals, their evil deeds."

As he spoke, Rafe noticed the sun was setting on the horizon and the shadows were falling in the cemetery. The patriarch's words made clear many of the events that had happened to Rafe over the last several weeks, but it did not explain the disappearance of Clare. His uncle's words continued to drone on as Rafe watched the gray shapes appear and spread across the green grass among the headstones. The words did not explain what the visitors wanted with him. He had gained some knowledge of what he was dealing with but still was in the dark on Clare, which filled him with a familiar, intense anxiety. *The hour is getting close, I can feel it. My last chance to save her will be coming soon. I hope I am ready.* As Rafe listened to his uncle, another sound entered his consciousness. It was like a low moaning sound, and it grew louder. Rafe looked around to try to find the sound's origin. It was coming from everywhere. Eventually Roman looked about as well, as he also heard the sound. Roman looked at Mikhail and said, "What is this, Brother?"

Rafe soon saw a golden crucifix of the Russian Orthodox style break the horizon from the village below. It was held on a long pole in front of a procession of people dressed in the traditional religious garb of the Old Believers. Rafe then noticed the same type of group was approaching from all four sides of the cemetery. The entire village was moving towards them and chanting. Soon the three men were surrounded. Mikhail was smiling and he finally answered

Roman's question. "They are here to support you on your journey, Rafe. They know the evil you are facing. They are here to pray for you, for your journey will be difficult. Your uncle Roman will be staying here with us. He has been in Moscow too long. It is time for him to join the rest of his family. However, you will be leaving tonight. Your presence here is too dangerous for all of us. You have to unfortunately move on with your journey. You will be on your own, but we will be with you in spirit."

At that moment, Rafe heard the neigh of horses. The crowd of Old Believers parted, and an opening was formed in their circle around Rafe. He saw a carriage being drawn by three horses approaching. Mikhail spoke again. "This man will take you back towards Anchorage, so you may find a way to leave us here in Alaska to fend for ourselves."

Rafe remembered what he had been told as a child about Russians and how they loved the number three. They kissed three times, and there were always three horses on the troika, or horse-drawn carriage, again referencing the Father, Son, and the Holy Ghost of their beliefs.

"Where shall I go from here?" Rafe asked.

"If I were you," answered Mikhail, "I would go to the farthest point of the former Russian Imperial Empire. I would go to California. There you will discover more of your destiny in this life. Go to Fort Ross in San Francisco and find out why the Russians abandoned her. That is where you will find your answers."

"Will I see you again, Uncle?" asked Rafe.

"I think not, my nephew. Not in this life. You may not see any of us again, but we don't believe in good-byes. It is time for you to leave." Rafe turned one last time to look at all of them then mounted the carriage and did not look back as the driver started his way north towards Anchorage.

Chapter Twenty

The carriage took Rafe only a few miles to the local airstrip near the community. Almost every remote village in Alaska had access to a fixed-based flight operator, or FBO. There were hundreds of them spread out throughout the Alaskan bush, funded by the state government. Nikolaevsk, however, was not far from Homer, on the Kenai Peninsula, which had a large, state-maintained airfield. The FBO usually operated the airfield frequency, where pilots announced their intentions on the uncontrolled strip. It also provided weather information, Notices to Airman, and other types of support for pilots.

Rafe was dropped off at the local charter service. He walked inside the small terminal as directed and waited to be called to board his taxi. Everything had been prepared ahead of time. The man behind the desk pointed to a raspberry pie sitting on the counter. The smell warmed the room. "Help yourself," the man said. Rafe took him up on the idea, and soon the raspberries were awakening his mouth with their taste. Small pleasures, he thought.

A half hour later, a native man walked in and pointed him to a small aircraft, which was being readied for flight. Rafe walked

214

out of the terminal toward the plane and sized up the gentleman who was walking around removing the aircraft's tie-downs, on his pre-flight checklist.

"Where are you taking me?" asked Rafe.

The man looked up at him as he reached to untie a rope attached to one of the wing struts, obviously annoyed with being spoken to. For a few seconds, Rafe wondered if the man was going to reply to him or not. Then he spoke firmly. "I've been paid to fly you to Anchorage, Lake Hood specifically, sport," said the grizzled, old man. He looked to be at least eighty years old and walked with a slight stoop as he shuffled around the plane, inspecting every inch of the aircraft. However, when needed, he exerted a quickness that belied his age.

"What are you looking for?" asked Rafe.

"Anything that could kill me!" answered the old man. "They say there are no old, bold pilots. Well, I'm a good example of that. Can't never be too careful!" he exclaimed. "Get in," he ordered tersely.

Rafe did as he was told and climbed into the four-seat, high-wing aircraft. He had been provided clothes and other items in a small bag by the villagers. One thing which bothered Rafe, as he strapped in next to the pilot seat, was the fact that the aircraft was a seaplane and two floats were attached where the landing gear usually existed. He surmised that wheels must also be protruding from underneath the floats somewhere. The gray-haired, elderly bush pilot deliberately climbed into the seat opposite him, put on headphones, and proceeded to fire up the engine. His hands were trembling, but when he placed them on the yoke, or controls, they steadied immediately. Rafe guessed the man must have had thousands of hours flying in the Alaskan bush. The small aircraft shook as the propeller roared to life, and Rafe tried to make out the man's words as he spoke silently into the microphone protruding from his headset. Only those tuned in to the frequency could hear. Rafe could make out nothing, as he had not been given one. They taxied to the runway and soon were roaring into the sky. The pilot banked north towards Anchorage, and the Kenai Peninsula spread out before them. The mountains surrounding Anchorage were visible ahead.

They flew for over an hour, and soon the mid-sized city was in sight, with the backdrop of the range rising behind it. The higher peaks were bathed in a white blanket of snow, but the "termination dust," or the first winter blanket south of the tree line, was long melted. Rafe marveled at the beauty of the landscape below. The pilot said not a word the entire trip, but as they neared Anchorage, he pointed down towards a body of water on the southwest side of the city. There Rafe saw lines of floatplanes adorning the water as they bounced up and down in the stiff wind, tied to their moors. Lake Hood had three landing areas as well as a gravel strip and was the busiest seaplane base in the world with close to two hundred takeoffs and landings a day. The seaplane base was located a close north to Anchorage International Airport, three miles from downtown Anchorage. The pattern was full, as Rafe could pick out traffic in all stages of their approach as well as aircraft driving towards the field, their landing lights on, mainly for others to see them rather than to increase visibility.

The pilot set up a pattern for an approach at one of the designated lanes and soon was slowing, descending to land. Half a minute later, they splashed down into the water and taxied to the nearby dock for Rafe to disembark. The pilot expertly guided the plane in place, gently touching the wooden platform, and then motioned for Rafe to get out. He didn't stop the engine. Rafe opened the door, grabbed his bag, and hopped down on the right float. He then jumped onto the dock, shutting the small aircraft door behind him. The pilot revved the engine and without looking back taxied out to the landing area outlined by buoys for takeoff. Soon the floatplane was racing down the water and eventually jumped into the air, headed back to the Kenai Peninsula. Rafe walked into the small flight office, not knowing what to expect next. Upon entering, a plump native woman behind the counter asked him to have a seat until his ride arrived. She was pleasant enough, although Rafe couldn't quite understand her through her thick Alaskan native accent. He sat down and thought about calling Neal.

Neal answered on the first ring. "We've been doing some further research," he said immediately. "We've detected a great deal of evidence of visitor activity over the last several decades in Europe and Russia. The pieces of a puzzle have been coming together if you will. By themselves, these events, murders, or reports to authorities of rituals or what have you mean nothing. However,

217

if you know what you are looking for, then you can see a pattern; you can connect the dots."

"Makes sense," responded Rafe, somewhat numb to the world.

"There's more."

"Go ahead and tell me, why don't you?" Rafe asked somewhat nonchalantly. Nothing would surprise him now.

"We've picked up a trail of activity in the United States. It's primarily been on the coasts. California, New York, D.C. Nothing is definite, but we think we have found evidence the visitors are becoming more active in America. And suprisingly, Washington D.C. is a hotbed of activity as well."

"I wouldn't doubt that for a minute. Where in California have you found this activity?" Rafe asked.

"Well, San Francisco to start. Interestingly enough, there is an old Russian fort there called Fort Ross. The name comes from the old Russian word Rus, or Ross. They controlled this part of the state for decades, leaving only after the Crimean War started raging in the nineteenth century. We've seen evidence of rituals there, 911 calls for unusual activity, et cetera."

"Well isn't that special. I think I could be on my way there now as we speak. I'm being flown down from Anchorage."

"Really? Why is that?" Rafe told Neal that his uncle had suggested it might be a good place to continue looking for answers. "Then I'll meet you there. Let's do this together," Neal added.

"Deal, done," responded Rafe, glad to have a friend on board his quest. He hung up the phone and thought about his plan for the next twenty-four hours as he waited for Neal to arrive.

Rafe sat again in the library, researching symbology. This time, he was in San Francisco at the main downtown branch of the public facility. The grand building had opened twenty years ago and was a massive, architecturally artistic building sporting a beautiful Sierra White granite facade; the interior totaled 375,000 square feet.

He had been driven from Lake Hood direct to the nearby international airport in Anchorage. The flight the day before from Alaska had been long but easy, and he had arrived in San Francisco some hours ago then rented a car. He slept most of the time on the flight, his body worn out from the stress he had experienced over the last few weeks. He grabbed a few more hours at a hotel near the airport. He was now somewhat rested but apprehensive. He didn't know what to expect next. *I must be experiencing some sort of post-traumatic stress disorder,* he thought. *But the stress isn't over yet.* Rafe had the rest of the day before Neal's plane would arrive from London in the late afternoon, so he intended to make the best of it trying to find out what he could about the visitors.

He leafed through several books on symbology, trying to make sense of some of the images he had noticed during the rituals and the attack on the village in Siberia. The image of the man's body with the lion's head he connected to ancient Mythraism; the same with the image of the soldier slaying the bull. There was not much

219

more known about these symbols. However, this was not the case with the all-seeing eye of God, or the Eye of Providence. The concept of an all-seeing eye began with the Christian time period and was usually surrounded by a triangle, representing the Trinity, or Father, Son, and Holy Ghost. There was much history associated with this image, and it could be found in various representations in Christian markings and relics around the world. Medieval priests used the eye as a warning to those committing sin, that they would be seen and punished. The design committee for the United States seal put the eye above an unfinished pyramid of thirteen steps, representing the thirteen original states, professing that God was watching over the creation of this new country and would see that is was prosperous and successful.

Rafe poured through more books, searching for any insight he could find on the three symbols. There was nothing new. He picked up the pile of reference materials and took them back to the shelf on symbology, where he had found them. As he placed the last book back on the rack, he noticed another title down below, at the bottom of the bookshelf. On the spine of the book was an all-seeing eye, although slightly different in style. He reached down and pulled the book off the ledge. The title read *Symbology of Satanic Cults*. Rafe flipped open the book and found the section on the eye. It seemed the all-seeing eye could be used to project the vision of the Devil as well. The eye supposedly originated with the Egyptian sun god Horus, and was continued as a dual satanic symbol into the present.

Am I dealing with Devil worship? I wonder if that is the connection I'm supposed to find? thought Rafe. *This is maddening. Maybe a visit to the fort will provide more clues.* He closed the book and left the library. The time had flown by, and he needed to head towards the airport.

The drive from the library towards San Francisco International took Rafe through the center of the city and then outwards to pick up Neal. The plethora of public service announcements on the radio made him chuckle as he drove. *The nanny state is alive and well,* he thought to himself as he negotiated the traffic. *I can relax now. I've been told to have a disaster plan and to watch out for chemicals in my kid's toys. Don't people think for themselves anymore?*

He couldn't help but feel a strange sensation being back in the Lower Forty-eight of the United States. The last time he was on American soil, before his recent stint in Alaska, had been a rough departure from a screwed up marriage. He longed to see his children again, and he was worried sick about Clare, as he had been for weeks now. He hadn't even had time to think about his other kids and how they were handling it. He picked up the phone and called his two older sons. The conversations were quick as usual, as they were involved deeply in their own lives, starting to grow away from their parents as they approached college. They gave him the latest on what the police had said on their last visit to their mom's house and updates on their sport activities. Rafe didn't ask any more questions, and they didn't really want to talk further. *I need to go see them after this is over,* he thought. A wave of sorrow washed over Rafe. He had maybe lost Clare, had lost Cecilia and parts of his newfound family. However, the event that had shocked him and destroyed his inner soul was the killing of Ksyusha. He couldn't get her out of his mind, nor could he Clare. *Figure this out! Be strong and save your daughter. It will be nice to have Neal here to help me with all of this, someone I can trust.* Rafe drove onto the interstate to the airport, oblivious now to his surroundings as he prepared his mind for whatever events the future held.

One thing Rafe did notice as he was driving through downtown San Francisco was the increase in the homeless population. They seemed to be on every street corner, drug paraphernalia scattered on the street beside many of them. The city just seemed much dirtier than he remembered. No one seemed shocked by this as they went about their day, walking around them on the way to and from work. *What is happening to my country?* he thought.

Chapter Twenty-One

Rafe pulled to the curb at San Francisco International in front of baggage claim. He looked for a place to park temporarily, out of the view of the police shooing the parked cars away from the front of the airport for security reasons. The terrorism threat had been raised recently due to events overseas, and the security personnel were nervous. Neal was waiting for him on the curb and hurriedly hopped into the rental car, slamming the door behind him after throwing his small bag into the backseat. He carried only a small briefcase otherwise. The two shook hands aggressively. "Good to see you, mate!" said Neal as Rafe pulled back into the active traffic lane and headed to the airport exit to go back into the city.

"Good to see you as well. How was the flight? Long I presume?"

"Yes, quite long. It's good to be off that bloody airplane. The business class ticket helped somewhat though. I thank the Queen for that small luxury."

"She always did take care of you," laughed Rafe. "Let's find a nice place to eat and grab a drink. Work for you?"

"Splendid idea!"

"We've got to get through the city first. I say we cross the bridge and find a place to eat in Sausalito. I've booked us a hotel there. Fort Ross is an hour's drive north of San Francisco. So staying in Sausalito, we will be closer to our destination once we decide to visit the fort, and we won't have to negotiate the traffic coming out of the big city."

"This is your country, sport!" responded Neal. "I trust you implicitly!" Rafe navigated the myriad of paths out of the large, multi-terminal airport, and soon they were headed north.

It was 7:00 p.m. when they arrived at the bistro overlooking the Sausalito section of the San Francisco Bay Area. They had crossed the Golden Gate Bridge, and the weather was clear enough to get a good view of Alcatraz in the middle of the bay to the east. Hundreds of yachts were moored off the coast, along with a large number of houseboats. Painters and other craftsmen were spread out along the plaza next to the water, hawking their wares. A small orchestra was playing chamber music on the waterfront as well. Sausalito was an industrial center during World War II but had morphed into an artistic, cultural oasis. It was quite bohemian with art and creativity everywhere. The warm evening was quite pleasant. "This is beautiful!" remarked Neal.

"Yes, isn't it? You've never been to the Bay Area before?"

"Never. I didn't know what I was missing. And what a great little spot to eat!"

"Yeah, I like this place. They say the word bistro comes from the Russian occupation of Paris in 1814 after Napoleon was defeated and put into exile on the island of Elba. The Russian word for quickly is *bystro*. It is thought the Russian occupying officers would force the Parisians to feed them and would say *quickly* in Russian. Hence, the term bistro was applied to small French restaurants that served food rather quickly. That's your trivia for the day."

"Interesting," added Neal, not really listening to Rafe as he gazed out over the water, lost in thought.

"So tell me more about the visitor activity around the fort," said Rafe, as he noticed he had lost Neal's attention and therefore changed the direction of the conversation.

Neal was jerked back to reality and replied a few seconds later after thinking about Rafe's question. "We've only got circumstantial evidence, you understand. Several of the residents along the coast near the fort have reported to police that they have seen frequent fires burning around the fort itself, multiple fires at once in fact, usually late in the evening. It could be torches from one of the rituals you have spoken of. Some of the locals have been quite upset and vocal about it and want it to stop."

"How often have you had these reports? And have the police found anything?"

"We've located a handful of eyewitness complaints thanks to the cooperation of your local police. And no, the police have found nothing when they checked them out. To them, it was just a false alarm. But to the trained eye, well it could be something else, couldn't it?"

"And this was enough for you to fly all the way over here?"

"Yes, it was. We don't have that much to go on. However, there is more. Your government has picked up signal traffic. You're very good at that you know. They've collected several conversations about events at the fort. It seems they've been monitoring some of the same people we have and passed on the information to us recently. It seems your NSA has been quite productive."

"Yes, we've become quite accomplished at spying on our own people. So some of the visitors mentioned these so-called events? In what manner?"

"They've been caught discussing going to the fort in San Francisco. It doesn't take too much to put two and two together now, does it? It's probably the visitors."

"Well that is interesting."

"And here's the mother lode. They've discussed tonight as a possible time frame for an event."

"Really? Do you have a time? That is something to fly all the way over here for!"

"Yes, I thought you might see the light."

"So where do we go from here?"

"Once it gets dark," added Neal, "we go to Fort Ross."

An hour and a half later, the sun was approaching the horizon, and Neal motioned for the waitress to bring the check. She returned shortly with the bill. Rafe nonchalantly threw some cash on the table to cover the dinner and drinks. After standing, he reached down to add a few one-dollar bills for the tip. Neal followed his movements and saw the dollars lying on the table with the back of the bills facing up. He became transfixed on the image presented to him on the back of the one-dollar bill. It was a pyramid adorned at the top with the Eye of Providence, or the all-seeing eye. Neal stared at the image for several uncomfortably long seconds.

"You okay?" asked Rafe, noticing Neal's trance on the image.

"Yeah, I guess so," responded Neal as he forcibly broke his gaze away from the dollar.

"You've never seen the back of a U.S. dollar before?"

"I'm sure I have, but no, can't say that I've ever noticed. Interesting design," said Neal squeamishly. His face had turned white as a ghost.

"First time for everything," added Rafe suspiciously. *What was that all about?* he wondered to himself. Something stirred in the back of his mind, and he became suspicious of Neal and his interest in the all-seeing eye.

Rafe and Neal drove the hour plus route up to the area on the coast where Fort Ross was located. The fort was perched on a flat cliff overlooking the Pacific Ocean. The view was quite stunning during the daytime. The site had attracted the early Russian explorers for its beauty as well as its natural security features. The fort sat in the middle of a large, grassy area, no trees or any other obstacles

227

around it. No one would be able to approach the citadel unseen from any direction, providing an extra modicum of safety.

It was a square, wooden structure surrounded by walls built with sharp, pointed poles, as forts were constructed in that era. Multiple wooden buildings were located inside. Guard towers were placed on the four corners of the fortress. There were several modern buildings outside the structure that housed tourist facilities and other commercial ventures, but the majority of the grounds were made to resemble the early nineteenth-century Russian stronghold.

Fort Ross had been a Russian outpost at the farthest reaches of imperial Russia as the tsar searched for lucrative fur pelts to line his pockets and finance the wars in Europe. The Spanish had claimed the land of California to the south,but the north was wide open to Russian explorers. The fort also helped supply the Russian Alaskan community as well with raw materials.

Relations between the Russian colonial rulers and the native peoples of Alaska were adversarial at best. Many of the groups were conquered by Moscow, but a few of the native Indian tribes held out against Russian rule. However, most were negatively affected by disease and outright brutality at the hands of the Russian occupiers. Moscow sold the fort in the mid-eighteen hundreds as they pulled back to preserve their Siberian empire as war spread in Europe and Asia. The sale of Alaska took place a few decades later, as the furs were over-trapped and the supply was dwindling. Russia never again ventured into North America.

228

As they arrived, night was setting in and the entire compound was dark. They parked in the tourist parking area, away from the walls of the fort, and began walking towards the ocean. The moon highlighted the way as they progressed slowly, not knowing what to expect. They both were apprehensive.

The two men quickly passed the compound itself and, not noticing any activity, continued towards the ocean and soon were standing before a guard rail, which prevented any further advance. They were completely alone.

"I guess we wait?" asked Rafe.

"Sounds good to me. I'm glad it's warm. It could be a while. Who knows what we are likely to see tonight. Let's stay alert. We should see anyone coming."

Rafe pulled a cigar out of his sport coat and lit it. He held out one for Neal. "Care for one?"

"Sure, thank you. I love surprises." The moon was high in the sky now and bright as a beacon. They were highlighted against the ocean. "Tell me about San Francisco," added Neal after lighting the cigar and puffing to ensure the tobacco was well lit all the way around the far end.

"What do you want to know?" asked Rafe as lit his cigar as well and drew the smooth tobacco smoke into his mouth.

"I want to know about the soul of the city."

"The soul of the city is dying," responded Rafe.

"Why do you say that?"

"Because I drove through it today. There are homeless everywhere. There is no work ethic. It's just anything goes it seems and someone else will pay for it."

"That's what happens when you promise a society everything they want," responded Neal.

Rafe looked at him for a few seconds, trying to understand his meaning. "Do you know something I don't, Neal?"

"Yes, I think I do, Rafe. And it's time you knew as well."

"What do you mean by that?" Rafe asked suspiciously, his spine stiffening, a sense of dread washing over him. His new suspicions about Neal seeming to be confirmed, his anxiety level for Clare increased as well.

Neal said nothing for several moments then finally spoke. "Why don't you follow me?" Neal hopped over the railing and started walking to the edge of the cliff. Rafe followed cautiously, his guard highly aroused. They approached the point of no return on the cliff, and Neal turned to Rafe. "What do you see below?"

Rafe walked to the edge and stood beside Neal. Far below, there was a small beach where the waves crashed into the land from the ocean, having whittled away the dirt from below the cliff over the centuries. Rafe leaned over the edge and looked down. A hundred feet below, he saw a large group of torches arranged in a circle on the sand. He could vaguely make out dark shapes around the fires. The people started chanting in some kind of dialect that Rafe couldn't understand. Neal spoke. "I think it's time we go down, don't you, Rafe?"

230

"I'll follow you from a distance," Rafe responded, being very cautious.

"Your call," replied Neal. The two started walking along the edge of the cliff. Soon Neal turned and spoke to Rafe, who was walking a few meters behind. "Follow me down these stairs; they've been carved into the rock. They are solid, but the lighting is not great as you can see, so be careful."

"I appreciate your concern," responded Rafe sarcastically.

"I thought you might," Neal said as he smiled politely. He started down the stairs and Rafe followed, slowly negotiating the rough, stone steps. Ten minutes later, they emerged on the beach; the waves crashed against the outlying rocks, creating a deafening sound. Rafe stayed a ways behind Neal as he walked towards the torches. Rafe could make out the altar in the center of the ring of fire, the hooded figures silently surrounding the area in a familiar arc. When he had reached the group of people, suddenly Neal turned towards Rafe and spoke. "Rafe, we've been waiting for your arrival here. We are glad you are finally among us, so we can talk."

"So you knew I would come here? Or better yet, you led me here?"

"Yes, you could say both statements are true!"

"So I guess the question is, why?"

"Because we want you to join us, Rafe!"

"Join you in what?"

L TODD WOOD

"We want you to join our little group here. We have a lot of fun at our recurring gatherings! Haven't you seen?" Neal said with a laugh.

"You forget the small issue of my daughter's disappearance."

"Well, I'm sure our leader can help with that. The real question is whether or not you will become one of us."

"Where is your *leader?*" asked Rafe.

"You will see him again soon enough."

"What are you trying to accomplish? What are your goals? Tell me what you are trying to do!" demanded Rafe.

"I think that is painfully obvious, and you know very well what we are trying to do! Just look at all of the poverty, joblessness, and corruption all around you in this city! Isn't it wonderful! It gives me a hard-on!"

Rafe looked into the eyes of the hooded figures standing around him in a circle. The torches flashed an orange glow into their faces. He recognized many of them, as they were frequent figures in government, academia, and in the media. He was among a group of very powerful people indeed. Rafe said nothing for a while.

"Let it go, Rafe! Join us! It's no use trying to resist. Everything has been planned! You are supposed to be one of us!"

"I guess I didn't get the memo. And besides, murdering families in the middle of the night just doesn't appeal to me!"

"That matter couldn't be helped! Sometimes things must be done for the good of the society!"

"Yeah, I remember Stalin said something like that."

232

"He was a wise man!"

"Whatever you say, Neal. So let's cut to the chase. There is no way I'm going to join your little band of marauders. It's just not my bag, baby. So why don't you give me back my daughter, and let's call it a day, huh? That way you can go back to England and continue whatever evil journey you are on, and I can get back to writing. How does that sound?"

"I'm afraid it's not so easy, my friend. And besides, I can't give you your daughter back. That will come from the leader, if he decides to do so. I was merely asked to invite you to join our group."

"Well, as I said, that's not going to happen."

"Suit yourself. But I must tell you, there will be consequences. It would be much easier if you just submit now and avoid all the unpleasantness! Speaking as your friend of course!"

"You are not my friend!" responded Rafe.

"That's where you are wrong. You see, I was given an offer I couldn't refuse as well. Now, I'm happy I made the right choice. It's not that difficult once you get the hang of it! Trust me!"

"I used to trust you. No longer."

"I had no choice, Rafe, and neither do you."

"We'll see about that."

"Yes, you are right about that one! The problem is, I'm not sure you'll get another chance."

"Well, your leader asked me to find something. Is this it?"

"Aaah, yes. You are correct. I'm not sure how to answer that. You will have to figure that out on your own, as he said. All I know is he will be disappointed in your answer tonight."

"I guess I'll deal with him some other time. So what do we do now that I have refused your offer? Are you going to kill me here on the beach?"

"Oh no! Nothing rude like that, I assure you. We are simply going to blindfold you and tie you up. That way you can't see us leave. We'll leave enough slack so that eventually you can get free, but it will take you a while. Good night, Rafe!" With Neal's comment, someone from behind Rafe put a hood over his head, and whatever light there was went out. Rafe was hog-tied and left on the beach. The crashing of the waves drowned out any sound of the visitors leaving and heading back into society.

Chapter Twenty-Two

The problem is, I'm not sure you'll get another chance. The words kept ringing in Rafe's mind as he struggled to climb the stone stairs back to the top of the cliff and to the car, if it was still there. His knees were bloodied, as he had fallen several times. It was much harder to climb up than it had been to walk down. Rafe's thighs burned as he pushed himself to put one foot in front of the other and inch his way towards to the top of the cliff. His legs were weak from low circulation, as the ropes had cut into him; Rafe kept moving. Soon he could at least see the top, and it gave him increased motivation to move faster.

He felt a giant loss. Although he had been betrayed, he felt a loss just the same. Neal had been a close confidant for years. Now Rafe was truly alone. He was truly alone in his fight for Clare. He was the only one who could save her. *And I will die if I have to in order to do so!* he thought to himself. *I will do anything to save her.* The panic returned with a vengeance. *Where is she?*

Rafe finally arrived at the top of the cliff and sat down facing the ocean. He had to rest, as he was breathing heavily and felt light-headed. It had taken several hours to free himself from the ropes, and he was quite tired. For the first time, he felt almost hopeless. The events of the recent past had taken a toll on his body and especially his mind. *I have to find the strength to go on. I am her only chance.* The light was beginning to peek over the horizon behind him to the east. The ocean lay undisturbed by human hands before him, violently crashing into the shoreline below, creating a crescendo of noise. It was a beautiful sight; he tried to allow the rhythm of the waves to soothe him. He lay back in the grass and tried to take a quick nap, as he was exhausted. It was no use. *Too bad I can't enjoy it!* After thirty minutes of contemplating his situation, his energy had returned. Rafe stood and made his way back to where they had left the vehicle. He felt slightly stronger now. He was overjoyed when he saw it was still there. *Thank you for small miracles.* Rafe took one last look at Fort Ross as the sun broke over the horizon then got in the car and drove back towards San Francisco.

Rafe didn't know what to do next. He stared out over the water at the yachts moored off the coast of Sausalito. The vessels drifted in the wind that had picked up as the day grew older. He had returned to the same bistro for something to eat after catching some sleep at the hotel. He had even managed to bandage his knees. Rafe had rapidly experienced all the different stages of grief for the loss of his good friend, Neal. Now he was just feeling anger, again. He was enraged at the betrayal but powerless to do anything about it. He drank quickly the cup of coffee the waitress had brought him and then asked her for another. The young girl returned shortly to refill his cup. She dropped a newspaper on the table for his perusal. "You look bored," she added. "Maybe this will help." She smiled and walked away.

Searching for inspiration, he spread out the paper on the table to take in the headlines. There were the usual school massacres and drive-by shootings, but immediately his eyes were glued to an article from New York City. It seemed that as the construction crews were digging the underground sites for the new Second Avenue Subway line, they found an archeological discovery that no one could explain. Experts were trying to determine how a two-thousand-year-old Roman Mythraic temple could have been built underneath New York. *This just keeps getting stranger. I guess I'm going back to New York immediately. I'm going home.*

The flight to New York City was a long one. Since he bought a ticket at the last minute, he couldn't get a direct flight and had to switch planes in Denver. The layover was maddening. He paced the carpeted concourse of the modern airport and waited for his connection. The plane for the flight was late arriving due to maintenance reasons, and his departure was moved back two hours, so he amused himself in the bar. Rafe didn't arrive at JFK until almost midnight. The familiar airport was empty as he walked through the terminal to the exit. After being in Europe, he was always shocked at the third world nature of the New York City airports. The infrastructure was old and lacking in any aesthetic appearance. One of the escalators was not working. There seemed to be no sense of urgency to fix it. There was no style, no class, just barely functioning steel and concrete. He hadn't checked a bag, so he immediately took a cab into the city. The traffic was negligible at this hour, and Rafe was in Manhattan within twenty minutes after crossing via the tunnel.

The extreme stress he had felt before in his life in New York returned just as fast as it had left when he arrived in Venice months before. That Italian existence seemed like another life now. He missed his garden of herbs on the balcony. *Maybe I can go back there when this is all over,* he mused. Rafe considered calling his ex-wife but thought better of it. Maybe I'll touch base in a few days, when I know more about what's going on here and hopefully have more information on Clare. He had booked a night at the W Hotel on Lexington in Midtown and upon arrival was shown directly to his room. The boutiquey, modern facility was a favorite watering hole for the after-work, banker crowd near Park Avenue. After dropping off the small bag he traveled with, Rafe quickly returned to the bar. There was too much on his mind for sleep at this point. Plus, he had gotten some shut-eye on the plane. He was wide awake and his mind was racing. Rafe walked into the dark, modern space near the west end of the lobby and ordered a drink. He sat at a shady, corner table, out of the way of most of the patrons that is those who were left at this hour. It was well after midnight and the crowd was thinning. Rafe contemplated his next actions silently. *Should*

I just show up at the temple? Would any of the visitors be there? Why have I been drawn here? What's here for me to find? The answers would not come, and slowly fatigue began to wash over him. *This last month has been a blur. I don't understand why I'm still alive.* He began to get up and then noticed two women in their late twenties and early thirties talking furiously and comparing notes as they sat next to each other in front of the bartender. They were quite attractive. Rafe stood up and walked over to the modern bar and sat down near them. He wasn't interested in them romantically but more in a curious, informational way. They were obviously discussing something of importance. The interaction was quite heated.

"He has to find a way to fend off the attacks from Butler that will inevitably come!" stated the older girl emphatically.

"Sure, but he also has to seem above the fray. We don't want him dragged down into the weeds, where he is not strong. We both know he's not a policy wonk."

"No, he's more of a sexual wonk. Wonking every new female intern that comes on board," laughed the other woman.

"Yeah, I think we've both been there, haven't we?"

"No comment!" laughed the older woman.

Rafe listened discretely for a few minutes and then decided to break into the conversation. He really didn't know why. "Sounds like you two are preparing for a debate or something."

The older of the two looked at him with a startled expression. "Why yes, we are. How did you know? Was it the exquisite way we dress or the intellectual quality of our conversation?" she said

239

sarcastically, her eyes undressing Rafe from top to bottom in an obviously flirtatious manner.

Rafe smiled. "I used to help with some political issues myself, back in the day. It's the same everywhere, you know. The incumbent has to be above it all, while at the same time not allowing any of the riffraff to get close to him. It's a delicate balance."

"I guess it is. And we definitely have riffraff, but he's ours." she replied, slowly letting her guard down. "Our candidate is debating the other side tomorrow. We were just wondering if our debate prep strategy was strong enough. We've been working on it for weeks but you always wonder. You always are worried you forgot to prep him on something or teach him how to respond to the inevitable difficult question. I guess we'll know very soon."

"Quite right! It's almost impossible to prepare for everything. Who's the candidate?" asked Rafe.

"Greg Bowker," she replied. Instantly Rafe remembered the face of the man who asked him to drink the sedative at Tsaritsyno, and he noticeably stiffened. He remembered the man walking over to him with the long blade, an evil glint in his eye as he hoped to be able to use it on Rafe's midsection. The thought of disemboweling Rafe gave him great pleasure.

"What's wrong? Do you know him?" asked the younger staffer.

Rafe regained his composure. "Let's just say we've met once in a dark alley."

"Hmmm. That doesn't sound good. He does have quite the reputation. I hope it wasn't anything too terrible. If so, we don't want to know about it! At least not now anyway."

"Yeah, and please don't tell the press, whatever it is!" laughed the other woman.

"What are your names?" asked Rafe.

"I'm Megan, this is Kathy. We've worked together on several campaigns, but this has been the most interesting to say the least!"

"So where's the debate?" asked Rafe.

"It's at NYU downtown. Do you want to come? I have some tickets here in my bag. It's quite an important race." She reached into her purse and handed Rafe a ticket.

"I'll be there," he said coldly. "Thank you." Rafe got up from the bar and caught the elevator to his room.

Rafe had booked a luxurious suite overlooking Manhattan. *I deserve it after what I've been through!* he rationalized as he kicked off his shoes upon entering. It was decorated in an elegant, modern design and had a large, floor-to-ceiling, glass window, which looked out over Midtown from the twenty-second floor. *This city really doesn't ever sleep!* he remarked to himself as he stood taking in the twinkling lights of the metropolis. A glass of single malt Scotch from the minibar finished the mood quite nicely. Soon, his eyes grew tired.

After a few hours of trying, Rafe realized he was not going to be able to sleep. The bed was incredibly soft and the bedding luxurious but it was of no use. His mind was still racing. He sat up in bed and flipped his legs over the side to stand then made his way in the dark to the desk, switching on the light. He opened the laptop that he had bought in San Francisco and searched for news on the Mytrhraic temple discovered in Manhattan a few days before.

The Second Avenue Subway, or SAS, had been a dream of New Yorkers since the turn of the twentieth century. That dream had been a long time turning into reality. The Lexington Avenue line a few streets over was the busiest in the United States with over 1.2 million riders a day. SAS was planned in 1929, but work was never started due to the Great Depression. The line was revived after the end of the Second World War, but funds were diverted to maintenance projects on existing routes. Digging actually was initiated in the early 1970s, and some progress was made, but the project was halted when New York City became insolvent. In the first decade of the twenty-first century, the project finally moved forward to reality with construction on phase one, which would connect 96th and 63rd streets. The few sections that were completed during the 1970s were to be tied into the new sections being built. Due to changes in design, a couple of the previously completed sections were to be abandoned. This initial tunnel on the new route was completed in 2011, with the tracks and other equipment scheduled to be completely installed by 2016.

It seemed the temple was discovered while excavating an underground storage area off the main tunnel, to be used for housing electronics to run the entire system. Federal law required work to be halted when a possible archeological site was discovered. Members from the State Historic Preservation Office were called in to begin

242

exploration of the temple. They were still trying to figure out how the temple came into existence, as it was obviously ancient. The entire known course of human history could be altered. Evidence of the Roman Empire in North America? Archeologists all over the world were salivating to get more information on the discovery.

There must be security down there, thought Rafe. *And how in the world would I even find it underground? It's not like you can just walk into a subway dig and know your way around. I'll have to figure something out. Maybe it will come to me tomorrow.* Rafe closed the computer, hopped back in bed, and closed his eyes. He thought about Clare for a few minutes then sleep finally came quickly.

Chapter Twenty-Three

Rafe woke late in the morning. The sunlight was streaming in the glass windows of his room, warming his face as he lay in bed. *I've overslept. Damn it!* He jumped out of bed in a panic, turned on the coffeemaker, and jumped into the shower. *Today is the day! I can feel it! I"m going to find Clare! One way or another!* he thought as the hot water drowned his groggy mind and refreshed him for the day. Upon exiting the bath, he felt like a new man and decided to make a phone call. An idea had come to him in the night.

David Wharton was a professor of history at NYU and had influence with the State Historic Preservation Office, who was conducting the temple examination. Their role was to ensure any archeological find. In the state of New York was properly examined and catalogued. In this way, important historical information would not be lost to the ages. David and Rafe had interacted on another scientifically important project years before. It was a find down in the Wall Street area, an original part of the Dutch city of New Amsterdam before the area was sold to the English. They had bonded during the experience, as they shared the same academic interests and a passion for history. If anyone could help, it would be David. *Maybe he can get me in! It's worth a shot.*

Wharton answered on the first ring. "Rafe, it's been a long time. To what do I owe the pleasure of speaking to an old colleague after all of these years?"

"Unfortunately this is not a social call, David. I need a favor."

"Just tell me, old friend. It's been too long. I'll help if I can."

"Well, I'm extremely interested in this new temple that's been discovered at the SAS. But the security, from what I can tell, seems very tight. Can you get me a way in? It's very connected to something else I am working on."

"Gotcha! Yes, what a fascinating story. The discovery may change forever how we view human history on the continent. But it's a tall order, as the interest is intense. Let me see what I can do. Give me your cell phone number. I'll ring you back when I have more information, okay? Most likely later today or in the morning."

"Sure, thanks, David!" Rafe punched in his cell number and sent it to David via text.

"Anytime!"

Thirty minutes later, Rafe was on the street, walking towards the 51st Street subway station. The Lexington Avenue line ran parallel to the new Second Avenue line but was extremely overcrowded, especially during this peak morning time. It was a rainy, dark day, and he did not have an umbrella, a must for any New Yorker. *Fitting,* he thought to himself. He ended up buying one from a street vendor who had conveniently set up a table with a great selection on the street. They always seemed to show up at the right places when it rained in New York, typically outside of the subway stations. *I guess there are some vestiges of capitalism left around here.*

He entered the metro station then closed and shook his new umbrella, all the while attempting not to stab a fellow commuter, and descended down the stairs to the tunnel that led across the street to the uptown track. Rafe couldn't help noticing the tile falling off the walls, and the orange stains of water damage draining down from the ceiling, creating stalactites of a frothy, chemical mess. The whole place smelled of urine and vomit. The escalators were once again inoperative. *What is happening to my country?* he asked again to himself. The homeless were everywhere, as the economic situation had deteriorated badly over the last decade. Getting a job was difficult, since no one was hiring. It was the natural result of overreaching government interference in the private market. Companies were not investing in new businesses. Innovation and risk-taking had been stifled. It had happened over and over again throughout history. *Right now, I'm only concerned about Clare.*

Rafe made the platform in time to see a train approaching the station. He saw several large rats rummaging around the trash thrown down to the railway level. As the train slowed to a noisy stop, he caught the uptown car and exited onto 86th Street in the Upper East Side, or Upper East as it was called. Soon he was heading east towards the shore of Manhattan that faced Brooklyn and Queens. Eventually the construction site for the Second Avenue Subway was looming before him, blocking his path.

The entire area was cut off up and down the street with fencing, and there were scores of men in yellow hard hats and orange reflector vests milling about. Police were also omnipresent guarding the entrances to the newly discovered archeological find, which sat directly below them. It seemed everyone wanted a look at the discovery. The press was everywhere as well. Their satellite trucks clogged the roadway. His phone rang in his pocket, and he ducked into an alleyway and answered quickly.

"Rafe, it's David. Look, that place is pretty highly secured. It seems the federal government is also getting involved to make sure no one gets in. I'm not sure what they've found, but I can tell you for sure, I can't get you in. But hey, if you do get a look, I want to know about it, okay? Sorry, Rafe!"

"No worries, David. Thanks for trying. Let's meet a little later in the week. I'm in the city for a few days, working on a project."

"I'd love to. Would be nice to connect. Ciao."

Rafe walked down the sidewalk opposite the construction and tried to find a way to enter that was unguarded; the fencing was visible for miles. However, it was no use. There were plenty of burly guys in suits with earpieces and bulges under their jackets to prevent this. Anytime he got close to an opening in the fence, one of them would approach him and he backed off. However, another idea popped into Rafe's head. He headed back towards the 86th

Street metro entrance. The rain kept coming, darkening Rafe's mood with foreboding of possible events to come. He shivered with the cold as he felt the presence of evil all around him. *I feel Clare calling me! She's still alive. I know it!* Rafe descended back into the cavern of the subway and navigated the underground maze until he was standing on the opposite platform from which he came. He stood back from the edge as he waited, as there had been multiple high-profile instances of passengers being pushed into oncoming trains. Rafe jumped on the next car heading downtown. During the forty-five minute ride, he was assaulted twice by panhandlers using the captive riders on the subway as their personal begging audience. It was not a pleasant journey. It seemed the experience of riding the subway was the canary in the coalmine of the health of New York City. When the ride was a pleasant one and the journey free from harassment, life was good in the Big Apple. When one feared for his safety and the subway cars were covered in graffiti and filth, the future of the city was not bright. He was happy to finally exit the metro in the southern end of the city.

Two hours later, he sat alone on a bench in Washington Square Park in downtown Manhattan. The New York University buildings surrounded him, along with a plethora of bohemian cafes and establishments catering to the university student crowd. The rain had stopped and the skies had cleared somewhat. Rafe was thankful for that. The sun's rays peered down through the leaves of the many large trees placed strategically around the square. The fountain in the center was the hub of activity. Rafe sat in one of the corners, under a shady oak, watching the people as they walked by. He noticed plenty of piercing, tattoos, and various other forms of mutilation of the body. *I don't recognize my country anymore.*

As the sun started its daily journey towards the west and the shadows began to fall, Rafe finally saw what he was looking for. Greg Bowker walked towards the event with his entourage, including the attractive, young women Rafe had met the night before. No one noticed him sitting alone, away from the auditorium entrance. The debate would start in two hours. Bowker was aiming for his tenth term representing this congressional district. He faced a strong challenger, and a commanding performance in the debate would be key to winning the election. The girls were right, it was an important event. There were media trucks everywhere, their satellite dishes protruding from the tops of the vehicles with military precision.

Once Bowker's group entered the building, Rafe waited for approximately fifteen minutes and then entered himself. He found the venue and selected a good vantage point, sitting in the rear of the auditorium. He waited for the festivities.

Over the next hour, one by one, the three candidates came up to test the microphone and get a feel for the layout of the event. They each took about five minutes alone with their individual staffs. Bowker was last and took about ten minutes total. Anger welled up inside Rafe as he viewed the monster who had knowledge of the whereabouts of his daughter and who had threatened him with death. Rafe no longer cared about himself or anything else. His only goal or mission in life now was to save Clare. He would do that he felt sure. Let the consequences to himself be damned.

Bowker was finishing up his time on the stage, conversing with his staff, and going over final points for the debate. The two women he had met were busy stuffing him with last minute bits of advice. He seemed to be the very arrogant type, dismissing his staff's concerns over several issues of style and presentation of the arguments. "I'll do it my way and I'll be fine!" Rafe heard him declare loudly. Soon they were obviously complete, and the team picked up their belongings to leave. *This is my chance,* thought Rafe.

Before leaving the stage, Bowker asked his assistant to point out the bathroom. The girl who had given Rafe the ticket waved her hand towards a flight of stairs to the rear of the platform. Seeing this, Rafe seized the moment and quickly made his way down the pathway to the stage entrance, unbeknownst to anyone. Everyone else was gone. He silently followed the congressman down the steps at the rear of the performing area to the toilet facilities.

Rafe slowly and without a sound pushed open the door to the men's bathroom The area was reserved for performers and was not noticeable to the general patrons of the auditorium. The two of them were alone. *Perfect!* thought Rafe. There was a ninety-degree turn in the entranceway, and Rafe peeked around the corner. The congressman had his back to him, relieving himself in the urinal. He finished and turned to leave. He was a large man but Rafe didn't care. He had the element of surprise.   At that moment, Rafe dove into him and slammed him back against the wall. Bowker's head banged against the tile and he was temporarily disoriented. Rafe had a piece of an iron rod in his jacket pocket that he had picked up at the construction site. It could easily resemble a weapon, and Rafe stuck the end of the iron into the man's gut with his hand in his jacket pocket. "Where's my daughter? You son of a bitch!"

The man was startled for a second and held up his hands to catch his breath and analyze his situation. Rafe could see the fear in his eyes. Then recognition spread over his face and after a few seconds, spoke, "Easy, Rafe! No need for violence. Your daughter is safe, I assure you." He started to lower his hands and smiled.

"Keep your hands up where I can see them, you piece of crap! That's not what I asked! I said where is she?"

"I can lead you to her. Just let me take you. Put down the gun, okay?"

"She's close by?"

"Yes," answered Bowker affirmatively.

"Then do it now!"

"Okay, okay! Follow me." Bowker lowered his hands and straightened his jacket. Rafe allowed him to move away from the wall and towards the doorway.

"I will, very closely!" said Rafe. They slowly walked up the stairs to the stage area. Rafe scanned the auditorium for anyone who could see them. He saw nothing. The bathroom door slammed behind them. He kept the rod pushed into Bowker's back. Upon arriving on the platform, Bowker started running, screaming for help. *I guess I didn't fool him with the fake weapon,* thought Rafe and he let him go. Rafe didn't see Bowker's security detail behind him. And he didn't see the taser. The electric charge raced through his body and he fell to the ground, convulsing. One of the men put his boot on Rafe's face. Spittle oozed from his mouth as Rafe lost control of his body. Soon he was handcuffed and lay prostrate on the floor. The police arrived ten minutes later. Rafe didn't care. All he could think about was Clare.

Chapter Twenty-Four

He was released into a holding cell in downtown New York City. It was not a nice place. Perhaps it was intended not to be a nice place in order to preclude someone taking a chance on coming back; Rafe didn't know. He did know he wanted out and never wanted to be here again, but that was beside the point. The point was Clare. Locked up in here, he couldn't find her. He had to find a way out.

Thankfully, he was alone in his cell, which he thought was unusual. The other cells he could see were crowded. There were lots of gangsters and other general thugs. He could tell by all of the tattoos covering their bodies.

Strange, he thought. *Why do I get special treatment? I guess I'll find out soon enough.* Rafe sat down on the metal bench to the rear of the small room. The cage he was in held little else beside himself, just a small toilet. The bench was cold and there was no blanket. He waited for a couple hours and had plenty of time to think. All he thought about was Clare and how being inside here was failing her. The hours drifted on and his hopelessness grew. He eventually stretched out on the hard bench and dozed off, waking up some time later. *I need to get out of here!* he said to himself when he realized where he was. Then finally, there was some movement out in the hallway by the entrance to the cell block. He heard the door open, and soon, footsteps echoed though the cell block, walking his way. Rafe stood to meet whoever was coming to see him. A few seconds later, David Wharton walked in front of the bars, and Rafe was truly surprised. "What are you doing here, David?"

"I could ask you the same, Rafe, but I won't, because I know what you are doing here. As your friend, I'm here to help."

"I don't understand. How can you help me?"

"I can get you out of here, for starters!"

"How could you do that?"

Wharton held up a key. "With this," he said.

"I don't understand. How did you get that and how did you get in here?"

"Now let's have a little conversation, Rafe. I think you know who sent me. He wants to meet with you. However, we need to have an understanding first. I'll take you to him, but I don't want any funny business, okay? Let's just keep this nice and peaceful, and we'll all get along fine."

The reality of the situation slowly dawned on Rafe. "So you are one of the visitors also?" he asked, dumbfounded.

"Yes, of course. I've been involved with them for years. We are making quite a difference, don't you think? Most of my senior academic friends are involved as well. Our work is never done."

254

"Making a difference in what? Involved in what?"

"I think you know what we are up to, Rafe. You've noticed what's going on around here. But I'm not going to discuss that with you. I'll let him do that. So do we have a deal? Are you going to be a good boy for me? I really don't want any problems."

Rafe thought for a moment and then spoke. "I'll agree to your terms."

"Good. I thought you might. Your daughter I'm sure will appreciate that. You do want to see her again, don't you?"

Rafe grabbed the bars with both hands in fury. "If I could break your fucking neck right now, I would!" he threatened.

"Aaah, but we have an agreement, don't we? So you won't."

"I won't right now. It seems I was wrong about you."

"I guess that's good enough for me. Don't feel bad, Rafe. We all have our reasons for what we do." Wharton put the key in the cell door and opened it wide. He stood back so Rafe could exit then walked somewhat behind him as they left the cell block and entered the guard room. The policeman waiting for them put handcuffs on Rafe and led him out onto a loading dock, where he was put in a police van. Before the door closed, Wharton called out to him. "This is where I say good-bye, Rafe. Have a good meeting! He's looking forward to spending time with you!" Rafe heard Wharton laughing as the door to the vehicle was slammed shut. He heard and felt the cop get in the front of the van and start the engine. It roared to life, and soon they were headed out into New York City. He could not see where they were going, but they drove for a good forty-five minutes, stopping and starting frequently, as the traffic was heavy. Finally the vehicle stopped for good and the engine was shut down. The rear doors were opened, and he was told to step out of the van. Rafe did as he was instructed.

He hopped down out of the vehicle and onto the pavement, the sunlight stinging his eyes temporarily. Rafe found himself wishing he had some sunglasses and immediately recognized where he was. He was outside the construction zone of the Second Avenue Subway, near where he had been the morning before. He guessed he was somewhere around 86th Street. "Follow me and no trouble or you go back. Do you understand?" said the cop.

"Yeah, I got it," responded Rafe dryly. The policeman grabbed his arm and led him through the entrance in the fence and towards a construction elevator, which had been installed temporarily to reach the subterranean work area below. The security guards milling around eyed Rafe suspiciously

"I've been instructed to take you only so far. The rest you will have to figure out on your own, capiche?" the cop said.

"I'll do as you say, boss," Rafe replied with an angry smirk.

"A wise guy, huh?" The cop said nothing else but accompanied him in the elevator, shut the metal door, and hit the button on the control panel to start down. Thirty seconds later, the elevator car stopped with a bang. The policeman swung the gate open and pointed towards a dark tunnel to the south with a small light visible at the far end. "Go that way," he said. "You'll find what you are looking for. There is nothing else I can help you with."

"Okay, thanks for the ride," Rafe quipped and held his hands up. "What about these?"

"Oh yeah." The cop took out his key and removed the handcuffs. "No hard feelings, huh?" the cop added. Rafe shrugged his shoulders and stepped away from the elevator; the cop swung the door shut then pressed the button to engage the motor. The elevator quickly began moving to the street level above. Rafe was left alone in the darkness. Suddenly he felt quite alone. And there was something else; he felt fear.

He stood there for a couple minutes, allowing his eyes to adjust to the lack of light. Slowly shapes in the distance became clear to him. There were large pieces of drilling equipment and electrical generators to one side and piles of train track on the other. Pallets and boxes of other equipment and materials were laid out as far as he could see down the freshly dug tunnel. Once his eyes were accustomed to the dark, Rafe started walking.

The ground was somewhat uneven so he had to be careful. Although there was the small light down the newly excavated tunnel off the main track area, there was not enough visibility for him to make out where he was going. He pulled out his phone and turned it on to use as a flashlight. The small penlight beam pierced the darkness. It was enough. Soon he was at the entrance of the small passageway. He hesitated for a moment then he entered. Thirty seconds later, he stood outside an opening dug into the side of the tunnel. It seemed to lead to another small passageway and then to a final opening. *That must be the temple,* Rafe surmised. A small, red

257

light flickered inside the space beyond, resembling a candle flame inside a tent. The deep red and orange light danced around the walls outside the tunnel entrance where Rafe stood. He noticed he suddenly felt cold and alone and scared. Fearing for his own personal safety for the first time in a long time, Rafe thought of his daughter, took a deep breath, and kept walking.

Chapter Twenty-Five

As Rafe neared the entrance to the temple, apprehension welled up inside him. It was like nothing he had ever felt before. He stopped walking. Why am I feeling this way? Am I afraid I will find out the truth of what has happened to Clare? What if she is gone? What if they killed her? He could taste the fear but soon started walking again slowly, not sure if he wanted to enter or not. And he felt cold, very cold and completely vulnerable. Rafe started shivering. He neared the entrance to the Mythraim, hesitated, and then turned to face the chamber carved into the earth.

The temple was built similar to all of the others he had seen in the last few weeks. There was the same table and the same bench facing each side of the elongated space. The roof was curved into an arch. At the far end of the temple stood an altar with the now familiar image of the soldier slaying the bull with a spear while riding him. But Rafe was not looking at how the temple was constructed or the now familiar accoutrements. Rafe was staring into the face of the man from the market he had seen weeks before in Barcelona and whom he had seen kidnapping Cecilia.

"Hello, Rafe," said the man happily. He was very well dressed and elegant; he seemed to be about sixty with salt-and-pepper hair. He was trim and confident and sported a slight beard. He wore a long, dark, leather jacket. There was a quiet power emanating from him.

Rafe was unable to speak. He should have been raging at this person and pummeling him to the ground with his fists to force him to tell him about Clare. But the only thing Rafe felt was fear and extreme evil.

"Don't you want to say hello?" the man said.

Rafe finally was able to get out in a hushed tone, "Who are you?"

The man stared at him for a while and then replied, "You know who I am." He paused for effect. "Don't you, Rafe?"

"I don't know...," Rafe stammered. He was unsure, but he felt as if he knew this person somehow. He couldn't quite put his finger on it.

"Well let me tell you. I've been in your dreams, your fears, your horrors. I've prodded you to make decisions in a certain way. Yes, you know me." He paused again. "I've been called many things: Iblis, Baphomet, Beelzebub, Mephistopheles. But you would know me as Lucifer."

Rafe struggled to understand what the man was saying and was at a loss for words. Standing in front of him was just a man, not a god, not a spirit. But Rafe could feel the danger, the evil. The being was who he said he was, and Rafe was even more afraid.

"I don't understand," said Rafe softly.

"No, you don't yet, *but* you will."

"Where is my daughter?"

"She is safe, for the time being. You needn't worry about Clare." Rafe felt a wave of relief and then fear, for he was not sure he could trust this man or whatever it was.

"What do you want with me?"

"You will know shortly. I want your help in a little project of mine."

"Why did you have to kill Cecilia?" asked Rafe.

"I'm not dead, I'm here, Rafe," a familiar, female voice said behind him. Turning, he saw Cecilia, or what he thought was Cecilia, standing in the opening to the temple. She looked the same but different, more beautiful but also more dangerous. She smiled seductively. "Nice to see you again. Don't be scared. It's still me. I won't hurt you." Rafe wasn't so sure. She leaned against the entranceway in a strikingly sexy, almost glowing pose. Too sexy for that matter, almost evil. Her skin seemed to glow with an unnatural radiance. Her hair flowed around her face although there was no wind. She seemed magical.

"Yes it's Cecilia, as you know her," said the man. Rafe turned back to face him. "Her real name is Lilith. She was Adam's first wife! Not that hag, Eve. Adam had great taste, don't you think? And yes, she is with me. She has been with me and done my bidding for thousands and thousands of years. I hope you enjoyed your time with her. She's spectacular! Isn't she? She did her job very well, I

261

think you would agree? Bringing you to me? You should feel very lucky to have made love to a demon."

Rafe felt as if he were spinning. He felt the world around him disappear. The arched roof of the temple was now open to the stars. Things slowly were becoming clear to him, but his mind wouldn't accept what he was being told. Finally Rafe gathered enough courage to speak. "My father always did tell me to try and find beauty on the inside as well as on the outside."

"Ahh, good advice from your father," said the man. "In fact, all of the people that have been pointing you in my direction recently work for me in one way or another. Whether they know it or not. Did you find what I wanted you to look for?"

"I think so." Rafe paused. "You wanted me to discover why societies fail."

"Very good, Rafe! I'm proud of you! You get a gold star for that answer! And why do they fail?"

"From corruption and greed. From removing the need for hard work. It seems there are many ways. If a society has nothing to work for, if everything is given to it, then it dies."

"Very good. You have learned from your little journey, as I had hoped."

"When can I see Clare?" asked Rafe.

"Yes, I understood your weakness very well, didn't I? Taking Clare was all I needed to do in order to make you come my way. You can see her when we come to an agreement."

"About what?"

262

"Strange as it may seem, I need your help. You do have free will you know."

"To do what?"

"Again, I'll get to that in a minute."

"And if I don't do as you ask?"

"Then of course your daughter will have to be sacrificed, and, I will make you watch." Rafe felt his knees go weak, and he reached out to the stone table for support. The limestone felt as cold as ice.

"Don't worry, baby," said Cecilia as she put her arms around his waist and kissed his neck. Her hand went slowly to his crotch. Rafe felt her electricity flow through him. "I'm sure you'll make the right decision." He tried to ignore her.

"Tell me what you want," said Rafe determinedly.

"Okay, Rafe, I'll tell you my request and then you can give me your answer. You see, I don't like it when societies do well and flourish. They tend to start achieving prosperity; they work hard, build self-confidence, and accomplishing great feats. I like to make things much more interesting." Lucifer smiled. "So since you humans have started to create civilizations, I have been trying to destroy them. And I've worked up a pretty good formula. Works just about every time."

"And what formula is that?"

"Why it's very simple, Rafe. I promise them everything they think they want!"

"That's it?"

"Yes, it is. Well, it's not quite that simple. There is a little more work involved, but that is it in a nutshell. You see I am the one who turned the Roman Empire into a corrupt entity. I am the one who helped concentrate power in one individual who was treated like a god and doled out favors only to those that were loyal to him. And, I made sure he gave the people just enough to keep them happy, happy enough to stop working. I killed their self-reliance, their freedom of choice. This destroyed the republic and their rule of law. It corrupted the military and weakened their defenses. The barbarians did the rest."

"That seems so easy."

"Yes, it is quite easy. You humans are very easy to manipulate. I made sure the Byzantine Empire fell as well, although it took a while longer. And when Russia started to become enlightened and powerful, well that was my coup de grace. You see, I made a similar deal with Lenin. He turned out to be such a wonderful protégé. It was so easy; the Russian people were so ready to be promised everything they'd ever dreamed of. It was a wonderful achievement, don't you think?"

"I guess for you, yes it was. Although tens of millions of people died in the end, and it didn't last."

"Well, of course it never lasts. I have to let you people win sometime, don't I? I have to keep it interesting!"

"So that begs the first question I asked. What do you want me to do for you?"

"Oh, Rafe, isn't it obvious? I want you to promise the people of your country everything they want. I want to destroy the United States of America. I want you to help me turn her communist. I can't let America become the fourth Holy Roman Empire. I want you to help me kill it!"

"Why me?"

"Who better than a famous writer. The pen is so much mightier than the sword. You can change minds, change hearts with your words. People respect you. You are famous. They will listen to every little word you say. Plus you are a descendant of the Old Believers. Where could I find a better pedigree? Yes, you are my guy. I can't think of a more powerful messenger to destroy any talk of a future Holy Roman Empire than a son of the original Russian Orthodox Church. "So now, Rafe, I need your answer. Will you help me or not?"

Chapter Twenty-Six

Rafe held Clare's hand as they walked through Central Park in New York City. The leaves were falling and created a remarkable palette of colors framing the stone walkway. Fall had arrived and winter was approaching. Hundreds of children ran and played, laughing on the Saturday afternoon, as they jumped in the piles of multicolored leaves along the pathway. Rafe was at peace, as Clare was safe and happy. She didn't remember much about the ordeal. She occasionally talked about the nice man but that was it. She had no idea her life had been in danger. Rafe was thankful for that. But there was something else, something that disturbed her, deep down in her subconscious. Perhaps even as a child she had sensed the evil. It was in her dreams that the man came back to her. She would wake up screaming with fear. Rafe would dash into her room and hold her for the rest of the night. He felt guilty, as he realized he enjoyed these times when she needed him so desperately. Rafe saw her only on the weekends, as he was so busy now with work. Rafe treasured his times with Clare and his older children. Today was a special day, as it was Clare's birthday, a Daddy and Clare day. He had her all to himself.

Except for one quick thing he had to do. The two of them continued hand in hand up the paved walkway and eventually came to their destination. The playground sprawled before them, the bright, colorful obstacles beckoned her. Clare squealed with delight. "Can I go, Daddy?"

"Yes, my love. Of course!" responded Rafe. Clare bounded from his arms and gleefully ran to the jungle gym rising from the soft, wood-chipped earth. She soon scampered up the slide the wrong way and came tumbling back down, laughing with delight, sawdust sprinkled in her hair. Rafe beamed with pride. *I made the right decision,* he thought. He glanced over at the bench located underneath one of the massive oak trees dotting the landscape of the park. There sat Neal smoking a cigar and waving at him. Rafe walked over.

"How are you, my friend?" asked Rafe.

"I'm great! Thanks for asking. It's good to see you again!"

"You as well. I've missed having a friend around. You are a friend, aren't you, Neal?"

"I have been always, mate! Want a cigar?"

"Yes, don't mind if I do! Time to celebrate I should say." Neal reached into his pocket, withdrew a nice Cuban, and handed it and a lighter to Rafe. "So I'll see you at the rally, right?" asked Neal.

"Yes, I'll be there. I'm rather enjoying my newfound occupation. How is the promotion for the event going? Do we have a head count yet? I really want this rally to be a rousing success!"

"I think we are up to around twenty thousand confirmed. I've got you speaking second in the lineup. Hope that's okay with you?"

"Sure, works for me. I'll give a fabulous speech!"

"Great. Then I'll see you next there. Be sure to get there early in case we have any last-minute hiccups we have to deal with. I want this to go smoothly. I don't want you know who pissed off again."

"Yes, I know what you mean! I'll be there early."

"Also, Rafe, I hear there is a possible government position opening up for you. A rather prestigious post I'm afraid. Don't let it go to your head! You know our leader likes to reward his supporters."

"So I hear. I'll believe it when I see it. See you at the rally."

"Great. You know, Rafe, I did what I had to do as well."

"I understand, Neal. We all do that from time to time."

Neal threw away the stub of the cigar into the bushes and got up to leave. He shook Rafe's hand and slowly started to walk away. "See you soon, let's have a drink sometime. What do you say?" asked Neal as he left. Rafe nodded in agreement.

Rafe watched him walk away but then called out to him one last time. "Neal. I've been wondering something. What was the offer you couldn't refuse?"

Neal turned and stared silently at Rafe for what seemed like an eternity, the color draining out of his face. "You don't want to know the answer to that question. Let's just say it was my worst fear. Don't ever ask me that again," the Englishman responded with a vengeance. With that, Neal turned and angrily walked away, his shoulders held somewhat less high than before. *Whatever it was, it must have scared him badly,* thought Rafe.

After Neal left, Rafe called for his daughter to return. Clare came walking up slowly, obviously tired from jumping all around for the half hour she was engrossed in the playground. Rafe picked her up and placed her on his shoulders, and they began to walk back down the hill to the exit from the park. She played their normal game of trying to fall sideways from his grip, but he stopped her at the last minute. "Do it again, Daddy!" she cried. This went on for several minutes.

"Clare, I have a special treat for you now." Ice cream was next on the agenda. She bounced on his shoulders with happiness as they walked, nearing the southern park entrance.

"I want chocolate! With sprinkles!" she demanded.

"Okay, okay! Today is your day, my love."

As they approached the ice cream stand near the subway station, Clare noticed a homeless man sprawled on the sidewalk. His meager belongings were stuffed into two plastic bags. A half-eaten plate of food was near his face, along with a few beer cans that were definitely empty. His head rested on a brick barrier that separated the sidewalk from the rest of the park. His hair was matted with dirt and his teeth were black.

"What's wrong with him, Daddy?" Clare asked innocently as Rafe lifted her up off his shoulders and put her back down on the concrete.

"He's homeless, my dear."

"What does that mean?"

"He doesn't have anywhere to go."

"That's sad. Is he going to be okay?" she asked.

"Don't worry, honey, the government will give him everything he needs. He'll be okay. I'm sure he's just not feeling well. And you know what the best part is, my angel? Daddy's been writing a lot of articles in the paper about how good it is for the government to take care of everybody. I'll make sure someone comes and helps him. Would that make you feel better?" Rafe noticed the pride in his daughter's eyes. It was nice to feel like he was doing something positive, even if the results told a different story. Clare enjoyed her ice cream, and Rafe enjoyed the day with his daughter.

Epilogue

The young man shifted the sands slowly and quietly with care, watching intently for any sign of something important as he worked. He operated in small, soft, delicate strokes. His team had discovered many significant artifacts during this excavation, and he was excited about what they would find next. The savage wars had long been over, and now that peace ruled the land, the people had an opportunity to learn about the past. This one area had been a gold mine of discovery. It was outside the capital city of the empire, where the cemeteries were placed, since the graveyards had not been allowed inside the city limits. The cemetery had yielded many secrets, but he was confident she had many more to give. Many of the common people were buried in this area. The discovery had given the research team insight into the daily lives of the empire's citizens. One couldn't understand a civilization by just studying the ruling elite. However, each discovery only whetted the team's appetite for more information. They were never satisfied, and there was much more work to be done. The young man was proud to be part of such an important effort.

His tool hit something hard. It was stone, but it looked to be a sculptured one, not natural. It was too smooth. He carefully dug farther around the edges. As he meticulously removed the soft material from around the large rock over a two-day period, it became obvious what he had found. Once enough of the earth around the stone was removed and the shape revealed, he called the rest of the team over to inspect the find. Over the next several days, they were able to remove the rest of the dirt from around the large, circular rock. He suspected it was another tomb, but there were no markings. It was a common, simple grave. His whole team was working on his find now. Several days later, they made room for the stone to be removed. The dirt to one side was extracted and they were finally ready. The moment was at hand. The young man quivered with excitement. He had studied for years about this place, and now he would witness the history for himself. He had heard of the wonderful and amazing things that happened here, long ago. How the civilization had formed a republic, and the people had ruled themselves for centuries, before being taken over by a corrupt dictator, and eventually overrun by the barbarians. He had heard of the magnificent discoveries and inventions this civilization brought to light. Scientists in this age couldn't even agree as to what secrets were lost when the empire fell. They only knew there was much to discover. There was so much to learn.

His superior was managing this part of the excavation now. It was too important a find to leave to a young researcher. Plus, the man wanted the credit for the discovery, which they all surmised would be a substantial one. The young man was okay with this. He was interested only in the science and the knowledge. He didn't care who took the credit or received the inevitable glory. And yes, there would be glory, as the find was significant. The young man was only dreaming of mingling with the souls of the past as he carefully excavated their bones and burial relics, saying a small prayer for each one as he did so. He felt connected to the remains in some way.

He was jerked back to reality as his boss called for all of the team to gather and help move the stone. Six of them now were ready to push the rock away and reveal the secrets of the tomb. He could barely keep his excitement in check. They began to collectively apply pressure and the stone moved, slowly but surely, inch by inch. Soon, the entrance was open before them. *It had all happened so quickly!* the young man thought to himself. *The moment is here!*

The team peered inside and shined a powerful search beam before entering on foot. There were safety precautions to be followed. It was indeed a tomb. Several white skeletons lay on stone tables, placed perfectly along the walls. They had obviously been carefully prepared for burial centuries before. However, one body lay on the floor, curled up near the opening of the tomb. The skeleton was in remarkable shape, considering it had been lying there for several thousand years. The young researcher perceived it was a female. After the technicians declared the tomb safe to enter, the young man stepped inside.

After a cursory walk-through, he turned to examine the interior of the rock that had guarded the tomb, for this piqued his interest. He carefully went over the entire surface, taking pictures, and then signaled his leader. His theory was right. There were scratches on the stone—most likely having been made by the female body that lay in front of them. She must have been buried alive and tried to claw her way out. *What a horrible death. I wonder what was her crime?* The young man looked at the carcass more closely, all the while taking more pictures. Then he noticed something else. There was an item that had been wrapped around her neck. It was a small, stone cylinder. He carefully removed and catalogued the find. The ends were sealed. He began to shake with excitement. This could be incredibly important! Perhaps this could be the breakthrough they were looking for all this time! He forced himself to remain calm and to follow procedure. Meticulously, he prepared the item for removal and inspection.

Several days later, the team was in the laboratory at the university. Every possible procedure was followed to ensure the item would not be harmed as they examined it more closely. The technician carefully removed the seal of the container with gloved hands. Inside was a delicate parchment, which he slowly removed with care and unfurled on the sterile table. One of them had a video camera and was recording the whole exercise. No one said a word as they stared at the remarkable words written on the parchment. They were amazed at what they said.

We the People of the United States, in Order to form a more perfect Union, establish Justice, insure domestic Tranquility, provide for the common defence, promote the general Welfare, and secure the Blessings of Liberty to ourselves and our Posterity, do ordain and establish this Constitution for the United States of America...

####

About the Author

L. Todd Wood is a graduate of the U.S. Air Force Academy. He has been an aeronautical engineer and an Air Force helicopter pilot. In the Air Force, he flew for the 20th Special Operations Squadron, which started Desert Storm. He was also active in classified counterterrorism missions globally supporting SEAL Team 6 and Delta Force. For eighteen years, he was an international bond trader with expertise in Emerging Markets. He has conducted business in over forty countries. Todd has a keen understanding of politics and international finance. He is a contributor to Fox Business News, The Moscow Times, NY Post, Newsmax TV, and others.

www.LToddWood.com

Other Works by L. Todd Wood

CURRENCY

SUGAR

Please post a review with your favorite online retailer if you enjoyed the book!

Find out about new releases by L. Todd Wood by signing up for his monthly newsletter!
http://eepurl.com/WJ7Kn

Connect with Me Online

@LToddWood

https://www.facebook.com/CurrencyLToddWood

https://www.linkedin.com/profile/view?id=50785725&trk=nav_responsive_tab_profile

Google+ LToddWood Author Page

Pinterest.com/LToddWood

CURRENCY

by

L Todd Wood

Prologue

Weehawken, New Jersey
July 11, 1804

The smartly dressed, older man came first, sitting erect and still as death in the rear of the long oar boat as it silently rowed across the wide river. The moon cast an eerie glow across the fast-moving, silky, black current.

He was balding, middle-aged, and had dark features. However, he was in a much darker mood, a murderous mood in fact. He was the kind of man who never forgot anything, especially the stain on his honor. His eyes bored holes in the back of the man sitting in front of him, and he did not notice his surroundings, as his mind was lost in thought. He was there to right a wrong he had suffered.

To this end he was joined by two other men seated near him, as well as two additional young rowers and his dueling second at the head of the craft, a total of five. The only sound was the water lapping like a running brook as the oars slipped in and out of the calm, silvery surface. Slowly the boat crossed the dark current. Preoccupied, the passenger did not hear. He was focused only on the task ahead of him.

They beached the long oar boat on the bank, and he and the three men quickly scurried into the woods as the rowers stayed behind. Immediately the four gentlemen began to clear the brush along the ledge facing the water. The birds awoke but no one heard. Their singing cast an odd, joyful sound, contrasting eerily with the morbid events unfolding beneath them.

A man younger by a year arrived a half hour later in a similar craft with a smaller entourage. He was a person of importance and seemed rather arrogant. In fact, he had a brilliant mind. Unfortunately he had a habit of taunting others with his brilliance, which is what brought him to where he was at this hour. His pompous mood seemed out of touch with the somber circumstances.

One of his party was a well-respected physician. His second, sitting in the bow, carried an ornate box the size of a breadbasket. Inside were two Wogdon dueling pistols, the finest in the world at the time. The pair of weapons had already claimed the lives of a handful of men. One of those killed had been the younger man's son.

The first party made themselves known, and the group who had just arrived made their way up the embankment to join them. Salutations were exchanged.

The seconds set marks on the ground for the two men ten paces from each other. The younger man, since challenged, had the option of choosing his spot and had already selected to be facing the river. The two antagonists loaded their pistols in front of the witnesses, which was the custom, and the seconds walked into the woods and turned their backs. This way they would not be party to the scene and could not be charged with a crime, as dueling was now illegal. The honorable gentleman was becoming a rare breed. Times were changing.

The blond man's second began counting down. Unknown to his charge's opponent, the pistols had a secret hair trigger firing mechanism; just a slight application of pressure would ignite the powder. This was a slight of hand to say the least.

A loud crack rang out. A few seconds later, another. Then a cry of pain. Whether the younger man accidentally fired due to the hair trigger or intentionally wasted his shot, we will never know. Historians have debated this point ever since. His shot missed his adversary and ricocheted into the surrounding trees.

The return fire from his opponent, however, was deadly. The ball pierced his abdomen and did mortal damage to his internal organs before lodging in his spine. He collapsed to the ground.

The acrid smell of gunpowder still hung in the air as the dark-haired man walked up to him writhing on the ground. He was confident in his errand as he stood over him and methodically reloaded his pistol.

"Where is it?" he asked as he calmly packed the powder down the barrel.

The seconds stepped forward out of the brush, but the older man waived them off with his pistol. The New Jersey woods were strangely quiet; the New York lights across the river twinkled in the background, soon to be obscured by the rising sun. Its rays would soon shine a bright light on the deadly events happening below.

"Where is it?" he said again sternly but softly, pointing his reloaded pistol at the man's head as he tried to lift it off the ground and speak. The long, highly polished brass barrel reflected the early morning sun.

Blood poured from an open wound in his gut. Although mortally wounded and lying in the dirt, he held his hand over the opening to try to stop the flow.

"Go to Hell!" he gurgled as his mouth filled with blood.

"I probably will but I think you will beat me there." The darker gentleman chuckled and knelt down beside him. He started going through the bleeding man's pockets. "I have heard you always carry it with you." Aaron Burr knew he didn't have much time before the surgeon and seconds gathered and pulled him off. Inside the man's blood-soaked coat, he found it.

"Ahh!" he gloated smugly. He quickly hid the pouch inside his own vest and stood.

"You will never find what you are looking for!" the wounded gentleman said in a whispering laugh. His strength was ebbing. He was going to die.

"We'll see," replied Burr.

"He's all yours!" he called to the second, and the wounded man's supporter rushed forward and tended to Alexander Hamilton.

Chapter One

June 10, 2015
Bahamas

The seawater thundered over the stern as the old fishing boat attempted to cut through the eight-foot waves, soaking everyone on board to their core. Connor Murray felt the impact in his kidneys as he held on to the ladder for dear life. The tuna tower swayed above him. His arm muscle burned as he prevented himself being tossed into the sea from the violent movement. Saltwater stung his nose. The new motor growled like a wounded bear as it strained against the onslaught.

How long can this go on? he thought.

Connor had puked twice and didn't relish a third attempt, but the nausea in his gut and throbbing in his head told him it was inevitable. The other two weekend warrior fishermen with him on the stern were leaning over the side as he contemplated his situation.

He heard them groan as they tried to empty their stomachs, but there was nothing left inside them. He was miserable.

The day had started easy enough in the predawn hours as they boarded the boat at the end of New Providence Island east of Nassau. The water was calm this early in the morning. This part of the island was protected by natural reefs. The rapid change in depth as the ocean floor rose to the island caused the ocean and the island currents to crash into each other and protected the east end from the ocean's wrath.

He had been planning this trip for weeks with his good friend. Alex, his Bahamian business colleague, had just finished overhauling an old, thirty-two-foot pilothouse cruiser, a labor of love for two years. The boat had been refurbished from bow to stern; many a weekend night they had spent drinking beer on the deck after a day's work on the "yacht, "as Alex's wife called it. Conner chuckled to himself. She was a little bit of a "wannabe."

The boat was not pretty, but she was strong. Alex had seen to that. He took very good care of her. When someone tears down and rebuilds something that intricate, it becomes part of them. The boat had become his passion. His wife didn't seem to mind; she had her yacht.

Connor had met his friend years ago when Alex was the head trader at a large hedge fund located in the tony Lyford Cay area on the west end of the island. Alex mingled with the movie stars. After trading together for several years and socializing on every trip Connor took to Nassau, they became friends and trusted one another completely. They took care of one another as they both moved firms several times over the years. Their careers flourished and their wealth grew.

This trip was a much needed change of scenery away from the Bloomberg terminal for both of them. The constant movement of the ocean was a welcome relief from the volatility of the markets. Stress relief was critical in their business. A day or two in different surroundings did wonders for one's trading acumen. "The three-day weekend was invented for Wall Street," Alex would often say.

The sun was rising as they cruised past old Fort Montague close to East Point. He could make out the row of old, British twenty-four-pound cannons lining the top barricade. The fort had held up remarkably well through the centuries, considering it was constantly exposed to the elements. The history here ran deep. Connor loved it. The islands were in his blood now. The open ocean waited for them ahead.

Today the only possible negative was the sea, as there was not a cloud in the sky. Their luck was not good.

The trip out of the channel was hellish as they crossed the churning waves. The barrier reefs produced a literal wall of water the boat had to climb, as the underwater structures halted the ocean's momentum. It was no better on the other side, but Connor knew Alex would not turn back. He had promised everyone on board some fish, and this was her maiden voyage. They all quickly decided it was too rough to make the two-hour trek to Exuma, which they had planned. Instead they would stay off Paradise Island. Connor was quietly grateful.

Later in the day, after they had landed three dolphin, a bull and two females, all mercifully decided that it was too rough to continue. Now they were making their way back to protected waters, but it wasn't easy. The waves beat the side of the boat and refused to provide a respite to the passengers and crew. The fishermen were still hugging the rail in case they had to empty their stomachs again.

Thinking he would feel better higher, Connor climbed up the ladder and leaned into the back support next to Alex. He could see a line of boats making their way into the harbor to escape the violent sea.

The tower swayed violently as Alex strained to control the craft as she muddled her way up and over the crest of the waves.

"Must have taken on some water," Alex growled. "I can feel it sloshing back and forth down below. It's hard to control this pig."

Connor wasn't listening. "Tell me the latest on our discovery," he said.

April 23, 1696

Captain William Kidd turned one last time and looked over his shoulder at the Plymouth land mass disappearing in the background. The city that produced the Pilgrims had long since lost its dominance as a critical port for the Crown. The coastal lights faded in the mist.

Kidd would not miss England. He would, however, miss his beautiful wife of five years, Sarah, and their daughter in the English colony of New York, recently acquired from the Dutch, which called her New Amsterdam. The city was on its way to becoming a cultural and economic center of North America.

Sarah was one of the wealthiest women in the New World, primarily due to her inheritance from her first husband. She had been already twice widowed and was only in her early twenties.

He had left them several months ago to fulfill his dreams. He would not see them again for three years. Such was the life of a sailor.

This voyage has started very badly, he thought to himself. Maybe it was a sailor's intuition, but he had an uneasy feeling in the pit of his stomach.

He turned his attention back to the Adventure Galley. He had overseen her construction himself in London. She was built in record time, so there would be leaks and other imperfections to deal with, but she would do the job. Kidd had sold his former ship, Antigua, in order to raise funds. The King was lusting for pirate blood and treasure. He made no secret of his haste for Kidd's voyage. The new ship would have to do.

She was a strong, thirty-four-gun privateer and would be formidable when he engaged pirates. Her design was elegant at 284 tons. Her oars would be an important capability when maneuvering against an enemy. His crew however, now, was another story.

He had tried to leave England several weeks earlier with an altogether different group of men. His mission was financially speculative. The men would be paid the prize booty they could seize from legitimate pirate or French ships. Therefore he wanted men of good character who were excellent seaman. Having personally chosen each of the 150 men, he took pride in his selections.

In a hurry to depart London, he had chosen not to salute several Royal Navy vessels leaving the mouth of the Thames. It had been a mistake. This was a long-standing tradition and a direct affront to the English Navy and the King. His men had even taunted the English yachts as they passed, showing their backsides. Hence the *Adventure Galley* was boarded, and thirty-five of her best seamen were pressed into the Royal Navy. It was another several weeks before he could get Admiral Russell to return sailors to him to fill his crew. He received back landsmen and troublemakers rather than the original able-bodied seamen.

He was now on his way to New York to fill out his crew with another eighty good men. Then he could chase pirates.

"My crew will not like to be sailing under an unlucky captain," he said aloud. Perhaps it was nothing to be worried about. "Maybe we have gotten the bad luck out of the way at the start."

He turned around and faced the bow.

The open sea helped calm his nerves.

Captain Kidd was very glad to be leaving England in command of his own powerful ship. The crew could be dealt with over time. He was a restless man.

He had desperately wanted a commission from the King to command a Royal Navy vessel and had sailed to London from New York in late 1695 in search of this honor. He loved the sea and had been a respectable member of New York society for several years. He had used his considerable maritime skills as a merchant seaman to build his wealth. Kidd was in love with his beautiful Sarah and their young daughter of the same name, whom he adored. But, his first love was the sea. He wanted adventure.

He had sailed to London with a recommendation letter to request an audience with the King in his quest to become a Royal Navy Captain. While there, he became involved in a scheme to help the monarch with his pirate problem while making money for himself and others. Several financial benefactors backed him in building a ship and outfitting it to sail against any pirate he could find with the booty paying the mission's expenses. The profits would be split among Kidd and the powerful English gentlemen. These included the Earl of Bellomont and other aristocrats. He never met the King, but he did receive a written commission to perform this duty. The King was to receive ten percent of the take.

This was a dangerous gamble, and Kidd knew he was sailing in treacherous territory. He was already at odds with the Royal Navy, who presumed it was their duty to deal with the piracy issue. It was an unlucky start indeed.

He had no friends at sea, and he suspected as much as he crossed into the Atlantic. The rewards, however, could be great and in his mind worth the risk.

Looking out over the vast ocean, he felt at peace for the first time in many years. His wife and daughter were the furthest subjects from his mind. He was with his love at last.

CURRENCY can be purchased/ordered at any online or physical retailer. The novel is also available electronically via most online retailers. The audio version is available via Audible.com, iTunes, or Amazon. Signed copies can be purchased at LToddWood.com.

SUGAR

by

L Todd Wood

Prologue

Saccharum officinarum

This story starts several hundred million years ago. The exact timing doesn't really matter. You only need to get the gist of what happened.

The day started the same as they had for tens of thousands of years. The sun rose and the temperature followed. The cold-blooded animals stirred. The heated air cloaked all life on Earth in an embryonic cocoon. And the air was warmer today, noticeably warmer than usual.

There were many more animals as of late, all different kinds. The diversity of life was exploding all around. That's what happens when an ice age ends, when the Earth warms. The resulting tropical conditions foster all kinds of evolutionary experiments.

It was the end of the Paleozoic era. It was one of those fulcrums in the history of the Earth, a springtime to end all springtimes, a great awakening.

Plants were large in this day. Giant ferns dominated the interior, but in the coastal plains near the oceanic waters, another type of organism thrived. These were the grasses. One of these specimens in particular grew in giant clumps. This invasive plant had large, noded reeds that reached to the sky. It was a perennial and therefore multiplied in abundance along the coast. It was the ancestor of what today we call sugarcane. However, this organism was much larger than the cane we are familiar with in the twenty-first century. The reeds were massively tall and looked like today's pine trees, flowing in the summer wind.

Millions of years later, this part of the Earth was to become known as Southeast Asia. To be exact, it would be called New Guinea. At this point in history, however, the area still shared a coastline with the landmass that would become Australia. But alas, this was not to last.

The animals became agitated. Something strange was happening. The large array of reptiles was moving to higher ground. Somehow that sixth sense that animals often possess had kicked into high gear. Something was going to happen. The air became very still.

There was a deafening crash as the natural dam made from glacial-carved rock in the mountains gave way high above the coastline. A few hundred thousand years of melted ice behind it had created enormous pressure. It could no longer hold. The water cascaded down from the higher ground like a prehistoric Niagara Falls, only bigger. The seas began to rise.

One particular clump of the cane was perched on an outcrop of rock overlooking the rising ocean. The water from the breached natural dam rushed over it and instantly knocked the entire plant into the sea. The resulting deluge of sediment from the oncoming flood covered the plant entirely. It had no chance to decay. Over the millennia, the layer of sediment above it slowly turned into rock, becoming a hard seal.

Layer upon layer of sediment was deposited above it across the ages. These too turned to stone.

Over a few hundred thousand years, the pressure began to build.

Part One

Chapter One

She was a Jatt of the Kharral clan. The time was the Christian year 1098 and it was no longer summer in the Punjab, the northwestern territory of India. The rainy season had just ended, and the cane was large in the lush, green fields. It was a time of harvest.

The Ravi River meandered like a snake through the valley near her home. It emanated from a confluence of five rivers of the Indus Valley, with the Himalayan Mountains decorating the horizon to the north. The territory was soaked with rain and runoff from the melting snow on the mountains. This provided ideal conditions for growing food. The abundant, flat farmland was extremely fertile. Things grew here, no matter what was planted. The Punjab was the breadbasket of the world, at least as the world was known at the time.

The people were happy. This was a celebratory time of year. They would garner money and staples from the sugar they would produce. It had been a grand harvest, and there would be plenty of food and shelter for everyone. No one would go hungry or cold in the following winter, the deadliest season of the year.

Historically the Jatts were nomadic herders but had settled in the Punjab and now were skilled farmers. They were a people that would be successful at whatever they put their mind to. This trait was in their genes. There was an unwritten rule that you didn't get in a fight with a Jatt, because they didn't stop fighting until they were victorious or dead.

Jatts were members of the upper castes. They were not Brahmin, but due to their technocracy, they were placed above many in the hierarchy. For instance, the girl's father ran the cooperative sugar mill, which serviced the fields arrayed around her village as far as the eye could see. The cane beautifully swayed in the wind as the warm breeze flowed down from the Himalayas.

Her name was Roopa, meaning "blessed with beauty." And beautiful she was, shockingly so. Like the other women in her clan, she had wheat skin and long, dark hair to her waist. However, her eyes were blue, which was very rare in her people. The contrast was mesmerizing. Many unmarried men in the village had been watching her for some time, dreaming of making her his wife. There was much talk among the village as to who the lucky man would be. Marriages were arranged in her clan, causing much consternation among the young maidens. Their lives changed forever with the decisions of their parents. The parents tended to look for a wealthy widower to provide for their daughter, whereas the young girls dreamed of a young prince. The parents usually got their wish.

Roopa had just turned fifteen and her body was changing. It had been changing for a while. She was a woman now, she could feel it. She had strange yearnings that she did not understand. Her life was blooming in the spring of youth, her future ahead of her. She felt immortal.

Roopa had been raised in a privileged environment. Everyone in the valley depended on her father. This gave him a position of prominence and respect. Her life was easier than most due to her parent's position in the clan, but she was still expected to work. The last few years had been tough on the sugar industry in the Punjab, so a successful harvest was a wonderful thing for the Jatts. However, there was always work to do, even for beautiful young girls. Besides, her father wanted her to learn the joy of creating something with her own hands.

Her family refined sugar, as they had done in this region for hundreds of years. In this way they had become important, even indispensable. If the mill was not in operation, the population suffered. Her father took this responsibility seriously and worked hard to keep the mill in working order and to improve its efficiency. He constantly looked for ways to increase the output from the raw cane, even inventing processes of his own to streamline and grow the operation. He was loved by the people that depended on him.

"You should put on your orhna," her mother scolded as Roopa left the house on the way to the sugar mill to do her job for the day. There she would help package the sugar loaves as they were taken from the molds at the mill. It was a critical job, to make the finished product attractive to their buyers on the Silk Road.

"You are a woman now!"

"It is too hot to wear it and work," Roopa retorted with disrespect.

"The men will notice."

"I am still a girl," Roopa said and stood to face her mother in the doorway to the outside world. The intricate, religious carving accentuated the entrance to the dwelling. Metal accoutrements adorned the exquisitely detailed wooden door.

She knew her mother was right. She could feel the men staring at her nowadays and rather enjoyed it, but she was rebellious in the prime of her youth. Soon I will have to start wearing it when I leave the house, she thought to herself. The orhna was a shirt but also a veil. It was worn over her angia, or blouse, and ghagri, or heavy skirt. Her mother said it was so that she would not have to worry about men looking at her., that is was a luxury. Well, she didn't want this luxury. Her breasts were full and the men loved to stare at them. Her hair flowed down her back soft as a sheaf of feathers.

Her family had very strict rules regarding women. She was a Muslim, but not all of the clans in the Punjab shared her religion. There were Sikhs, Buddhists, and some Hindu.

She left the house with her mother still preaching behind her, her voice trailing off in the wind.

Chapter Two

Roopa paused to take in the view from the garden in front of her home as she walked away from the entrance. The blooms on the colorful flowers were wilting as the air slowly cooled and winter approached. The view of the valley always amazed her at this time of the year. The house was set on one of the foothills leading up to the Himalayas. In front of her, the Punjab valley flowed with the green fields of sugar cane as far as she could see. The waves were mesmerizing as the breeze wove its web among the tall grasses. As a child, she had attempted to find images of local animals in the moving grass. She would keep this habit for life, as the cane would always be with her. It was also one of the last moments of childhood she would enjoy, though she didn't know it yet.

After she had drunk her fill of the view, she made her way down to the structure that housed the sugar molds. The ancient stone stairway that she negotiated down the hill to the village was also a childhood friend. She knew every step, every crack. The familiar surroundings comforted her. She had played among the mill buildings as a child and knew them like the back of her hand. Blissfully, she had not a care in the world.

The men of the village were in the fields for the harvest. This was backbreaking work to say the least. The men worked tirelessly for many days to bring in the cane, bending over and hacking the base of the tall plants. That's the thing about sugar cane: when it's time, it's time, and when it's cut, it has to be processed right away, or the sugar will change into a less valuable fructose within forty-eight hours. It was a brutally busy time of year for the farmers, but days of celebration always followed when the sugar was in its final form. Then the village could relax and the fun could begin.

The cane, once hewn, was taken to a mill where it was cut into short lengths and crushed by a stone grinder to extract the liquid. Wind or water usually powered the mill in the eleventh century. Water was plentiful in the Punjab and so was the natural choice. The fiber was then pressed again with a beam and screw press to obtain any remaining juices. This was where Roopa's family came in. Her father owned the mill that was supplied by hundreds of small farms in the area. India never developed the plantation system that was famous in the West Indies and elsewhere. It was every family for itself, but it was a collective effort.

In the end, they all had to come to Roopa's father. He was the expert. He possessed the vast store of knowledge that had accumulated over the centuries on how to refine sugar. It was passed down through the ages in his family. He had even made his own adjustments to the process to increase the yield and the quality of

310

the final product. There were always improvements to be made. That's how humans made technological progress.

Once the cane was pressed, the juices were boiled down to crystals in vast, copper pots. To filter impurities out of the mixture, ash or a similar material was added, which attached to foreign elements and forced them to the bottom of the container. The material skimmed off the top was molasses, a byproduct of sugar production but useful in its own right. The remaining liquid was placed in baskets or pottery to dry and harden. The mold was usually in the shape of an upside down cone with a hole in the bottom small end. Repeated draining of the refined sugar would result in a cone of white material. It was called a loaf. They were very valuable. Small cutting tools called sugar nips were manufactured to break off minute chunks of the hard sugar from the loaf to be used in cooking or just to please the palate. These chunks were called khandee, the origin of the western word candy.

Once finished, the loaves were groomed for sale to the highest bidder. This was Roopa's duty: to prepare the loaves in an attractive way for sale to the wealthy foreigners of the West. She used a brightly colored wrapper from paper, which had been introduced and supplied by the Arab caravans decades earlier. The Persians to the Egyptians were already well versed in the use of paper packaging at this time. Her father loved her designs, and that is why she was given this job. Many girls from the village found work in this part of the process.

Roopa entered the structure that housed the finished, unwrapped product. The sweet smell was overpowering. The heat from the refining process hit her full in the face. She began to sweat as she made her way to the table where she worked. She was glad she had not worn the veil.

With fresh energy, she immersed herself in the task of creating designs for the sugar loaves that had cooled and were ready for packaging. The cones were like great white canvases with which to work. The only thing holding her back was her imagination. She enjoyed transforming them into something that would catch a customer's eye. This always brought her pleasure. She had a way of bringing different colors together that was inviting to the traveling merchants. She was a creative girl and often lost herself in the task, ignoring the goings-on around her and the actions of the others in the room.

About an hour into her work, she noticed the boys who were working on the molds stop chatting and turn to look at her. She could feel their stares. Her mother was right; she would have to start wearing her veil. For the first time, she felt naked with her hair, arms, and neck exposed, not to mention the cleavage of her breasts. Suddenly she felt very alone and vulnerable. She had crossed some sort of rubicon and there would be no more childhood. She was an adult now.

She saw the boys making suggestive jokes about her and laughing amongst themselves. They were looking straight at her and making crude gestures with their fingers and hands. Horrified, she ran from the storage hut back up the hill to the house in shame.

Chapter Three

Roopa sprinted up the stone stairs and back into the house, slamming the ornate door. Her mother looked at her knowingly, but Roopa ignored her. Her face burned with shame. She ran to one of the back rooms of the relatively large structure and, once alone, put her head in her hands and wept.

She was so confused and upset. Why should those boys get to act like that? she thought. Then she understood what her mother had told her. Wearing the veil was a luxury. Young girls didn't have to put up with the staring, the mocking. Muslim boys were scared of the female, her mother had said. They are threatened, so they attack. Her shame turned to apprehension as she thought of the future.

She had overheard her parents talking about marriage-her marriage-several weeks before. Once they thought she was asleep, they discussed which one of the families in the local area would be most beneficial for them to marry Roopa into. Since her father had wealth, she did not have to worry about being sold into one of the temples as a concubine for a priest. That was a horrible fate. After the priest tired of her, she would be sent to a brothel. Yes, at least she didn't have to worry about that. But to whom would she be married? The thought terrified her. She didn't want to leave her parents, and she definitely didn't want to be married off to some old, overweight merchant. She felt she had no choice but to trust her parents. They wanted what was best for her. They loved her very much, and she loved them. Together, they had a nice life, the only life she had ever known. Her pleasant yet simple existence among the mill and the village was coming to an end. Alas, she sighed, all things must change in time. She vowed to enjoy her remaining time at home.

She was a woman now. It was time she started acting like one. She would be more careful. She started to calm down as a sense of confidence swept over her. She washed her face from a bowl the servant had left near her bed and prepared to leave the room and face her mother. After all, she was a Jatt.

Then, in the back of her mind, she knew something was wrong, terribly, terribly wrong.

The first thing she noticed was the sound, a very frightening sound. It was the sound of the mountains moving. She could feel the ground shaking under her feet. Roopa was bewildered at first then very afraid, terrified in fact. She rushed to the window in her room and craned her neck in the direction of the fearsome noise. The hair on the back of her neck rose in horror.

"No!" she whispered to herself.

She was so frightened she was paralyzed. She knew deep in her soul at that moment that her short life was about to change forever in a way she had never expected. She could not move and stared out the window.

First she noticed the elephants. There had to be one hundred of them at least, all pounding the earth into submission as they thundered toward her village. The beasts wore armor on their fronts. On their backs were elaborate fortresses, which carried a handful of men armed to the teeth and yelling excitedly at the top of their lungs. The dust swirled up behind the mob of creatures as they tore up the earth with their soles. The elephants provided the shock of armor that military commanders would use tanks for in the future

Behind them were the horsemen, hundreds of them. They were swirling their swords high in the air and yelling war cries as well. Roopa was petrified. Their chain mail armor reflected in the sun, and the contrast with the leather coverings was unmistakable. The horses wore armor as well. Their riders' faces were covered with grotesque, fearsome helmets.

She broke from her trance. What should she do? Whatever it was, it had to be done quickly.

Roopa knew who they were. They were the Ghaznavids. She had never seen them before, but she had heard stories. They were the Turkic nation that had absorbed the Persian realm and its way of life to the north and west. They had controlled most of the mountains and deserts to the west, also occasionally the northern part of India, the Punjab. Their western lands had been lost over the last few decades; however, they frequently reinvaded the Punjab in order to plunder the wealthy villages and exact tribute from the Indian kings. Little did Roopa know that they were the reason why she was a Muslim now. The Ghaznavids had spread Islam throughout their empire over the last few hundred years.

The empire descended from slaves of the Turkish regime who fought their way out of bondage and gained their freedom. They had succeeded in conquering Persia, known today as Iran, and present-day Afghanistan. However, the heirs to the throne were not as cunning and ruthless as their elders. Much of the kingdom had been lost. They were fearless warriors and enslaved Afghan and Indian warriors to flesh out their armies. India foremost was a ripe target for pillage and plunder. The women were especially valued for their beauty. Roopa understood this. The empire now depended on raids into India to maintain their sultan's lifestyle and to fund his armies. They were here for no good purpose indeed.

What should I do? she screamed to herself without uttering a sound. She decided to hide. There was a crawl space above her room, which no one could find. She had hid there as a child and even her parents could never find her. Although much bigger now, she managed to squeeze her way through the beams into the small space between the floors. There was even a thin ray of light coming through a seam in the building where the walls came together. She worked her way towards it so she could see outside and watch what was going on.

Roopa feared for her family.

The rows of elephants stopped short of Roopa's village. They ringed the mill and the surrounding structures. No one could enter or leave. The horses began to graze as some of the soldiers dismounted and began to search the homes. Young men and boys were marched out and put into a group in the center guarded by infantry. The young ones were crying. They would never see their families again. One of the soldiers grabbed a young teenage girl and carried her off to his horse. The girl's mother ran out to try to stop what was happening. She was cut down with a swipe of a sword, her head severed from her body. The girl screamed in horror while the horsemen in their saddles laughed.

Roopa's house was searched. All of the inhabitants including her family and servants were lead out into the common area of the village and guarded. She was not found but shook with fear.

The soldiers reached the sugar mill and the cooling houses. All of the sugar loaves were taken and loaded on the elephants. It was a fantastic haul, since the harvest was near completion and the refining was mostly done as well. The sugar was worth a small fortune, and the military commander intended to sell the sugar to the west for weapons.

That was more than Roopa's father could bear. The sugar was his life and the lifeline for his clan. He broke free from the soldier who was guarding him and rushed to the foot soldiers loading the sugar onto the beasts. Roopa watched in terror as an archer on a horse drew his bow. "No!" she screamed.

Upon hearing her scream, they turned to reenter the house to look for her. She saw them look up toward the area of the house in which she hid. Her heart sank.

The arrow left the archer's bow and penetrated her father's back, piercing his kidney. He collapsed to the ground. Roopa bolted from her hiding place and rushed out the door of the home to the astonishment of the soldiers. Her beauty entranced them, and they did nothing but watch as she ran to her dying father. She caressed his head as the life ebbed from his body. No one disturbed her for a few moments. Tears streamed down her face and he died in her arms.

The ranks of the elephants broke, and a single rider emerged. The foot soldiers gave way and bowed to him as he passed. He trotted over to where Roopa lay on the ground, sobbing, cradling her father's head. She looked up at the figure cloaked in armor and was terrified by the sight of him.

He said nothing.

He reached down and grabbed Roopa under the arm with incredible strength, lifting her up to his horse to ride behind him. She could not resist. She was broken.

Then he rode away. The army with their spoils of war, including new forced recruits, followed. The captured young girls were thrown in a wagon. Mercifully the remaining villagers were left alone in their grief.

SUGAR can be purchased/ordered at any online or physical retailer. The novel is also available electronically via most online retailers. Signed copies are also available at LToddWood.com.

Lightning Source UK Ltd.
Milton Keynes UK
UKOW01f1111210716

278917UK00001B/20/P